T0090236

Praise for *Alentejo Blue*

"The grace of Ali's words is dazzling." —*Time Out New York*

"Ali is an expert with gesture; even minor characters appear in attitudes that are particular and unforgettable."

—Nell Freudenberger, *The Nation*

"The 'novel in short stories' is no new trick but Ali adapts it in a distinctive way, making it her own. . . . These stories are absorbing and beautiful . . . legitimately gripping and lovely prose."

—*The Baltimore Sun*

"Ali evokes the village of Mamarrosa the way the American novelist Sherwood Anderson did the town of Winesburg, Ohio, in 1919."

—*The Philadelphia Inquirer*

"Ali is masterful in writing about her characters' lives."

—*Los Angeles Times*

"While Mamarrosa is a village of fiction, travelers could only hope to find a place so real."

—*The Oregonian*

"Spellbinding . . . In *Alentejo Blue,* a human tale akin to *Brokeback Mountain,* Ali immediately establishes the strength and maturity with which she writes."

—*The Buffalo News*

"Monica Ali has created a memorable cast of characters here."

—*Minneapolis Star Tribune*

"Beautifully written, a tour-de-force." —*BookPage*

"The voices are vivid and resonant . . . a more structurally ambitious, more nuanced book than *Brick Lane*."

—*Chicago Tribune*

"A master of concision and suggestion, [Monica Ali] says volumes about characters and situations by what she does not say. It does indeed take a village—in this case, to show the fundamental universality of all human predicaments."

—*Booklist*

ALSO BY MONICA ALI

Brick Lane

Alentejo Blue

fiction

monica ali

SCRIBNER
New York   London   Toronto   Sydney

SCRIBNER
A Division of Simon & Schuster, Inc.
1230 Avenue of the Americas
New York, NY 10020

This book is a work of fiction. Names, characters, places,
and incidents either are products of the author's imagination or
are used fictitiously. Any resemblance to actual events or locales
or persons, living or dead, is entirely coincidental.

Portions of this book have been published in *The New Yorker*
under the title "Sundowners."

First Scribner trade paperback edition June 2007

SCRIBNER and design are trademarks of
Macmillan Library Reference USA, Inc., used under license
by Simon & Schuster, the publisher of this work.

For information about special discounts for bulk purchases,
please contact Simon & Schuster Special Sales:
1-800-456-6798 or business@simonandschuster.com

Designed by Kyoko Watanabe
Text set in Aldine 401

Manufactured in the United States of America

1   3   5   7   9   10   8   6   4   2

Library of Congress Cataloging-in-Publication Data
Ali, Monica.
Alentejo blue : fiction / Monica Ali.
   p. cm.
   I. Title.
PR6101.L45A44 2006
823'.92—dc22   2006042380

ISBN-13: 978-0-7432-9303-7
ISBN-10: 0-7432-9303-7
ISBN-13: 978-0-7432-9304-4 (Pbk)
ISBN-10: 0-7432-9304-5 (Pbk)

For SCT

Villages are like people, we approach them slowly,
a step at a time.

—José Saramago, *Journey to Portugal*

Because I do not hope to turn again
Because I do not hope
Because I do not hope to turn

—T. S. Eliot, "Ash-Wednesday"

One

At first he thought it was a scarecrow. Coming outside in the tired morning light to relieve his bladder, blessing as always the old Judas tree, João turned his head and saw the dark shape in the woods. It took some time to zip his trousers. His fingers were like enemy agents. They pretended to be his instruments but secretly worked against him.

João walked out beneath the moss-skinned branches thinking only this: Eighty-four years upon the earth is an eternity.

He touched Rui's boots. They almost reached the ground. "My friend," he said, "let me help you." He waited for the courage to look up and see his face. When it came, he whispered in his lacerated old man's voice. *"Querido,"* he said. "Ruizinho."

Standing on the log that Rui had kicked away, João took his penknife and began to cut the rope. He put his free arm across Rui's chest and up beneath his armpit, felt the weight begin to shift as the fibers sprang apart beneath the blade.

The almond blossom was early this year. The tomatoes too would come early and turn a quick, deceiving red. They would not taste of anything. João took Rui's crooked hand in his own and thought: These are the things that I know. It was time to put the broad beans in. The soil that had grown the corn needed to rest. The olives this year would be hard and small.

He sat in the long grass with his back against the log and Rui resting against him. He moved Rui's head so it lay more comfortably on his shoulder. He wrapped his arms around Rui's body. For the second time he held him.

They were seventeen and hungry when they first met, in the back of a cattle wagon heading east to the wheat fields. Rui pulled him up without a word, but later he said, "There's work enough for all. That's what I hear." João nodded, and when the hills had subsided and the great plains stretched out like a golden promise, he leaned across and said, "Anyone who wants work can find it." They moved their arses on the wooden slats and pretended they weren't sore and looked out farther than they had ever seen before, white villages stamped like foam on the blue, the land breaking against the sky.

On the third day they put down at the edge of a small town and the children who ran up to meet the wagon were bitten hard, no different from João's brothers and sisters. João looked at Rui but Rui set his mouth and swung his legs over the side the same as the other men. The older ones got called and went to cut cork or plow the fields while João and Rui stood up tall with their hands in their pockets. João was so hungry he felt it in his legs and his hands and his scalp. They walked through the hovels, the women lining the doorways, the dogs nosing the gutters, and came to the center. "We'll stick together," said Rui. He had green eyes and a fine nose and white skin, as though he had never been out in the sun.

"If someone wants us, he'll have to take us both," said João, as if he were master of his destiny.

They scrounged half a loaf at the café by scrubbing the floor and humping the rubbish to the tip, and slept on the cobbled street with their mouths open. When he woke, the first thing João saw was Rui's face. He thought the pain in his stomach was pure hunger.

Side by side they scavenged and slept. They milled about with the other men waiting for work and learned a lot: how to eke out a few words to last a conversation, how to lean against a wall, how to spit, and how to fill up on indifference.

At the top of the square was a two-story building with bars on the bottom window. João had never seen a prison before. The prisoners sat in the window and talked to friends or received food from relatives. One day a dozen or more people had gathered. João and Rui had nothing else to do.

"He talks about sacrifice. Who is making these sacrifices, my friends? Ask yourselves."

No one looked at the prisoner. They were just hanging around waiting, though there was nothing to wait for.

The prisoner clutched the bars and pressed his face to them. His nose escaped. "Salazar," he said, "is not making sacrifices."

There was a general stirring, as if fear had blown in on the dry wind.

"Listen to me," said the prisoner. His face was thin and pinched, as though he had spent too long trying to squeeze it out of the narrow opening. "In the whole of the Alentejo, four families own three quarters of the land. It was like this too in other countries, like Russia. But now the Russian land belongs to the Russian people."

Each man averted his face from every other. It was not safe to read another's thoughts.

João glanced at Rui. Rui did not know what the others knew, or was too reckless to care. He looked directly at the prisoner.

"The people make the wealth, but the wealth does not belong to the people."

Men withdrew their hands from their pockets as if emptying their savings before leaving town. The prisoner slid his fingers between the bars. "It is forbidden for us to go barefoot. Salazar forbids it." The man laughed, and the laugh was as free as the body was caged. "Look, this is how we must bind our feet. As long as our feet are in slippers and rags, our bellies must be full."

An old man with a bent back, obliged to gaze at feet the long day through, grunted a loud assent. A younger man, blinking back tears of fury, said, "It is true."

The prisoner tipped back into the dark cell as though wrenched by some unknown force, perhaps by the darkness itself. Each free man discovered he had something to do elsewhere.

"Rui," said João, "we better go."

Rui stood with his hands on his hips and tossed his head like a bullfighter. "It's finished," said João. He grabbed Rui's elbow and dragged him away.

Later a man came to the square and beckoned João. "You want to work?"

"Anything," said João. "Please."

"Come," said the man and turned around.

"My friend," said João, looking over at Rui, who whistled and kicked his heels against the wall.

The man kept walking.

"Wait," called João. "I'm coming."

He looked up and saw Rui's hat on a large stone, bathed in a circle of milky light. He imagined Rui sitting there, taking off his hat for the last time.

João's spine was stiff and there was an ache in his chest. He shifted in the damp grass and looked across and saw how oddly Rui's legs were lying. His trousers were hemmed with mud. One boot faced down and the other faced up. For us, thought João, there can be no ease.

He had been there as usual on Thursday, outside the Junta de Freguesia for the game. Everyone was there: José, Manuel, Nelson, Carlos, Abel, and the rest. Only Mario did not come, because Mario had broken his hip. "That Manuel," said Rui, "is a cheating bastard." "That Rui," said Manuel, "is a stupid donkey." Everything went on the way it had for the past eighteen years, since Rui turned up in Mamarrosa, though Rui and João had been the young ones then.

"Carlos," said Abel, "you bowl like a woman." "Shut up," said Carlos. "What do you know about women?"

Malhadinha was the best way for men to talk. You rolled the balls out onto the green and rolled the words out after them. You didn't have to face each other.

Afterward they locked the balls in the Junta and went to the café to drink.

"My granddaughter wants to go to Lisbon," said José.

"My son left London and went to Glasgow," said Rui.

"My daughter," said Carlos, "says she will throw me out if I cough once more in the night. But she always says that."

When it was time to go to bed, João walked with Nelson, and Rui walked with Manuel. Sometimes João walked with Manuel. Sometimes he walked with José or Antonio or Mario. But in all those years he had never walked alone with Rui.

João thought he did not want to be the one to return Rui's hat to his wife. He thought and thought about what to do. A bird flew down and landed on the hat's ridge. It was gold with a black head and black feet. João had never seen a bird like that before, and he knew it was a sign that he should keep the hat. Then he remembered about Rui's wife. Dona Rosa Maria had died not last year but the year before that. The day they buried her was a scorcher. July the fourth: memorial day of Isabella of Portugal, patron saint of difficult marriages and the falsely accused.

<hr />

When they met for the second time, they were men.

João passed the greenshirt parade in the Praça Souza Prado and climbed the steps up to the Rua Fortunato Simões Dos Santos, heading for his favorite bar. At the top of the steps, he turned and watched as a boy marched out of the ranks and raised his right arm in the infamous salute. João went into the bar and saw Rui. His skin had darkened and his nose was no longer fine (it looked as though it had been broken), but João knew it was Rui because he brought back the pain in João's stomach.

He was talking, drawing people in from the corners of the room. "All I am saying is that a man who owns ten thousand hectares or more and dines on six courses twice a day is living a life of excess. Doesn't the Public Man himself tell us we must restrain our desires?" Rui wore a checked shirt, a frayed jacket, and his hair dangerously long: It came to within an inch of his collar. "Nobody can contradict Salazar."

"But you speak like a . . . a . . ." The man sitting opposite Rui dropped his voice. "A Communist."

"'From each according to his ability, to each according to his needs.' That's what *they* say." Rui waved his hand. "Whoever heard such nonsense? Why should a man work according to his ability? Why should a man receive according to his needs? Imagine what would happen if people took this nonsense into their heads! Álvaro Cunhal"—he let the name of the Communist Party leader hang for a while—"must rot in his cell forever."

João knew what Rui was doing. He could see by the way the others shifted and glanced around that they knew too.

"We are with the other side," said Rui. He looked up and saw João, and something passed across his face. "Blackshirts and greenshirts stick together."

"Excuse me," said a little vole of a man sitting by the window, "but do you accuse Salazar of fascism?"

"Accuse?" said Rui. "I certainly accuse him of nothing. In 1945, when he decreed all flags to fly at half mast as a sign of respect for our dear departed Hitler, I saluted him. We supported the Germans, so of course it was a sad day for us all."

"But no," cried the little man with his lips aquiver, "we weren't with anybody."

"Oh," said Rui, stroking his nose, "I forget. But nevertheless, I am sad when I am told to be sad."

★   ★   ★

It was 1951, the third year João passed in Lindoso with his sister, her husband, their four children, and the husband's brother, mother, and aunt in a long low house with three doors and one window. In the season he cut cork, and when the season was over, he did whatever he could. Over the years he had been a grape picker, an olive picker, a goatherd; a tanner of hides in Olhão, a laborer on the roads in Ourique, and a gutter of fish in Portimão.

He tried to warn Rui. "There are spies," he said. "Informers. That little man with the shrunken head, how does he make his living? Nobody knows."

Rui shrugged. He felt his nose, pinching down from the bridge to the tip. He could never get used to his nose. "The PIDE pays him, I am sure. These secret police are not so secret."

"Please," said João. "Be careful."

Rui cast his line again into the dark waters of the Mira. "Nobody speaks more highly of Salazar than me."

He had been in France after the War, with all the other illegals, working the construction sites. He learned to read and write. "Liberté, egalité, fraternité," he said. "In France," he said, "a man has rights. He has dignity. He has respect."

"He has freedom," said João. He sat down on the riverbank.

Rui sat next to him. In the cafés and bars, you could not talk freely. Out here there was privacy.

João could hear Rui breathing. He could hear his heart beating, or perhaps that was his own heart, banging in its cage. He looked in Rui's face, and for a long moment they held each other's gaze. Rui looked away, as he always did.

"For the love of God," said João.

"Tell me about Portimão," said Rui.

In the months since they found each other in the Rua Fortunato Simões Dos Santos, João had told it many times. Rui wanted to know everything about the sardine-processing factory. The worker who read out articles from *Avante!*—who had snitched on him? What, exactly, did he look like? Was João sure he did not come from Aljustrel, because he sounded like a Comrade that Rui had met there. He wanted to know as well: Did the men respond? Were they interested in joining the Party? Did they see that the means of production should be owned by the people? Did they understand about surplus value?

João did not like to think about the factory. Rui kept making him describe the workers' barracks. The smell there was, if anything, worse than in the main building. The floor was a permanent slime: the result of loose tiles, faulty drains, blocked souls.

"There's nothing more to tell," said João. What would happen if he put his hand on Rui's cheek? Just to think about it made him tremble.

"The barracks," said Rui, "did it bring men closer, living together like that?"

"No," said João harshly. He thought about the men he had known there who came to his bunk at night, who had wives waiting at home, children to be fed.

"All right," said Rui. "Let's be quiet, then. We are not afraid of silence."

They looked down at the Mira, the never-ending pilgrimage of water, moving blindly, relentlessly on. A rowboat went by. Rui touched his hat.

João turned his head to Rui. Rui would not look at him. João kept waiting, out of spite. If he put his hand between Rui's legs, if he led him up a dark alley and turned around, if he took him into the woods and dropped to his knees and kept his eyes down—these things Rui would accept. João wasn't having it. His desire was so strong it felt like hate.

"Salazar," said Rui, who was, after all, afraid of silence, "has not told a single truth from the day he was born. If he tells you that the sun will rise in the east, you know it will rise in the west. But we keep pretending to believe his lies. That's the problem with our people. If you pretend for long enough, you forget you were only pretending in the first place. The illusion becomes a kind of reality." He looked underneath his jacket where he had thrown it down and found the tin of bait and then began to wind in his line. "It's like me. I didn't start coming to the river to fish, but now I think I'm a fisherman."

"Why did you come, then?" said João, wanting to hear it.

"I'll tell you something," said Rui, finally letting his eyes meet João's. It was safe now that he was standing. "Salazar has told so many lies that his tongue has begun to rot. Really, it is what I heard. That's why he likes to hide away. Yes, my friend, it is true. This is true: Salazar's tongue is black."

Not long after, they took him far away, to Porto. Within a day or two it was known over the town that the address of the PIDE headquarters in Porto was 329 Rua do Heroismo. It was said that the back door connected with a cemetery.

João's nephew, who was in the Portuguese Youth, drilling every Wednesday and Saturday afternoon with a wooden gun, said, "Will they nail his wee-wee to the wall?"

"Get out," said João. "Is that what they teach you? Get out."

Everybody knew the stories. They beat a pregnant woman on the belly. They burned a man's hands and threw him out of the top-floor window. They made prisoners do "the statue," standing by a wall for ten days at a time with only their fingertips touching it. Everybody knew the stories. The children seemed to know them first.

João was getting a cramp. He needed to stand up. He pushed Rui's hip gently to roll him off. The bone was sharp beneath his hand. He slid his palm up beneath the undershirt and felt the stomach, the ribs, the looseness of the skin like a newborn calf's. The scent of eucalyptus anointed the day as the heat rose up from the ground. Somewhere a dog began to moan. The cork trees kept their counsel. It was two hundred years old, the tree that Rui had chosen. Eighty-four years was barely a beginning.

João went over to the large stone and picked up the hat. The felt was warm between his fingers. He sat down on the stone and put the hat on his head. Where were the tears? Why didn't they come?

He looked down at some old goat droppings and thought about the posters all over the village. PCP, they said in large red letters. A hammer and sickle sat proud in the top corner. VALEU A PENA LUTAR!

The struggle was worthwhile! Fifty years ago men died for the right to say so. Even those who remained alive died a little. What did the young ones think? What did they think when they looked at Rui, his squashed nose, his whiskery ears, the humble bend in his back? Of course they never looked; and the struggle belonged to them now, and it was not of a kind that João could understand. João lifted his eyes. "What do you think?" he asked Rui. "Shall we say this, as our last rites, that it was all worthwhile?"

They had one night together, when Rui brought his broken nose and his bruised limbs and heart and his green eyes that had lost their lashes back from Porto and knocked at one of the three doors on the long low house. The others moved out of their way, and João held Rui afterward, their feet pushed up against the rusting iron bed frame, knowing they could be heard, that his sister and brother-in-law would listen in the dark and hold their breath and think that the weeping was for the torture that had been, when it was only for the torture that was about to begin.

Rui would not be alone with him after that. Within six months he had married. Dona Rosa Maria was the local mortician's daughter. She had an overbite and a way of holding her hands behind her back that made it look as if she were hiding something, a pancreas, perhaps, or a kidney. Two months later they moved away. That night a man followed João out of the bar, and they went together into the woods.

*　*　*

A cuckoo called out, fell silent, and began again. A bird, thought João, never has to think about what to do next. This reflection struck him now with tremendous force, as if it had never before entered his head. A bird always knows how he feels. If he is hungry he will look for food. If he is frightened he will fly away. If he needs a mate he will find one. He is either hungry or not hungry. He is either frightened or not frightened. He knows when to be quiet, and he knows when to sing.

João went to lie down with Rui. He closed his eyes and put his hand along Rui's shoulder and stroked at his collarbone; he put his fingertips on the rope around his neck; he followed the bruise spreading like an ink stain up to his ear, which was cool and soft as a puffball; if he pressed down hard, it would explode in a gentle cloud. Rui's papery scalp showed through his thin white hair, spotted brown with age and red, perhaps, with death. João inched his head closer to Rui. He wanted to smell him. All he could smell was the life of the forest floor. "So many lies," he said to Rui. "Every day and every day, the lies."

For a long while he lay there against the body. "Let me feel something," he pleaded, as bitterness welled like blood in a deep white wound. When desire is gone, he thought, this is all that remains.

Before Rui moved to Mamarrosa, João saw him only once again. João was in São Teotónio visiting his youngest brother. He walked through the little town looking for something and saw a woman scrubbing clothes in the *tanque* outside the Casa do Povo. Dona Rosa Maria straightened up and slipped her hands behind her back.

She led João the two miles to the house, balancing a large basket on her head and speaking barely a word. There were rows of tomatoes and beans outside the house and, as well, a row of children who tugged at her dress as she passed.

Rui sat at a table fashioned from rough planks. He stood up when he saw João, then sank back down and said, "You've come."

Rui was a truck driver's assistant, and his work took him away from home for days at a time. "When I am at home," he said, "I sleep." He looked at the children who had gathered around, the youngest still unsteady on his feet, as if wondering where they had sprung from.

They drank rough red wine while Dona Rosa filled a large iron with hot charcoal and worked on the end of the table.

"My woman," said Rui, pressing at his nose, "works as a maid at the doctor's house. This is her day off, but she is ironing their clothes."

They finished the wine, and Rui roared at Dona Rosa to walk back to the town to buy more. He leaned forward and clamped his hands on his knees. His eyelashes had grown back white. "I'm still part of it," he said. "Those bastards."

"You are careful, I hope," said João.

"Yes, of course." He shook his head. "A change is coming. This is what I know. A change is coming, my friend, and then it will no longer be our turn to be careful."

They drank more and spoke less, and João spent the night on a rag rug in front of the hearth with a dog curled up on his feet and the sound of five small breathing bodies in the room.

In the morning Rui went out before it was light, and Dona Rosa kicked João's shoulder to wake him. It was raining, and Dona Rosa pulled a shawl over her head and locked the little ones inside to keep them dry while she went to cook for the doctor and his wife and their children.

João looked up at the tittering leaves. I am old and I am calm, he thought. It is not wisdom. It is not experience. It is the passing of desire. Change had come, was still coming. To think that change was once something to be struggled for!

The cork oaks that had stood two hundred years, how much longer would they stand? João had not seen it with his own eyes, but he had heard that there were plastic corks for wine bottles now. No, nothing was safe from change.

The big estates broke up, as Rui said they would, after the revolution he had always known would come. But the workers' collectives were mostly gone too. The landowners, born to win, bought the land back dirt cheap. And now they were selling it. There was talk of a six-hundred-bed hotel down at the coast, a golf course, a park with water slides. Some said Japanese owners. Some said Marco Afonso Rodrigues was coming back and it was he who would build this hotel.

Rui used to say, "We should drive them out of their *quintas*." The Germans, the Dutch, and the British were taking care of that.

When Rui and Dona Rosa came to live in Mamarrosa, all their children, the three who had lived, had gone to work abroad.

"They are good children," said Rui. "Real workers."

João was shocked at the thinness of his hair, the slope of his shoulders.

"They never forget us," Rui would say, meaning they sent money back.

And at other times, "They have forgotten us," meaning they did not often come home.

They met every Thursday for the game and in between in the street and in the bread shop. "Oh," complained Rui once when the bread was baked too hard, "things are not the same anymore."

João cradled Rui's head in his lap. Rui was never afraid of death. That he had proved long ago. There was only one thing that scared him; one thing he would never say. João smiled now because he finally understood that in death Rui had spoken. He looked up at the branch, the lovely moss-skinned branch that Rui had chosen on this tree in this place and no other, where he had, in silence, told the truth at last.

João looked into Rui's face. One eyelid was nearly all the way down, as far as it would stretch across the eyeball, which seemed almost to burst from the socket. The eyebrows were long and white and curling. There was a purple bruise across his nose. Rui's mouth had fixed open to make his final admission. The tongue, his tongue, was turning black.

Two

The Potts girl walked into the café preceded by her reputation so that everyone was obliged to stare. Even Stanton, who had not been in Mamarrosa a month, looked her over once more than was strictly necessary. Vasco, stuffed behind the grand Formica counter, served her with pineapple Sumol and unsmiling vigilance. The girl sat on the edge of the pool table swinging her legs and examining her navel stud. Her hair fell forward, revealing an ugly brown hearing aid, and Stanton averted his eyes.

Conversation spluttered and died on the lips like a lie discovered and was just as suddenly resurrected. The old men stood at the bar caressing their Macieiras and coughing up memories. In their black felt fedoras and black waistcoats, red handkerchiefs tied at the neck, they appeared to Stanton like postcards from the past, as picturesque as the crooked streets, the whitewashed houses, the doors and windows framed gaily in blue and yellow.

A young mother scolded and slapped and kissed her child, the love exhaled as palpable as the smoke from her cigarette.

"Always they are hitting," said Dieter.

Stanton looked away, out the open door, at the sun riding high over the far ridged hills. It couldn't be long before noon. Even eleven-thirty was respectable for beer. He waited for Vasco, cleaning ashtrays with a damp rag, to look his way, but Vasco kept watch over the Potts girl. Stanton went up to the counter and nodded to the old men. *"O Escritor,"* they said, as if for the first time. It was a fine joke.

"Yes, sir?" Vasco addressed Stanton warmly as a fellow man-of-the-world. He wiped the counter with commendable vigor, particularly for a man of his girth. Vasco was always wiping. It was a habit acquired from his legendary stint as a barman in Provincetown, Cape Cod, the United States of America. He had made his own innovation, though, in using the same unwashed rag for all purposes, shifting ash and dirt from surface to surface.

Stanton ordered two Sagres and was grateful to the Potts girl and her soft white belly for Vasco's preoccupation.

"I was thinking," said Dieter, stroking an eyebrow, "if you make the final payment in cash, you can forget about the EVA, the tax. Save a lot of money." He shrugged. "If you like, I will come with you now to the bank."

"But the *fossa,*" Stanton said. "It leaks. The work's not finished."

Dieter worried tobacco into a paper skin. His fingers were callused and nicotine-stained. "This is a—what do you say?—bad understanding." He had a tall man's slouch even when seated, and his chest, though broad, appeared concave. His hair, dark full curls, was cut into layers falling almost to his shoulders and brushed to a sickening sheen. Without glancing across the room, Stanton thought of the Potts girl's mousy strings. "The septic tank is an open system," Dieter went on. "That is what we call this. Solid waste is kept inside. The water passes outside through a filter. No, it is a bad understanding."

"Misunderstanding," said Stanton. "But it isn't. I didn't choose to have that system because it was more expensive. I didn't have enough money for that."

Dieter produced a smile. "Lucky man," he said. "You pay for closed, but you get open. For you this is very lucky."

"The damn thing leaks," said Stanton. He knocked a fly away. "And there are no tiles on the bathroom floor."

The builder shook his head. The curls bounced indecently. "The work is good. You don't want to pay, but the work is good." He lit his cigarette and sucked hard. He shook his head and sulked.

My new friend, said Stanton to himself. He thought with bitterness of the friends he had left behind, though he had not been sad to part. Dieter touched his arm. "Look," he said, indicating the men at the counter. "Brandy before noon. Impossible in this country to get anything done. In Germany—the workers, they work. Here . . ." He flicked his hair back in an oddly feminine gesture, using the back of his hand. "You see the problems. You suffer, my friend, and I suffer also."

"So you'll get it fixed?" said Stanton. "And the tiles. You know none of the internal doors are on?"

"Bastards," said Dieter. "Another drink?"

Stanton looked at his watch. "Why not?" The day was ruined anyway. He would go back, tussle briefly with the computer, develop a fever, prescribe an afternoon of research, spend a listless couple of hours with his books, go for a walk to clear his head, and return in time for sundowners. Each stage would develop inevitably into the next, all with equal futility. "If you don't have any work to do," he said, not caring to hide his tone.

"Too much," Dieter complained. He picked up the beer glasses, and Stanton saw that the calluses were beginning to soften, white rings around the yellow. There was a commotion at the back of the room. Stanton turned and saw the Potts girl move across the café, something insolent in her walk. Behind the counter, Vasco waved his short arms.

"Ladra!" Vasco screamed. Thief. He lifted a hatch and squeezed out, the operation hampered by his considerable size.

The girl turned at the door, donned a monstrous pair of sunglasses, flicked a V sign, and disappeared. Vasco stood panting. He had to have his trousers specially made, but they did not seem large enough now that his belly heaved and shook with exertion and emotion. His customers—those who had risen—retook their seats, clicking their tongues. Vasco trembled his way to the revolving rack over by the cigarette machine. He passed a hand over the postcards, comics, chewing gum, toy guns, and sunglasses, perhaps to divine what else was missing, perhaps to comfort his remaining stock. It was some time before he grew calm enough to serve beer again.

"But they do not go directly to the police," moaned Dieter. "In Germany it would be—*ja, ja*." He broke off as if even he had heard it too many times. "But do you know about that family? They live one, two kilometers from your house. English neighbors."

Stanton had heard some things. "Not really."

Dieter rolled another cigarette, spilling tobacco over his jeans. "The father is, you know." He tapped the side of his head. "*Louco.* When they came here, he had money. Maybe drugs money, who knows? He asks me to build a swimming pool. They are living in a caravan, but he wants a pool. So I bring the diggers, and before the pool is finished, he says now we build the house. I stop the pool and I start the house, but before the roof is done, money has gone. The wife is like . . ." Dieter thought for a moment. "What do you call this piece of material for cleaning the plates? A dishcloth, yes, dishcloth. There is a boy, about eleven, twelve," he said quickly, eager to pass on to the main topic, "and, of course, this girl Ruby. She has left the school, she has nothing to do but make trouble. There was a fight between her and the whores up at the brothel. Know where it is? By the GNR. The police look out for the girls. This fight—I heard it was really something—the whores said she ruined their business, giving it away for free." He shifted his knees and bumped the table and steadied it. "That is the story. Probably it isn't true. But it is the story."

Stanton pictured the girl, her T-shirt sawn off below the breasts, her fuck-you walk, the ludicrous stolen sunglasses crusted with butterflies. Fifteen, maybe sixteen. Anemic skin and dimpled knees. Unattractive, uneducated, disabled. That hearing aid was prehistoric. "Poor bitch," he said and got up, deciding against another beer and for a Macieira.

Stanton went outside to the pickup and pressed his hand against the door panel where the sun had glazed the red metal white. He drove out of the village, past the lines of orange trees that bordered the narrow sidewalks, past the water pump where a bent old woman filled plastic containers, past the small square with garish flower beds and dark green frog-plagued pond, and turned right after the traffic lights, which were there not to control the traffic (of which there was a dearth) but to raise a flag to the future.

He entered the house and went straight to the computer in the bedroom. All the furniture had ended up there, apart from a couple of chairs and a stool on the terrace. In his mind, a correlation had grown between the emptiness of the house and the quality of his work, the sparseness of one promising the fullness of the other. He read over the last few pages on the screen, making deletions and additions and willing himself into the story. He stood up and sat back down. He set his jaw and willed himself submerged. It was hopeless. It was like deciding to commit suicide and trying to drown with your face in the washbasin.

He closed his computer and resolved to suffer no more interruptions to his mornings. Taking his book, he went to the terrace and looked out over the garden to the cork oaks beyond, the rich earth-red trunks where the bark had been harvested, the spreading mossy branches that reached back to some ancient time. Stanton sat down and opened the book and was immediately distracted by a lizard flickering in and out of an empty flowerpot. He returned to the book, trudged through half a chapter, then hurled it down into the garden.

It was possibly the worst book he had ever tried to read. He decided this and instantly felt bloated with research. He was like a sumo wrestler stepping into ballet shoes and hoping to pirouette. What more, in any case, could he learn about Blake? If he knew *less* about him, it would be easier to write the novel. Hell, he might even be able to make some things up.

Without locking the door, a habit he had forced himself to break, he went down the steps from the terrace and turned out of the garden and past the tender-leafed eucalyptus that said shush-shush and were still and stirred and quieted again. He walked his usual track into the cork oak woods that began where the eucalyptus left off, with no sense of relish except for the gin he would pour when he got home. There were pines dotted among the corks, and he picked up a cone, carried it for a while, and let it drop.

The trees spread thinly, giving way now and then to grass and sheep. Over his shirt the shepherd wore a sheepskin, a hole cut for his head and a string tied in place around the middle. Stanton waved. All day—the man spent all day watching sheep. The thinness of his own endeavor was shaming.

Coming into a clearing where some old trees had been felled and the spring flowers grew more intense, he paused. There were anemones here, cistus and soapwort and wild geranium. The gorse spurted yellow over the tree stumps.

"You're English," said the boy. Stanton had not noticed him approach.

"Hello, compatriot," he said.

The boy grew unsure. He beheaded flowers with his stick.

"We're both English," said Stanton.

"Watch this," said the boy and threw the stick. It arced high and landed a distance off in the *silves*.

"Good throw."

"Yeah," said the boy. "Thanks." He smiled and rubbed a hand over his head, which was just about shaved, the scalp showing pinkly through. Lice, thought Stanton. A sneeze of freckles covered the bridge of the boy's nose and strayed to his cheeks. It was a nice face, open and willing.

"You write books," said the boy. "I like your truck."

"I'm heading back," said Stanton.

"Me too."

They walked together in the rutted track. The boy stamped his feet in the grass to make the crickets jump about. His shoes looked as if they might not last the journey home. He found a piece of marbled stone, swooped, and put it in his pocket.

"What's your name?" asked Stanton.

"Jay," said the boy. "Jay Potts. We used to have a truck like yours."

"What happened?"

The boy raised his thin arms. "Crashed it."

"Dad or mum?"

"Me." He left a long pause, and when Stanton did not fill it, he went on. "I only drive off the main roads. You know, on tracks like this 'round our house or in the field. Don't know what happened, really. All I know is it ended up smashed on a fig tree and I had to have one of those neck things for weeks."

Stanton laughed. "What you driving these days, then?"

"Well, me dad had a tractor and he used to let me drive that sometimes but now he's turned it over in the ditch and we can't get it out. And we've got the Renault Four, but I don't drive that. Don't ask me why."

"Why?" said Stanton.

"I don't know," said Jay. "Don't ask me."

An owl flew across the trees, coming low against the path. "He's up early," said Stanton. He thought about having orange with his gin this evening, getting some vitamin C. "So, do you go to school, or do you have more important business to attend to?"

They came up to the shepherd, and Stanton exchanged *boas noites,* and the boy spoke Portuguese, his accent so thick that Stanton could not understand. They went up the hill toward the house, the eucalyptus coming into view, watery now in the lowering light. The evening lay in prospect, and Stanton began to sag.

"We don't have to keep talking," said the boy. "I'll just walk with you."

A pair of rangy cypress trees marked the entrance to the property. "Funeral trees," Dieter had said when he came to give his estimate. They flanked every cemetery, growing tall and fat on the underground deposits. Jay stood with his hands on his hips. He stared at the ground and kicked his heels in the dust. "Well," said Stanton. Jay looked away as if a difficult issue had been raised.

"I might have some Coke in the fridge."

* * *

They drank on the terrace and watched the sun slide down the sky. At first Stanton was glad of the boy's presence, as if there were something unpleasant he should be doing that he could put off for a while longer. Jay sipped his drink, making it last. His bare arms were thin but sinewy, blueprinted for muscle. He didn't speak, barely moved, hoping perhaps to be forgotten.

Nothing changed, but everything began to look different. The boy was in the way. Stanton focused on a distant hill, the one shaped like a pyramid, and tried to block out this singular oppression. Slowly the feeling grew that the boy was preventing him from getting on with his evening, though in truth he had nothing to do. He was about to speak when Jay jumped up. "Best be off." On the steps, he turned. "I like your truck."

"You can ride in it one day," said Stanton, restored and generous. "I'm driving."

He opened a bottle of *vinho verde* and went to the bedroom. Sitting on the edge of the bed, he drank and watched the shadows on the wall. If a man is to have success, he thought, it is better for it to come later in life. Not so late that he has too little time to appreciate it. But not so soon that he has too little experience to appreciate it. It was not the first time he had thought this, but it was the first time today, and that, he considered, was a sort of progress.

Stanton worked. As he had no curtains he woke with the sun, and instead of turning the sheets up over his head, he rose and went to the table. The days lengthened. Soon it seemed that he had hardly gotten to bed before the sun came calling. Still he rose and would not be beaten. In the afternoons he reviewed what he had written and held despair at bay with savage cuts and a bottle of the local brandy. Dieter learned to stay away until after five. Sometimes they drank on the terrace; more often they went to the village. Dieter found a woman. Dutch, big-boned, with a disappointed face. "It is ridiculous," she would say. "These Portuguese." Tapping two fingers on the table, Dieter nodding along. Stanton's silence, he supposed, appeared as affirmation, but he did not care. All their complaining was a tonic, an inoculation against this *estrangeiro* malaise.

The Potts girl haunted the village. She was always on her own. Even when she was with people, she was by herself. Stanton saw her in the bar next door to the Casa do Povo, sitting on a table, feet on a chair, pretending not to notice the local lads looking up her skirt. She wore tie-dyed skirts with tasseled fringes wrapped low on her darkening belly, a charm bracelet on each wrist, and always the sunglasses. She never looked too clean. Stanton saw her in the pharmacy buying bandages, and when he heard her speak, it took a few seconds before he understood that it was not only her accent that thickened the words. She turned around and stepped right up to him. She smelled of earth. The sunglasses hid her eyes. There was a little mole right beneath her nose. She spoke to him in English. "You seen enough now?" Congested vowels and macerated diction. She must lip-read, thought Stanton. "Yes," he said, without making a sound.

For a while Jay seemed to live in the woods. Stanton had to walk the other way if he wanted to be alone. Then school finished for the summer, and the boy started dropping around to the house. "I'm working," Stanton said. "I know," said Jay. "I'll just be in the garden." Stanton did not want him in his garden. "I'll do some work for you," Jay said. "Clear some weeds or something." They looked down into the garden, the small orchard of lemons and oranges and peaches choked with brambles, the oleander collapsing under its own weight, the rest of the ground rubbed red and brown in the heat. "Or I can get your shopping for you. I'm good at shopping."

Sometimes he hung around climbing the fruit trees or bouncing a ball on the terrace. Other days Stanton sat with him and talked about football or Spider-Man or animals. "When I grow up," said Jay with doomed earnestness, "I want to work with animals."

"Vet?" said Stanton, being unkind.

"No," said Jay. "I don't think I'll get all them exams."

Stanton was sorry. "Ah, well. There's lots of ways of working with animals. I bet you're good with animals."

"I've got a puppy. Do you want to come and see it? I take the goats out sometimes, you know, graze them, and I feed the pigs. Me mum feeds the chickens. Don't ask me why."

"Why?" said Stanton.

"I don't know," said Jay, creasing his toasted freckled face. "Don't ask me."

He always left before Stanton said it was time to go, as if he could see the clouds gathering. And he said little about his family. It was pleasant, Stanton guessed, to take a break from being the Potts boy.

Chrissie came looking for him one day. Stanton watched the Renault 4 splutter over the gravel and knew it would be her. "I'm Chrissie," she said, "Jay's mum."

"Yes. Harry Stanton."

They stood there. Chrissie held her head to one side as if listening for an announcement. She swayed slightly on her feet, though this may have been an illusion, a quality of her paper-thin body and the air she carried with her, that she might at any moment melt away.

"He's not here, is he?" she said at length.

"No," said Stanton.

Chrissie perched on the stool. There was a light sheen of sweat on her upper lip and in the cleft between her breasts, her shirt unbuttoned almost below the bra. "He's been bothering you. I've spoken to him about it." She was, Stanton realized, taking pains with her speech. Talking posh to the writer.

"Not at all. Drink?"

When he came back with the beers, Chrissie was scratching her forearms. They were pitted with scars and traversed with red and purple welts. She tugged her sleeves down. "He's not such a bad kid. But he's got no discipline. I try to tell him. But does he listen?" She sniffed to indicate that he did not. "I do tell him to go to school," she said peevishly. "Did he tell you he's being kept down a year?"

"Oh ... well ..." said Stanton. "He ... loves the outdoors. And animals." He thought if you fed her up and put her in decent clothes, she would not be bad-looking. Her mouth was fashionably wide and her cheekbones high. She was perhaps ten years younger than him, mid-thirties. In another setting, with another attitude, she could be attractive: fey and otherworldly rather than blown about. What was the word Dieter used? Dishcloth. Not the right word but not a bad try.

"You don't want to end up like your sister, I tell him, but what good does it do?"

"Ruby, isn't it?" Those arms, though. What would you do with them?

"Ruby," said Chrissie. "You know."

"She'll grow out of it," he said. How banal he had become.

Chrissie looked at him sharply, then lapsed into self-pity. "I've had a hell of a time with her."

"It's difficult," said Stanton, wondering how to get rid of her. "These days it's difficult."

"You got kids, Harry?"

"No. No kids."

"Just as well," she said. "You being a writer," she added. "Need your peace and quiet, I expect."

"Actually—"

"I thought it would be better out here. It has been better," she improvised, "in some ways. Have you met my husband?"

"Ah, not yet," said Stanton. There was a fly crawling down her neckline and onto the curve of her breast. Four months since he'd had sex. There was nothing you could do with those arms.

"He don't . . . he doesn't go out much. You'll have to pay a visit. You know where we are."

He could have walked her to the car then. Instead he fetched another beer and let her talk. It could have been the sweat gathering in the hollow of her neck. But it was not that. He wanted something from her, and it was not sex but something baser. One day, he knew, he would write about this place.

She appeared once more at his door, and this time it was morning and she was not interesting. "I'm interrupting," she said, miserable, when he poked his head out. "He's not here," he told her. She swayed and rubbed her arms and gave off such a general air of hopelessness that Stanton wanted to kick her. "If you see him," she said and ran down the stairs to the car. Stanton went to his cell cursing the whole damn family.

In the evenings Vasco produced white paper tablecloths and three dishes of the day, which were always piri-piri chicken, pork with clams, and a grilled fish with boiled potatoes. "Mr. Stanton," he said, "what do you think of this war in Iraq? Everyone here is against it, apart from the government, of course." He handed out the menus. "Terrible business," said Stanton, pretending to study the items. "Exactly," cried Vasco. The way he squeaked still surprised Stanton, who always expected a baritone from a fat man. "Exactly, terrible business, but has to be done. Everyone is saying to me, 'Oh, they make the Empire, these Americans.' And I tell them, 'Shut up, what do you know?' Of course they make the Empire. United States of America will not be threatened. We had a big empire too—" Vasco turned purple and began to wheeze, tears in his eyes. It dawned on Stanton that he was laughing. "Five hundred years ago."

Dieter and his Dutch woman had chicken, and Stanton had a fish that kept watching him as he ate it. "I heard," said Dieter, "that Ruby is pregnant."

The Dutch woman said, "Who is the father? She probably doesn't know." She snorted and tapped the table.

An unbidden image entered Stanton's mind: the Dutch woman astride Dieter, tensing her buttocks, shaking her breasts, snorting. The couple spoke briefly together in German. He touched her knee and she stroked his hair, which Stanton found repulsive.

There was the brothel next to the GNR. Dieter went there sometimes, only for a drink, he said. Portuguese women—Stanton had decided years ago and confirmed it many times since—were not beautiful. Even the best-looking ones had something wrong, some fatal flaw: bad teeth or eyebrows that met or a figure that would be perfect save for the pigeon toes. It marred their beauty, but it did not always make them unattractive. Sometimes it was precisely what made them desirable.

The Dutch woman said, "I am sick to death of seeing all the donkeys here."

"Oh, absolutely right," said Dieter.

"The way they tie them, back legs like this," said the woman. She brought her arms parallel and close together to demonstrate. "It's so cruel."

"The dogs too," said Dieter. "So badly treated. In Germany you would be locked up."

Vasco came personally to clear the table, an honor he reserved for Stanton. "In Provincetown we did four, five hundred covers a night." He looked around at the empty tables. "Imagine. Four, five hundred." He rolled away, balancing the plates.

"I think," said Stanton, "that Ruby has an addict for a mother."

"Chrissie? You mean her arms, *ja*?" Dieter unfolded his legs and stretched out. His crotch bulged. Stanton wondered what his story was. To ask would break the agreement. It was comfortable to drink with a man who didn't bother you that way.

"Needle marks."

Dieter shrugged. "Maybe. I don't think so."

"What, then?"

"Fleas." He smiled. "Go to the house. Then you see what I mean."

"But the boy doesn't have them," said Stanton. "Or the girl."

"I'll ask you—do you get mosquito bites?"

Stanton said that he didn't, not very many.

"Me, they leave alone also. But some people"—Dieter raised his beer—"they fall in love with. What I mean is, some people just have bad luck."

The Dutch woman pursed her lips. "There is a reason for everything," she said with false humility. "Even if we do not know it. You say bad luck. Better perhaps to say bad karma."

There were few interruptions to his days. He saw less of Dieter, preferring on many evenings to share his sundowner with the shepherd, with whom conversation was not required nor, indeed, possible. He had reached the part of Blake's life that he called the country interlude, a three-year stay on the Sussex estate of William Hayley, the poet's patron. Stanton invented a milky-skinned maid with startled eyes and gave her to Blake as an experiment in passion that exceeded all visions. This morning, though, the work faltered. Breaking his rule, he left his computer and walked out into the garden under the hammering sun. The earth, dry and dead, crumbled beneath his feet. He walked to the far boundary, where a wild vine covered the stone wall. The grapes were small but soft. He tasted one and spat it out.

At the northeast corner of the garden was an olive tree. It was a hideous old thing, twisted and scarred and clinging to life. Stanton walked to it. He had been twenty-eight when his first novel was published. *Paradigms in Eight Tongues*. How much easier it was to write then, thinking he knew about life.

If a man is to have success, he thought now, it is better that it comes later, when he can really appreciate it.

A handful of succulents dotted the stony ground, timid little blue flowers among the spiky leaves, but most of the earth here was exhausted. Stanton surveyed his domain, black sunspots dancing in his eyes. He pushed on around to the far side of the house and slid a short way on loose clods, down to where the septic tank was buried and the grass grew long and lush.

*   *   *

The next day was Sunday. Stanton rose early, as usual, but decided to rest. He lay all morning on the kitchen floor, where it was coolest. He read four short stories from a collection of New Writing that had been sent by a newspaper shortly before he left London. They would have another reviewer by now, of course. What would he have said in a review? He could barely muster an opinion. It was too hot. He dozed on the floor and dreamed of a dog with orange eyes that stole into bed with him and closed its jaws around the back of his neck.

He woke in the afternoon with pain shooting from his shoulder down his right arm. He was filled with remorse for the wasted day. Rubbing his arm, he went to wash and accused his reflection of many things. He brushed his teeth, drank a beer, and brushed his teeth again. Then he drove to the village, parked outside Vasco's place thinking he would come down soon for a drink, and walked up the narrow streets toward the church. Two cars passed him, Stanton flattening against the walls to let them through. When he got to the marketplace, a patch of rough ground bisected by the steeple's shadow, people were still setting up. It was billed as a *festa,* a fete, but in England it would be called a car boot sale.

Some people had tables; others put their wares on a blanket or directly on the ground. An old man sold wood carvings. Another sold herbs grown in sawn-off plastic bottles. The local crafts cooperative displayed rugs and hand-painted tiles. There were piles of secondhand books and comics. There were glowing jars of honey and glinting bottles of olive oil. A woman with a gold brooch and silver sandals sat behind her scales weighing out bread and cakes. There were families who had cleared out their junk and spilled it in front of their cars. A vase, a radiator, old shoes, wooden bowls, lidless teapots, broken furniture, mysterious plastic objects of indeterminate use. These same families wandered the market acquiring other, equally useless possessions with which to replace those they hoped to sell.

All the *estrangeiros* are here, thought Stanton as he watched Ralf pressing orange juice on his bizarre contraption. Several of the German crowd hung next to him, trailing children in combat gear or miniature hippie dresses. Ralf had an old sewing table that he had converted into a juicing machine. With his feet, he worked the treadle, which spun a rod, which pressed a lever, which pumped up and down on a little plastic orange squeeze. To fill one cup took an age. Ralf charged one euro per cup.

"Now, why is that so fucking beautiful?" The voice had that dragging time-lag quality peculiar to the hardened drinker.

Stanton became aware that he had fallen into a kind of trance, watching the treadle move up and down and the rod go around and around. The heat could do that to you.

The man who had spoken sniffed loudly. Out of the corner of his eye, Stanton saw that the sniff had come too late. A long string of snot fell from his nose to the ground. The man turned and offered his hand. "Michael Potts. Everyone calls me China. Call me whatever you like. Who said that thing about a name being like a torch?"

"I'm afraid I don't know," said Stanton, shaking hands. Potts wore the filthiest pair of jeans he had ever seen.

"Might have been me. Got a pitch over there, mate. Come and see us."

Stanton wanted to get back to Vasco's, but Jay got to him first. "Bought anything?" Stanton shook his head. "Thought I might get some things for the kitchen. Plates, you know, and things."

"Got this." Jay held up a little glass ball filled with colored water. "You hang it on a string and it keeps the flies away."

"Oh," said Stanton. "How does it work?"

"Dunno. Probably doesn't. Look who I found."

Chrissie sat in the open hatch of the Renault 4. On a blanket at her feet she had arranged a few pans with broken handles and some rusting agricultural equipment. Her skirt looked like one of Ruby's, swirling patterns in purple and pink. She had better legs than Ruby. "Don't be a pest, Jay."

Stanton picked up a tool, a clipper or shear of some kind with a semicircular aperture. "What's this for?"

"Bullock castrator," said Chrissie. "China wants to ask you something."

China came up with a bag of cakes. He gave it to Jay. "Make yourself sick now, carn'ya?" He had red eyes and blasted cheeks. There was something about the way he stood that made Stanton think he had once carried muscle, though that time had long since passed. Another burnt-out case. "Listen, mate. I need a favor. Need to borrow that lovely truck of yours."

There was no way he was going to the Potts house. Stanton sat on the terrace nursing a gin and orange and looking at his truck. He didn't mind doing anyone a favor. But he could not get involved. Once he went over, they would start to assume. A pair of jays danced over the hood and went off squabbling into the woods. He had come out here to work. He had come to be alone. They cared nothing for that, and he—the heat of indignation rising now—did not care to be involved.

He drove over around five o'clock, a bottle of Macieira on the passenger seat. The house was in a valley at the end of a track that took senseless sharp turns, twisting first one way then the other. There was bamboo down here and a weeping willow and a false pepper tree by the first outbuilding. The light showed gold through the corks on the hillside. This place could be beautiful.

Stanton passed the wrecked truck. The boy had been lucky. There were several other cars down here, carcasses really, brambles growing out of their ribs. He parked a short distance from the house. The smell was terrible. Beyond the house was a series of caravans and some more outbuildings. A calf wandered up from behind the van and poked its head through the window. It made a tragic noise.

China came out from the house. Stanton climbed down and walked through a cowpat. "Shit."

"Mind yourself."

China led him through the manure. "There she is," he said, bending into the trench. "Apple of my eye, she was. Cracker."

The air was thick with the stench. Stanton could hardly breathe. "I've brought a rope," he said and went back to the truck, gagging.

The rest of the family gathered. "Want to hold her?" asked Jay, offering his puppy. "Knew you'd like her."

"Trust you to get in the way." Chrissie had slides in her hair. Lipstick on her mouth—a bad color, too orange.

Ruby sat on an old crate holding her nose.

"Jay," China bellowed. "Get out of the fucking way."

The cow had fallen into the trench at the back of the house and broken her back. China had dug it, he explained, because the house was getting damp. "Drainage, like," he said. The plaster had come away from the outside wall, exposing the clay bricks beneath. Stanton wondered about the foundations.

"Fucking council," said China. "They're supposed to come and take it away. You can't leave a fucking dead cow like that. Fucking health hazard."

"How long has she been there?" Even supposing the truck would take the weight and pull her out, what then? Was he supposed to take her away with him? Tow her back to his house?

Jay stood at Stanton's elbow, away from his father. "Five days. No, six. Took her a day to die."

"Jay," said his mother in a warning tone, unable to specify a crime.

"Right, that should do it," said China, patting the rope where he had tied it around the cow's neck. "Better back the truck a bit closer."

Stanton looked in the rearview mirror as he started the engine. The Potts family lined up at the edge of the trench, bathed in syrupy light. Sadness, like a rolling fog, closed in on him. I must stay away from them, he thought.

China banged on the side of the truck. "Mate," he shouted, as if proposing a pub crawl. "Let's go." Stanton put the engine into first and let the truck crawl forward until he felt the resistance. "Let's go. Go!" called China. Stanton moved into second and pressed gently on the accelerator. The truck made a sudden lurch.

"Good fucking God!" China yelled. Chrissie covered her face with her hands. The puppy jumped out of Jay's arms and ran for the house. Ruby moved forward with a curious expression, as if smiling through a great amount of pain.

"Christ," said Stanton when he saw what had happened.

"Cool," said Jay. "Look at all them maggots."

China began to laugh. He bent double and held his knees and laughed until he caught a coughing fit. The cow's head lay on the ground with the rope around its neck, spilling maggots and a fat black tongue.

"They went *flying*," said Jay. "Maggot bomb. You should've seen it."

Ruby crouched over the head. She seemed to be speaking to it. Little rolls of fat splayed out under her knees. Abruptly she got up and walked away.

Chrissie finished vomiting into the trench. She wiped the sides of her mouth with the back of her hand, tugged her skirt down, and smoothed the lap. "I don't know about anyone else," she said, patting her hair like a hostess whose guests have arrived a little early, "but I could use a drink."

They sat inside on high-backed leather-padded chairs and drank Stanton's Macieira. Ruby disappeared, and Jay played on the floor with the puppy. China smoked a joint and spread himself across his seat like a man preparing to hold court. "I'll tell you something," he said and tapped ash on the floor. "People look at me and they think"—he made a humming noise—"they think what a washout. What a sad fucking sack." He held up a hand as if to stay protests. "I know that. I ain't stupid. But I tell you something for free. All the things I wanted to do, I gone and done 'em. I never said to meself, 'Hang on, China, what's Auntie Maude going to say?' Fuck Auntie Maude, if you'll pardon the expression." He lifted the puppy on the end of his foot and tossed her gently back toward his son. "All right, some of the things I done are not that clever. Drugs are not clever.

But I done 'em because *I* wanted to, my choice, like. Cleaned me act up now, of course." He leaned across and poured another drink. Chrissie kicked off her sandal and massaged her foot. Her eyes met Stanton's for a moment, then they both looked away.

"'What does he want all them goats for?' That's what people say. Forty goats I got. You'll see 'em later. They know their way home, and when it starts to get dark, they always find the way. Jay'll go and get them if they don't. Won't you, Jay? I had the money, so I got 'em. People don't like that. You see—" He paused to toke hard and keep the smoke held in. Stanton thought, This is his favorite speech and it has to be savored. "If you have a desire, act on it—my personal philosophy of life. How many people do you see what are happy, truly happy?"

Stanton showed his palms.

"No, mate. You don't. You don't see 'em because they're grave-diggers. Burying their desires, the whole fucking lot. So fuck Auntie Maude, I say. Fuck the village. Fuck the lot. My personal philosophy. That dog's just pissed on the floor, Chrissie."

"Jay," said Chrissie, flexing her ankle.

"Run and get the goats, Jay," said China. "I'm going to show our guest around."

There was a pig in the first caravan. A little sink in there and a folding table. The windows had curtains too, a sophistication that the house lacked. The pig was expecting, China explained. He had to take her away from her mate, give her a little privacy now. The other two caravans were entirely derelict, but the way China saw it, they'd get restored, get back on the road one day. They picked a path through goat dung, cowpats, and chicken shit. Stanton was beginning to itch. He thought of Chrissie's arms. Three sheep stood uncertainly at the edge of a makeshift wooden pen, as if they had forgotten what they were supposed to be doing. China was going to kill one next week. If you had animals, it wasn't right to let someone else do the killing.

First time he'd tried to kill something, it was a duck for Christmas—there's one there now—he'd used an air rifle, thought a single shot would do it, but no, he'd filled it full of lead in the end, fucker wouldn't die, their internal organs are that small, hard to get a direct hit, you see, Chrissie wouldn't cook it, they had hot dogs out of a tin. The swimming pool had become a landfill, the rubbish piled almost to the top. There were another two pigs chained to a pole outside a falling-down outbuilding, performing a porcine maypole dance. "That's it," said China, his eyes even redder from the grass. "The chicken house is up the other end, but you don't need to see that."

"Nice place," said Stanton. "It's got . . ."

"Potential," said China. "Hear that? Jay's back with the goats."

The bells were low and rich and full of honey. Stanton and China walked back in time to see Jay run down the slope and through the herd, flapping his arms and grinning. Ruby was there, wearing a cleanish dress and the butterfly sunglasses, though it was nearly dusk. Stanton faced her directly, the others at his back. He was close enough to smell her but for the stink from the cow and the shit. There was something about this place that made you stop caring about anything. Her tongue flickered out and touched the mole above her lip. "Are you going somewhere?" said Stanton silently. She watched his lips. "Yes," she said in her ugly nasal voice. "I'm going."

Chrissie came outside. "One of these days," she said, petulant, "she'll get herself killed." She had a bucket of chicken feed in her hand. "Want to come with me?" Chrissie gestured vaguely at China and Jay moving among the goats, meaning they were occupied.

Stanton walked behind her, watching the way her backside moved beneath the thin fabric of her skirt, the ridges rising and falling on her calves, the red rings of bites around her ankles. His throat began to ache. They passed around the side of the willow to the farthest outbuilding. The sky was turning red. Her lips were hideous orange. She put down the bucket and took a step back, kicking it over. He kissed her without taking her in his arms. She did not seem surprised. She did not attempt to hold him, but her tongue was active, forceful. Brandy and a sharp tang of vomit. "Back there," he said and went up to the wall. He turned her around and lifted her skirt and made short work of it. He reached forward briefly and circled her wrists with his hands, the scabs pressed into his palms. She did not cry out or move her hips or even deepen her breath. "Thank you," he said and zipped his trousers. Behind them the chickens pecked the ground. When he went to the truck and untied the rope, the calf stood over the severed head and cried.

He went straight to his notebooks and flicked back and forth to find the place where he had listed Blake quotations, all those he thought he might be able to use. Here it was, on the fourteenth page: *Sooner murder an infant in its cradle than nurse unacted desires.* He poured a drink, turned on his computer, and worked long into the night.

Jay came the day after next. It was the usual time, but Stanton was still writing. "I'm getting behind," he said. "Tell you what, give me a few days, I'll come over and see you."

"Don't matter," said Jay, turning. His Manchester United top hung almost to his knees.

Stanton followed him out. "You understand, right?"

"Don't matter."

"It's not that I don't want you to come."

Jay stopped. Without turning, he said, "Yes it is."

Stanton suppressed a sigh. How had he ended up looking after this boy? He'd had enough. "Listen, the reason I came out here . . . Look at me. Jay. Look."

But the boy would not.

Stanton squeezed the back of his neck. Too many hours in front of the screen. "Actually," he said, "I think I could use a break. How about a Coke?"

"Don't matter," said the boy.

"Will you stop saying that? Stop being a baby and get yourself a drink. It's *doesn't,* anyway. And it does."

They sat on the terrace steps, not speaking. Jay pulled a long string of gum out of his mouth, wrapped it around a finger, and sucked it back for another chew. He crouched low to watch ants. He turned over a beetle that had gotten stuck on its back.

"How's the puppy?" asked Stanton.

"She ran away." Jay scratched in the dust with a twig.

"She might come back."

"No," said Jay. "They never do."

Stanton searched for something wise or comforting to say. "Got any spare gum?" he said.

"No. Tina's having babies soon. She's the pig."

"Great." He wondered if Dieter was right about Ruby, and if Jay knew. "Jay, don't you have any friends around here? Your own age, I mean."

"At school," said Jay. "Only see them at school, really. Thought you said it's *doesn't,* anyway."

"What I said . . . never mind."

Jay stood up. "That's me mum's car."

Chrissie had on a floppy straw hat and a long skirt. She's dressed up, thought Stanton.

"I've told you about bothering Harry."

"I invited him."

"Watch this, Mum." Jay ran up to the terrace. "I can walk on my hands now. Been practicing."

"Don't show off, Jay," said Chrissie.

"Look, Mum. See this."

"All right, Jay. We've all seen it."

"Very good," said Stanton. "Well done."

"Your dad wants you," said Chrissie. "He needs some help."

"What with?"

"How should I know?" said Chrissie, whining. "You best get going."

Jay rubbed his head. "How about you?"

"How about me? You can walk back. I'm on my way to the shops."

"How about you?" said Jay.

"Kids!" She tried a laugh. "I'll be going in a minute. I'm just having a word with Harry first."

Jay stayed where he was.

Stanton smiled and rocked on his heels. Someone told him once that the children of alcoholics become adept at sensing mood swings, reading body language.

"I'll wait for you at the car," said Jay. "You can give me a lift back to the road."

"Well," said Stanton. Thank God the boy had stayed.

Chrissie tipped her head to one side. "I could kill him."

"So," said Stanton, "you're going shopping."

Chrissie rubbed her arms. "You bastard," she said softly.

A forest fire burned for three days and nights on the hills that hid the sea. A firefighter was hurt, only slightly. The newspaper reported sixty-seven dead in the heat wave. Stanton kept a bottle of water on his desk, and it grew warm before he had finished a page.

Eventually he came to a lull. He went out and bought a football for Jay and a vase for Chrissie and a bottle of cachaça and a bag of limes to make caipirinhas. He picked up a pair of sunglasses with diamante studs along the arms but put them back again.

"Mate," said China, who had come out at the sound of the truck, "let's have a fucking drink."

Stanton had thought of it as a visit to see Jay, but he realized now that it wasn't.

"Been out all day with the goats," said China. "Something special like. People don't realize."

Chrissie took the vase without a word. Jay whooped at the sight of the football, which made Stanton feel bad. Ruby, thankfully, was out. He explained how to make the caipirinhas with lime juice and sugar and plenty of ice, and Chrissie went to the kitchen. She set doilies on the tray, one under each glass.

"Blinding," said China. "Jay, take that fucking ball outside."

"What do you like about them?" said Stanton. "The goats." He watched China spread against his chair, the slight tremor in his hand as he brought the glass to his lips. It was China he had come for: some atavistic instinct the man appealed to, a desire to see the demons at work.

"Goats," said China, his voice dragging like a broken muffler, "you look at 'em long enough, you see the universe. Good and evil, love and war, God and the devil. Know what I mean?"

"For God's sake," said Chrissie.

"Shut up," said China, not quite shouting. "Who asked you? Where's my lighter? There's one billy . . ." He leaned forward so that Stanton could see the scarlet rims of his eyes. "He don't know when to stop. He's so horny, I daren't turn my back on him." He slapped his thigh and hooted, a little spray of snot landing in his lap. "We think we're that much better than animals, but I tell you something for free—you watch 'em long enough, you learn a lot. A goat with the horn is like a man with a mission. Made by the same Creator to the same design. Yes, you certainly learn a lot." He lit the joint and passed it to Stanton.

Stanton took a hit and managed not to cough. He passed it to Chrissie, and their fingers brushed together. *The lust of the goat is the bounty of God.* The quotation entered his head, and he saw at once how to rework a passage that had given him trouble.

China got out of his chair. He looked around, picked up a filthy T-shirt, and blew his nose on it. "I'm going to check on Tina. She's a little darling, she is." At the doorway he looked over his shoulder. "Listen, mate, my home is your home. Anything you want, you take it."

Stanton followed Chrissie into the kitchen. The roof was plastic sheeting over untreated wood beams. There was a puddle of something—it had not rained for weeks—in the middle of the floor.

Chrissie put more ice in a plastic bag and smashed it with a hammer. Stanton slipped his arm around from behind and held her wrist. He felt her grip tighten on the hammer before she let it drop. It was over quickly, and this time they did not kiss. When they went back to the sitting room, Ruby was there, hugging her knees to her chest.

He was drinking in the bar next door to the Casa do Povo, thinking it had been a long time since he had driven home not drunk, when he noticed her. He ordered a pineapple Sumol and took it over to her table. She had a pink satin handbag with a stain on it and a beaded scarf that she had placed on the chair opposite, as if reserving the space. Stanton knew she would be alone. He moved her things and sat down.

"Do you mind?" she said, her voice coming out gassy.

"Not at all," said Stanton.

She turned her head and chewed her lip and then flashed back at him. "If you're going to sit there, I'll have a beer."

"I'd be delighted to buy you one," he said, "when you're eighteen."

"Ha, ha, very funny, my name's Bugs Bunny."

"Good one," said Stanton. "Look, I'll move when your boyfriend gets here. You're meeting your boyfriend, aren't you?" He glanced at her stomach, but there was nothing he could tell from that.

Ruby looked out the window. She reached up and tucked her hair behind her ears. "I know what you're doing," she said. "Deaf doesn't mean stupid."

"I know," said Stanton, speaking the words aloud this time. "I'm sorry." The shame seemed to spread from his anus, which contracted and released and contracted again. "I'm sorry," he said again. She kept her hearing aid turned to him like a steady reproach. "I'll buy you that beer, if you like." Nothing. In the pit of his stomach there was a deep absence. He was sorry for her and he was sorry for himself. He thought of the pub at the top end of the Archway Road, and the horse brasses around the fireplace. He could walk in there most evenings and find someone to talk to, Roger or Connor or Sinead or a whole bunch of them to bitch and moan and sneer with.

"Not much to do, is there, in the village? Not at your age."

Maybe she really could not hear him. A light down spread out from the hairline at her ear to the puppy fat along her jaw. The mole beneath her nose looked ticklish, like a crumb sticking there. Have it your way, thought Stanton, shaking it all off.

She heard him standing up or saw from the corner of her eye. "You can always find something," she said. "If you try hard enough."

"I expect so." He sat down and wished he had moved faster.

"Party in Milfontes tonight. Should be good." She did the thing with the tip of her tongue reaching up to the mole.

Christ, he thought. Here I am.

China came through the door as if he meant to take it off its hinges. He was drunker than usual. His jeans looked as if they would stand on their own. "Mate," he bellowed, "let's have a fucking drink." He noticed his daughter. "Get yourself home now. It's late."

"It's not," said Ruby. "And don't fucking shout. Showing me up, as per usual."

China leaned over the table, hulking his shoulders forward. "Showing you up? Showing you up? You've shown yourself up. A long fucking time ago, my girl." His jaw hung open, and Stanton gazed inside at the red and the black. China straightened up, the fight gone out of him. "Ah, well, fuck it. Do what you like."

"I will," said Ruby. She gathered her bag and scarf and went out, everybody watching the swing of her hips.

"I don't mind telling you," said China when he had lined up the brandies and the beers, "I don't mind telling you that in the old days, I'd have knocked her for six. Not my style anymore." He lifted his drink and spilled a little down his chin. "You got to let things be."

Stanton was weary. "Your philosophy of life."

"That's right," said China. It was just about possible to make out the whites of his eyes beneath the web of red veins. "When I was big

on control, I was really big on control, know what I mean, and I con-
trolled a patch of Yarmouth, ran nearly over to fucking Cromer,
know what I mean, and what I said"—he slammed his glass on the
table—"went."

My muse, thought Stanton, stabbed through with resentment.
"What brought you out here, then?"

China smiled, loose-lipped, slack-jawed. "Mate," he said slowly,
as if to comfort a dying man. "Mate. What brought any of us? On the
run, ain't we? On the fucking run."

Connor at last sent a letter: six pages of black Montblanc rollerball
on pale blue Basildon Bond. Five pages of dreary news wittily ren-
dered, and on the sixth page this:

*Roger, you may recall, was due to publish his masterpiece in July. Well, that
should have told him everything he needed to know. Eight long years of toil and
his publisher decides on July? The month for chick lit, the collected bons mots
of prepubescent columnists and monographs on crop rotation in fourteenth-
century Westphalia. Of course he hasn't left the house since.*

Stanton lay back on the bed. He looked at his toenails, ingrained
with dirt, the right big toenail chipped and peeling away at the corner, the nail on the little toe black, though he had not noticed banging it. He lay there gazing at his feet until darkness took them and the
cicadas made audible his thoughts: insistent, streaming, unintelligible.

He had taken the truck to the garage to get the clutch looked at.
When he got back, Chrissie was waiting for him.

"I'll have to start locking the door," he said.

She had her arms wrapped around her chest, her hip bones were
a pair of razor shells, and her pubic hair was surprisingly dark. "I
thought we should. At least once. You know, with our clothes off."

"Chrissie," he said, unbuckling, "do you think Ruby saw us?"

She turned on her stomach and spoke into the pillow so he could not catch the words. He ran his palm down the ridge of her spine and onto the shallow slope of her buttocks. She put her arms behind her back, wrists together. There was a spot of blood on the sheets from her forearm. "Turn over," he said.

She obeyed him, but when he looked into her face, there was nothing he could read except a kind of helpless defiance. He had seen once a picture of a protesting nun in a distant country who wore a similar expression as the flames licked up her robes.

"I don't care," said Chrissie.

"Do you think she saw us?"

"I can't help it," she said, and pulled his head toward hers.

She came nearly every day. When she was not there, he sat on the terrace spitting olive pits into an old can or shuffling a deck of cards, or he chopped wood and stacked it in the shed for the cool winter months, which were not far off. He did no writing.

They got into a rhythm. When he heard her car, he went to the bedroom and lit candles, though the flames disappeared in the sunlight. He liked the way she dozed on her side with her hands between her knees. He liked the way she shivered when he ran his hand down her back. She always sighed as she took off her bra.

"What's the point of these?" she said, blowing out one of the candles.

"It's romantic," he said. "You're supposed to like it."

Whatever pleasure she took, she kept largely to herself.

"Run away with me," he said.

She was making the bed. "I've got to get going."

"Venice," he said, catching her around the waist. "Monte Carlo. Rio."

"I've lost my hair slide," she said. "Did you see me put it down?"

He asked about Ruby. "She was," said Chrissie. "But she isn't now. Miscarriage."

"I'm sorry," said Stanton.

"Don't be."

She scratched her arms until they bled.

"What are you doing?" he said. "What are you doing?"

Jay came only once when she was there. Stanton pulled on his trousers and went to the door. "Come back in a couple of hours, can you?" The car, he thought. Jesus. "Your mum came round. She's in the woods. Thought she might find you there."

"Tina," said Jay. He put his hand up to shield his eyes as he looked out toward the corks.

"She had her litter?"

"Yeah," said Jay. "She's ate 'em, though." For a moment he looked solemn, and then he began to giggle. "They'd have been et in the end anyway. That's what me dad says."

Chrissie was dressed and sitting at his desk. "English," she said, "was my best subject at school."

They ran out of steam, got to the end of each other. They both knew it. Still, he had to say something, and it would be a delicate business. He sat out on the steps shuffling cards and waiting.

When she got out of the car, she checked her reflection in the side mirror. She carried a basket of eggs.

There was a cold rinse in his chest that might have been mistaken for fear.

"Chrissie," he said, "I need to bury myself for a while."

She set down the basket. "They've started laying in that old Citroën."

He took her hand. "Do you see what I'm saying?"

"For some reason," she said, "we're getting a lot of double yolkers."

She made it easy, really. He was grateful. "You've got your work, Harry," she told him. "Need your peace and quiet. And I've got my husband." He kissed her on the nose. "I'll still see you," he told her. "We'll have coffee." "I don't drink coffee," she said. "Tea, then," he said, "or a beer."

Later he met Dieter at the café and attempted a discreet celebration. "A bottle of red—the best you have."

Vasco wiped their table and tucked his filthy rag into his belt. "You would like something special? Expensive, yes?"

"Okay," said Stanton.

"Okay," wheezed Vasco. "I charge you more."

Dieter's subject was Portuguese bureaucracy, an old favorite. "All these obstacles they put in your way. They do not really want you to work."

Stanton nodded. The work on his own house would never be completed.

"In Germany they will be fired. The officials are there to help you, and if they do not, they will be fired. Pure and simple."

"Pure and simple," said Stanton. "Why don't you go back to Germany? Seems everything would be easier."

Dieter sat up and clutched the arms of his chair. "Germany?" he said. "If I never see that country again so long as I may live, so much the better for me. Germany? No. Never."

Vasco came with a bottle of the usual. "Very expensive, this. Very good wine for celebrating. Wait, I bring a glass and make a toast with you . . . So, what do we toast?"

"Long life," said Dieter, sounding pained.

"Life and liberty," said Stanton, raising a glass.

They stayed late, and Vasco was waiting to close. When Stanton went to pay, he was reading glossy brochures at the counter.

"Going on holiday?"

"Listen," said Vasco. " 'Treasures of the ages await at Hotel Luxor's Giza Galleria. Located on the main level of the East Tower, enchanting fountains, beautifully sculpted statues, and elegant stone walkways greet visitors when shopping Luxor-style at Giza Galleria.' " He passed a fat hand over his mouth. "Only in America, yes?"

Stanton conceded this to be so.

"But maybe also in the future in the Alentejo. Nothing is impossible."

"True," said Stanton, taking the easiest course.

"You have heard of Marco Afonso Rodrigues?"

"Remind me."

"A very big name in the tourist industry," said Vasco. "Luxury resorts in Thailand and Singapore. So I have been told. I believe he also has interests in London, Tokyo, and Macau."

"Of course," said Stanton, attempting to stem the flow.

"Do you know who he is?"

"Do now."

"He is Eduardo's cousin," Vasco said, inflating a little, if that was possible. "And he is coming home to Mamarrosa. Imagine that."

"Well, I'll try," said Stanton, more irritably than he'd meant. "He's been away a long time?" he added as a countermeasure.

"Twenty years or more," said Vasco proudly. "Of course, if he wants to do business here he will need a partner. Local knowledge—you cannot make a business without that."

"Anyway," said Stanton, taking out his wallet, "when are you going to America?"

Vasco closed the brochure. "Oh, I cannot travel. The asthma. It is not possible."

"Ah," said Stanton. "Then why . . ."

"Why?" squeaked Vasco. "Why? It is a good joke. The writer asks why I should read."

Ruby looked like a waxwork in the headlights. She stood still when he pulled in and she did not move when he opened the door. "Give you a ride home," he called. "Come on, get in." She got in without a word. She had the sunglasses in her hand. "Good night?" he asked. She leaned her head against the window. Finally she said, "I'm really, really tired."

A little way along the track that led down into the valley she said, "Let me out now. If Dad hears, he'll come looking."

Stanton stopped the car and cut the engine.

Playing it back later—in bed, entombed by the noise of cicadas—he could not recall who made the first move. She smelled of freshly dug earth, and her skin was all goosebumps, and when she came she bit his ear until he cried out and pinched her hard to make her let him go.

He spent two nights at his desk and on the third day slept in his chair and woke with his head lolled back, a demon pain laced at the neck and one hand on the keyboard.

He heard Chrissie's car and the soft click of her sandals on the steps. He heard the sigh of the door handle and the resistance of the lock. Ruby came the next day and knocked on the door and then the window and then circled to the back and stood outside the bedroom. He crouched in the bathroom next to the stack of tiles that would never be laid and noticed for the first time the mesh of fine lines through the clear glaze. He watched her go from the sitting room window, and when she got to the cypress trees, she looked back and raised one finger in the air.

It was the second week of October, and Dieter came to say goodbye. His Dutch woman had already left. "Maybe one day I will go to India too. This country—" He paused and flicked back his hair with that strange feminine gesture. "This country is getting on my nerves."

"Well," said Stanton. He felt the redundancy of anything he might say. "I wish you luck with everything."

"Thanks," said Dieter.

For a moment Stanton thought he was going to be enveloped into that concave chest. "Hope the work situation there is more satisfactory."

"To speak the absolute truth," said Dieter, "in the Algarve everything will be the same. But you know when it is time to go, and for me it is time."

"Whenever you're in the area," said Stanton, hoping that would wrap things up.

The rain came and turned the world to mud. Stanton took his boots off at the door, but still the mud insinuated itself into the house. If it carried on this way, he would be forced to clean the place. The oranges began to drop, but they could not, Stanton discovered, be eaten. The peach trees in the little orchard turned out rotten. They sagged beneath the weight of water and split and rested their branches on the ground. At dawn—sometimes he was rising, sometimes going to bed—the eucalyptus drifted ghostlike in the mist. A fox visited every evening, and Stanton began to put out his scraps.

The shepherd moved on without goodbyes. Stanton walked in the woods and saw hunters, once with ancient guns, and another time he thought he saw a boy, but when he came to the place there was no one. His mother wrote:

> I am sorry to tell you that your father has given up the allotment. I said to him, but you love gardening! And do you know what he said? No I don't, Joan. And I don't like it either.
> What are we to make of that? I expect you've got quite a lot of experience out there now yourself. I expect you're a dab hand now with trees and plants and growing things.

Four more weeks and he had a complete draft. He drove half an hour, the windshield wipers sticking and dislodging and sticking again, to the nearest town where he knew he could buy Glenfiddich and returned with two bottles.

He poured a generous measure. A fire, he thought, would be nice. The wood caught on the third attempt, but it was still damp, and the smoke hurt his eyes and made him cough.

He was sick of these four walls. In the last month he'd spoken barely a dozen words.

He thought about Jay. It would be good to see the boy again.

Chrissie. Lovely Chrissie. She wouldn't be angry. Chrissie could hardly complain. They'd said they'd have a beer.

Ruby. Well, Ruby. Ruby would be all right. She'd made the first move, remember. Been around a bit.

How many visitors did they get over there, anyway? Let's have a fucking drink, mate. Yes, let's have a fucking drink.

The whiskey bottle bounced off the passenger seat as he swung a sharp left on the descent into the valley. He sang an old tune, pulling up by the chicken shed. "'You can blow out the candle but you can't put out the fire.'" As he opened the door, he noticed the calf, much bigger now, bandy legs and bloated stomach, standing by the house with the rain running from its nose and tail and its hooves in plastic bags. The wind howled through the bamboo and sent a curtain of water off the roof. Chrissie answered the door and backed away from him, and he went in and found that all the Pottses were there and that none was ready with a greeting.

"What kind of man are you?" China had spoken quietly. Chrissie stood behind Ruby and stroked her hair. Stanton, needing salvation, tried to smile at Jay, but the boy would not look at him. "What kind of man are you?" That was all. Chrissie did not speak and Ruby did not speak and Jay did not speak and Stanton had no answer. He waited for China to call him every name under the sun, but China did not oblige. China was on his feet, and there was hope at first of a fight, but this too was clutching at straws. Long after all hope had gone, Stanton stood there and waited for something to happen and nothing happened at all.

On the drive back, he swerved to avoid a tractor he had not seen coming. The pickup skidded into the ditch, and two wheels sank without hesitation into the mud. It was not far to walk home. He drank a good measure before removing his clothes, and he found that if he just maintained a constant sipping, very evenly spaced, taking very small sips, he could keep all thoughts from his head. The whiskey was warming. If he observed very closely, very carefully, the way it traveled out from the solar plexus along all the major arteries and branched off along each individual vein, he could feel it as a kind of calm radiating out from the core of his being.

He woke in his chair, naked and half frozen, and when he went to boil water he could not feel his toes and his fingers were too stiff to strike a match. His head hurt. His back was broken; if not broken then something worse. When he bent to get his socks on he nearly cried. He set off to walk up to the telephone box and on the way he thought about how beautiful the place was and how much he would miss it. The rain had stopped in the night and the sun played in the treetops, scattering diamonds here and there and emeralds. It teased purples and scarlets from the plowed-up field and burnished the far-off hills a fine shade of nostalgia. He breathed deeply, and it was good to smell the eucalyptus and the pine, and he thought of the air making him clean inside. As he came up to the road he saw an old man in a black felt fedora and waistcoat leading a cow along the opposite track, heading for the village at such a slow pace, as if they had all the time in the world, as if arriving were nothing and the journey everything. He raised a hand and the old man raised a hand and they passed each other and Stanton went on his way.

Three

It is late and it is hot and the groinsweat makes bold with his thighs as he wipes for the last time the counter and turns over in his mind, now and now again, his grandmother's phrase: We live our lives. What a way she had of complaining! There. Pretending she would never grumble and turning her whole life into a complaint.

Vasco shakes the cloth over the sink, wipes the cash register, and stuffs the cloth in the drawer with the travel brochures. What a tedious thing to say. More interesting to say we don't live our lives, the ones we meant to have. He hitches up his trousers. When he got too fat for belts, he began to live in fear of his backside becoming exposed. He has suspenders but no faith in them. More interesting to speak of life as a spectator sport: We don't live our lives; we wait and watch and judge.

His legs ache. He would give anything—this café, the apartment above, his savings, his Yankees baseball cap purchased at the actual Home of Champions—for someone to come and rub his legs. Damn that Joelly, shirking off again this morning. He should go over and bang on his door. Joelly, I want you to massage my calves until the muscles are soft enough for a baby to chew. What do you mean, *poorly*? In my opinion a man, or even a boy like you, is fit for three things only: work, hospital, or the grave. A *bit* poorly? That is wonderful. That is superb. Absolutely prime.

His breath is becoming labored. Vasco switches off the lights and stands in the blue-purple glow of the Insect-O-Cutor, listening to it hum like a man in a state of perpetual indecision. This is what Vasco is going to do: light a candle, take the last cake from the display case (an almond tart), sit down and enjoy it, and then go up to bed.

Cake, fork, spoon, and candle are before him on the table. Vasco sees that he has forgotten to cover the display stand, a procedure imported from the United States of America, where he learned his trade. It is supposed to be a security measure. He looks at the dark and ragged outline made by the sunglasses, postcards, teddies, and toy whistles. They are safe enough. But they have been in that rack, most of them, for a long time, and he will not neglect to cover them for the night. A child spinning the stand: This is what stock turn-around means in the Alentejo.

What about that Eduardo! Vasco has never liked him. You can't trust a man who mumbles. Speak up if you have nothing to hide.

Vasco picks up the fork and holds it above the cake. Sugar glistens in the candlelight, beautiful as young love and as cheap.

Three days ago Eduardo said, "My own prize bull. Give me one of those *empadas*. I'll risk it." And hasn't been in since. Vasco hopes he never comes back again. He can do without customers like that.

He looks closely at the cake, the small landslide of pastry at one edge, the pearly nuts studding the surface, the dense brown syrupy sponge, the sugar flashing its heart out. He puts down his fork. Oh, that Eduardo, a friend for twenty years, and if he never crosses Vasco's mind again, it will be too soon.

"Will I eat this cake or not?" Vasco says it out loud. He picks up the spoon. The table shakes. These damn plastic tables; all day Vasco puts up with their trembling. These damn plastic chairs. He never dares sit in one until after he closes. When he stands up again, the chair will be stuck to his backside, and he will take hold of the arm-rests and prise it off and pretend that it could happen to anyone.

He will not eat the cake. The very idea fills him with disgust. He is not hungry at all. Well, perhaps just a little. If he eats the cake he will feel remorse. But there will be pleasure too. Nobody is going to come and rub his legs. Tomorrow the delivery from Lindoso will be here. Why leave one cake from the old stock in the display case? He strokes this thought like a dozing cat until it purrs right back at him.

Yes, silly not to eat it.

Although why should he force down this stale cake? Is he a dustbin? A man without refinement? *I'll risk it*. Eduardo! What a toad that man is. Everyone knows that Vasco's food is always fresh.

Vasco picks at the pastry and rubs it between thumb and finger. All this reasoning is useless. He is going to either eat the cake or not. Reason has nothing to do with it. For every argument there is a counterargument. If it were not so, the world would be a happy place.

If he eats the cake, he will go to bed with a full stomach and sleep soundly. Or the sugar might keep him awake. What are a few extra calories to a man of his size? On the other hand, only a slim man should be eating sticky puddings late at night. You see, there is never just the one way to look at things. Some people are blessed with partial vision. They are the ones who achieve greatness. The rest of us— Vasco turns his head and sees himself in the plate-glass window, floating with a candle in a black sea—the rest of us muddle through.

Vasco stares at the fat man with his neck spilling over the white chef's coat and it seems that he is drifting, that the blackness will drown him. "What do I know?" he says out loud, quickly. His voice is too high and too thin. He needs his inhaler, but his legs ache and he does not want to climb the stairs. He looks away from the window and sets his hands on the table.

His grandmother was under five feet tall and she knew practically nothing. She had only four teeth. In her entire life, she never went farther than Santa Clara. She could eat a whole raw onion. She could cut the head off a chicken and hold it down so she never lost a drop of the precious blood she used to cook it in. She could cure any woman (or goat or cow) of mastitis with her poultice and wouldn't share the secret ingredients with anyone. Her achievements were not large, but she was proud of them. She liked to pretend that whatever she knew, she knew with certainty.

When Uncle Humberto packed his spare pair of trousers (with cuttings from his favorite vine wrapped inside) and set off for a new life in Mozambique, of metal mines and miscegenation, she said, "He has answered a call."

When her youngest son, Henrique, answered another call two years later, this time to fight the savages in Angola and save them from themselves and international communism, she said, "It is the Lord's will."

When they learned Henrique would not be coming home again, while Vasco's mother sank to her knees and wept, his grandmother said, "What is meant to be, must be," and went out to feed the pig. But when Vasco broke her teapot, she beat him with the big wooden spoon. Vasco sobbed. "I couldn't help it. It slipped." She cracked the spoon down on his head. "Help it! Why was it in your hand in the first place? No, my boy, didn't the Lord, through His grace, give us free will? When Eve tasted the apple, she did not say, 'But I could not help it.' Put your arms down. Do you think I would beat you on the face?"

What a joke. Vasco digs his fingernail into the warm pool of wax gathering on the table. With teapots you are free to choose, in matters of life and death you are not.

He holds his finger, with its cracked wax globe, up before his face. In the morning, when he wakes, his legs will feel like that: stiff, bloodless remains.

He never was able to believe. All those mornings spent on his knees, smelling the polish and the dust, pushing his head against the pew in front as if he could force his way into the Light. "Oh, Lord," he prayed, "make me believe." Father Quintão's eyes watered when the young girls took communion. Vasco saw him in the sacristy with Laura Meireles, her skirts up around her waist. He prayed again, "Oh, Lord, please try harder."

★   ★   ★

That Eduardo is like a bad case of the piles: the last thing you want to think about and the first thing on your mind. What did he mean, anyway? My own prize bull—what kind of insult is that? A prize bull is a fine animal, and Eduardo has never come close to owning one. If you wish to insult a man, do it properly. That is Vasco's opinion, and he will not waste any more time on Eduardo.

Only a couple of weeks ago, he was in here snorting and mumbling when Vasco was discussing certain matters with Bruno.

"The United States," Vasco was saying, "is the policeman of the world. Like it or not, it makes no difference."

"This a free lecture?" said Eduardo, taking a stool at the counter.

Vasco ignored him. "The United Nations cannot fart without permission from them."

"Emissions and permissions," said Eduardo. "Who has the license here?"

Vasco should have said something then and there.

"A beer," said Eduardo. "When you have a moment."

The thing about Eduardo is that he eats his words. By the time you realize what he said, he is on to the next thing.

But Vasco should have spoken up, and then one thing would not have led to another like this.

He breaks the wax off his finger. Some of it falls on the cake. It is not as though Eduardo is one for holding back on opinions. But it makes him uncomfortable when Vasco talks about certain matters of world affairs because Eduardo—and Vasco knows this for a fact— does not even possess a passport.

Vasco rolls his shoulders. The bones click. How would it ever be possible, he thinks now, for me to decide to eat this cake or not to eat it? As if this is an isolated act, unconnected to all other acts that have gone before. As if history does not play its part. As if one thing does not depend on another. As if there is no chain. As if everything is random.

His aunt Joana was fat. Vasco never knew her, but Mãe used to talk about her all the time. She'd pinch his cheeks, his arms, his belly: "Just like Joana. The pigs went hungry when she was around." He was a fat baby. Mãe said, "God in heaven, you near split me apart." He was a fat child. "See that? Fat on the back of his *head*." He was a fat teenager. "*Don't* sit on that chair."

Yes, Vasco, he's the fat one, look at him eat. Have some more, Vasco. He can put it away. See, he's finished it already. But he'll have some more. Vasco, have some more. Eat. Go on, eat!

Probably Mãe did not love him enough. If your mother does not love you, you fill the hole with something. Mãe was always fussing around, pinching him and kissing him. She could never leave him alone. Probably she loved him too much. She made him needy. A needy person never has enough. There is always a hole to be filled.

This much is sure: One thing follows another. "I'll do this," we say, "because I feel like it." We think we live like kings, but we are puppets on the throne. We send out proclamations and fancy we are making History and forget that it has made us.

If I eat the cake, thinks Vasco—he bows his head toward it—I'll say it is because I am hungry. If I don't eat it, I'll say it is because I am full. It will become the truth. If Dona Marisa had taken this cake along with her coffee this afternoon, I would not even be here. I would be in bed resting my legs instead of sitting at this table, putting off the climb with this silly business about cake.

He lifts the plate and resists the urge to throw it across the room. The tart would fit in the palm of his hand. The pastry is roughly fluted and of mouth-drying thickness. The sponge is perhaps darker than it should be. It has spent too long in the oven or sat too long on the shelf. But the sugar winks at him and makes shiny promises: Give me your tongue and forget; give me your tongue and be free.

Vasco sets down the plate. He looks around the room at the plastic tables and chairs, their dull white sheen and sullen stance. He twists to see the long dark counter crouched beneath the indigo halo of the insect annihilator. The pool table stands close to the door. He was so proud when he bought it. When anyone played a game, he had to take two puffs on his inhaler. The baize is worn now, the victim of time and cigarettes and spilled drinks. A car goes by, heading out of the village, sluicing the walls pale yellow, the Moorish design on the tiles coming up and receding like a dream on waking, half lost, half held. He listens to the engine diminish. The sound grows fainter and fainter but does not disappear. It is coming from his chest. It will not disappear unless he fetches his inhaler or quits altogether this breathing.

"Well," says Vasco to himself, "what is life without the time to sit alone and contemplate?" This, at least, is something that the Portuguese understand. He listens as the lantana taps furtively at the window.

In a moment he will get up and fetch a small glass of whiskey.

To sit alone and think like this—every man should do it, but not every man will risk it.

He has made big decisions in his life. He is not incapable. There are people in this village whose biggest decision has been whether to paint the door frame yellow or blue. But Vasco went to America. Not even twenty-one when he left. We live our lives, his grandmother said. But Vasco made his. Mãe gave him a cross to wear. She had the chain specially lengthened. In Provincetown, Cape Cod, all the Portuguese wore crosses but didn't know if they were saved. Vasco left his in a kidney dish in Falmouth Hospital. A nurse ran after him down the corridor, saying here, here, you lost something.

Damn Eduardo. Damn him. Everyone listening and Vasco didn't say a word. He shifts his legs and the table quivers. He begins to knead his thigh. Next time that man comes in, Vasco will say, "You are welcome here, of course, but in my opinion you would be happier at Joaquim's. So much more to complain about there."

He begins on the other thigh. He will not waste another thought on Eduardo. The way he tosses peanuts into his mouth is quite sickening. Ever since he got the position on the Junta, he has been unbearable. He is certainly not as clever as he thinks he is. And now, with Marco Afonso Rodrigues returning, he believes he is a cut above. The worst thing about him, really, is that he never can speak straight. Oh, he's a sly one, that Eduardo, and not worth his weight in swill.

Marco might be Eduardo's cousin, but if he has any sense, it will be Vasco whom Marco decides to approach. The one businessman in Mamarrosa who knows anything about business at all.

A whiskey would go nicely. He was sweating before, and now he is chilled. Only his armpits are hot from the work on his thighs, and if he were to walk in here now from the street, he knows that he would smell them. He would like to let go of a fart but can't ease it out. When it comes it will blow the chair off. There is a pinch in his neck, bubbles in his stomach. His body never ceases to amaze him. He is supposed to be in charge of it, but this notion is absurd. In all that churning and creaking and bloating and leaking, he has no say.

Yes, he went to America. Got the idea God-knows-how and did it. He must have been insane. The insane are not responsible for what they do. They can get away with anything. Everyone is mad, thinks Vasco. Most of us can hide it. In private, we are all insane. Those travel brochures in his drawer—why doesn't he throw them away? Some are ten years old. He will never go back to America. He does not even want to.

Something is happening to his anus. It is fizzing. He squeezes his buttocks together. The fizzing stops. Vasco puts his elbows on the table and clasps his hands. What he hates most about being fat is the way his hands and feet have shrunk. No, what he hates most is the chafing inside his thighs and groin. It is a problem that no amount of talcum powder will solve. If he were in America right now, he would hardly be fat at all. In America they had to take the side of a house right off to get a man out of his own home.

Twelve years he spent in Provincetown. He learned his trade. The first restaurant he walked into he got a job, peeling potatoes, humping bins, scraping crap off toilets, and stuck it until the place closed down. He walked into another job as bartender, Manhattans and Long Island iced teas, and went on with it until he got laid off. He was in a pit-stop diner circling want ads when the owner shouted over, *"Quer trabalhar?"* and hired him then and there as a fry cook. Eggs and bacon, eggs and sausage, eggs with more eggs. A guy at the counter, yolk on his mustache: He was opening a smart new joint down by the harbor, needed a broiler man, how about it? His suit was blue velvet with thin lapels. It looked expensive. Vasco didn't say yes, didn't say no, but things took their course. The next five years he charred steaks the size of Castro Verde at the Blue Boy Inn on the corner of Commercial and Carver.

What a place! Three, four, five hundred covers a night. A ship could set sail in the lobster tank. Oak tables and fine linen and mirrors in curly frames that came all the way from Paris. It was sweet hell in there, roasting his forearms over the broiler, the fat spitting up in his eyes.

And there was Lili. He received her like he received everything else in those years, with gratitude, with surprise. The waitresses wore yellow dresses with full skirts, as if they were going on first dates. Lili tied a lilac sash around hers and said, "Jeez, look at me, prom queen." She smoked cigarettes in the kitchen and stubbed them out on mounds of carrot peel. Her grandparents were from Calabria, but she was New Jersey born and bred. She called all the chefs Tarzan and the customers Captain and the maître d' she called Mein Führer, but only behind his back.

Vasco got the idea she was watching him, but it was difficult to tell with her lazy eye. She might have been looking over at the salad station, or even up at the ceiling. He was not as fat as he is now. Some of the customers made him feel slim. It was a lot to hope, but certainly she kept looking, if not at him then in the general vicinity.

"What you doing Sunday?" she said, shouldering a tray of T-bones.

"Sunday?" he said, shaking with fear.

She wiggled her hip and her shoulder to get the weight of the tray loaded right. "You obviously don't know, so I'll tell you. You're going to Herring Cove Beach to make out with a girl. She's bringing the picnic." Her lazy eye had slid up nearly all the way beneath the lid, but the other one held his gaze. "Ask me how I know, Tarzan."

He opened and closed his mouth.

"I'm the girl, Tarzan." She smiled her tight-lipped smile. "I'm *the girl*."

Pai courted Mãe through a window. That was how it was done. *Namorar a janela.* Vasco told Lili about it. "A brick wall," she said, "great prophylactic." His grandmother's marriage was arranged formally when she was twelve years old, but she always knew that she was meant for Pedro, just as everything else in her life seemed to her foretold. Vasco's marriage too was arranged. Lili arranged it all.

"Let's not beat around the bush," she said. "I think this is it for me and you."

She was buttoning up her blouse. It was 1976. Lots of the girls were going braless, but Lili wore a kind of armor plating beneath her clothes. When Vasco managed to get his hands on her breasts, it was like feeling a pair of hubcaps. She smelled of cinnamon, though, and rose water, and it was all he could do to keep from fainting on top of her.

"Lili," he groaned, "don't say that."

She bedded down on his stomach. "This is it, Tarzan. We are going to get wed."

What he could do with, actually, is a beer to wash down the cake. This pastry will definitely be on the dry side. He raises one foot and turns his ankle. Eleven hours on his feet. Whose legs wouldn't ache?

All this women's liberation has gone too far. Lili had no time for it. She didn't need it, that's what she said. Now it's gone too far. Only the other day he was saying to Bruno that in his opinion, it has gone too far. In America now romance is dead. The feminists killed it and the men are scared. If a man opens a door for a woman, he will end up in court. Sex discrimination.

"You think it could never happen here?" he said. "These crazy Americans? Let me tell you, in my opinion, it is only a matter of time."

It's the way the world is. Even the Alentejo cannot escape. The United States of America is the Superpower, and it is not just a question of guns. He said to Bruno, "What language do you think your grandchildren will speak?"

Bruno pushed up his cap and grunted. Bruno is not a great thinker.

"English, my friend. With an American accent."

Vasco sighs a long, wheezing sigh. "Oh," he says to himself, "what do I know?" Not as much as Bruno, even. His grandchildren and their grandchildren will speak Portuguese. Such a beautiful language will never die. His eyes begin to fill. He is so tired he feels hollow. There is nothing inside him, nothing. Why does he say all these things? Such a beautiful language. Even when he said it, he didn't believe it. Why must he talk and talk and invent all these things? America this and America that. Twenty-two years since he's been there. He does not give a rotten acorn's worth for that place.

What a fool I am. Vasco focuses on the flame, which is beginning to burn low. Stripped to the core, this is what I am. Yet he holds himself apart, as if there are two Vascos, one passing judgment on the other.

"Talk to me," Lili would say, propped up in the hospital bed, three pillows behind her back, two more beneath her knees. "Tell me things. Tell me about Mamarrosa."

She swelled up like one of those magic beans you drop in a bowl of water. Her hands, her feet, her legs, her face. She was just into her third trimester.

The hospital chair was so low he had to reach up to hold her hand. Every time he stopped speaking, she said, "Don't just sit there. Talk to me."

"Everything will be all right," he said. "I promise."

She rolled her good eye. "I know that, you dope. Tell me something interesting."

Out in the corridor, the doctor had said, "The only cure for preeclampsia is delivery. Bed rest. That's the best we can do."

Vasco hunted him down and held him by the shoulder. "Take it out," he said. "Take the baby out."

The doctor looked at Vasco, considering, it seemed, whether to press charges. Then he laughed and clapped him on the back. "Can't do that, buddy. It ain't cooked yet. Another couple a weeks."

"I'm bored," said Lili. She wore a nightdress printed with teddy bears. She said the baby would like it. Her face was all stretched and shiny. The way her cheeks puffed out, she looked like a kid with a birthday cake. "What's a girl got to do to get a cigarette? Start talking fast or I'm going to roll down off this perch and bounce right out of here."

He told her about his grandmother and how, many years ago, Senhor Pinheiro had paid to have two windows put into her house and how she, unable to get used to it, boarded them back up again. Mãe had told Vasco about it, shaking her head to show how far she herself had come into the light. It was the same day she told him about Pedro Gomes getting an inside toilet. "What could he be thinking of? To bring it inside! A dirty thing like that." Mãe always stood a certain way, with her hand on her hip, to let everyone know she wasn't falling for it, whatever it was. She spread her hair once a week to dry in the sun and said, "I'll give you five escudos if you find a gray one and pull it out."

"Do you think she's going to like me?" said Lili.

"No," said Vasco, mock sad. "I don't think so."

Lili pulled her hand away.

"I was making a joke," said Vasco.

"My chest," said Lili. "It burns."

They put her on an IV drip and listened for the baby's heartbeat. Every time he heard the baby's heart beating, Vasco felt sick. Lili woke from a nap the next day and said, "What are all those little black things floating around the room?" She had the worst headache. By evening she couldn't feel her face.

Vasco prayed. He knelt down in a toilet cubicle and clasped his hands in front of his chin. "Please, God. Please." There was a wet patch under one knee. He tried to ignore it. "Help me." He was kneeling in urine. *Hail Mary, full of grace.* The tiles were freezing. *The Lord is with thee. Blessed art thou among women.* On the door someone had written "Springsteen sucks." *And blessed is the fruit of thy womb, Jesus.* Another pen had added "cock." *Holy Mary, Mother of God, pray for us sinners.* Cigarette ash on the tissue dispenser. *Now and at the hour of our death. Amen.*

The candle has burned itself out. Vasco looks across to the big window, but there is no reflection now. He picks up the spoon and the fork and puts them on the plate. It is time to go to bed.

"Lili," he whispers. "I'm sorry." How rarely he remembers. He thought his love would stay pure, the silver lining. But what remains? Disappointment, maybe; a little guilt.

A man can decide to do this and not do that. But feelings, thinks Vasco, are not in his control. I want to feel happy! This is the new madness. Everyone wanting to be happy. In Vasco's opinion they are crazy.

He breaks off a small piece of pastry and puts it in his mouth. He does not feel happy and he does not feel sad. These things he has lost. Belief he never had. It always eluded him. And what does he know? Not much. When he adds it all up, it does not amount to much. All I have, thinks Vasco, is my bloody opinion.

"God," he says, and bites on his fist. There is a throbbing behind his eyes. He gnaws his hand and stares at the table. Somewhere in the night a fox screeches. A mosquito whines close to his ear. The lantana brushes the window. For a long time he sits and thinks of nothing at all.

When he stirs, it is because he must shift his legs. The table shakes, and the fork and spoon slide off the plate.

Well, of course a man must have opinions. What is a man without opinions? He's Bruno, that's what.

Customers, Vasco knows, want conversation. They want jokes. They want comment. They want to be entertained. Eduardo, the old goat, will be in tomorrow, picking a fight and picking his nose. "Eduardo," Vasco will say, slapping the counter, "we've missed you. Though it's been cooler in here without all that hot air you blow around."

Yes, that's what he'll do, and that's what he'll say. Vasco smiles, his lips slightly parted. It is very fine, it is, to sit alone and contemplate.

The mind is a marvelous thing; no end to it at all.

He should get one of those jukeboxes. The cigarette machine has been jammed for two days. He needs to order more napkins, and the butter is running low. In the morning he will make a list.

Now it is time to go up, but first he will have a taste of that cake. Because—why not? Why shouldn't he? He will have just a taste and leave the rest. He thinks that is what he will do.

Four

The gate was open, so he zoomed right on in. He eased one leg over the crossbar, waited for the bike to slow a little, then jumped and ran along holding on between the bell and the knotted Benfica scarf. Perfect. He allowed himself a glance toward the bench, a quick one so it didn't seem like he was showing off. Pedro, Fernando, and *o treinador*. This was bad. Last week there had been six of them, and all they got was a lecture and sent away. It was the ones what didn't show up needed chewing out.

He dropped the bike on its side just off the field and jogged over. Pedro said, "Well, that's gone and done it."

"Yeah," said Fernando, "it's finished. No one's going to turn up."

"Kiss of death," said Pedro. He was two years older than Jay and attempting to grow a mustache. His father was a local hero. You saw posters of him all over, as far away as Santiago do Cacém and Colos: NELSON PAULO CAVACO—ACORDEONISTA E VOCALISTA. In his pictures he was always resting his chin on clasped hands and raising one very thick eyebrow.

Jay gazed out over the tarmac. It looked fit to melt. He kicked a pebble and bent down to pick up a discarded box of matches.

The coach got to his feet and threw the ball to Jay, who slipped the matches into his pocket and juggled the ball thirteen times without stopping.

"See that," said the coach to Pedro. Pedro raised an eyebrow, just like his dad. "Right," said the coach and looked at his watch, "when you see your *friends,* tell them that this team has one more chance to pull itself together. Now get lost."

Fernando tilted his head as if to say something but changed his mind. He had a big pimple on the end of his nose, all charged up with pus. Ruby said you should never squeeze your pimples, but this one looked ready to explode at a single touch.

Jay threw the ball high and straight. When he looked up to find his target, the sun burned everything out, and he thought he might as well die right here and now, there was no way he was going to head it. He got a foot to the ball, though, and sent it out across the field into the penalty box.

Running over to fetch it, he thought maybe the boys would play with him anyway. Only so they could go on his bike. He wasn't about to kid himself.

They passed him on his way back to the bench, but Jay knew he would catch up with them. Pedro's sneakers were white as prayer and his shirt as red as sin. "You know what's happened to this team?" he said to Fernando. "Yeah," said Fernando. "I know."

The coach took the ball and tucked it under his armpit. Jay waited to be sent away. The coach put one foot up on the bench and squinted at Jay. He looked puzzled or worried or something. The coach was called Senhor Santos. He was pretty old and his gums bled. When he spat—in football you always have to spit—you could see the red blood in the white spittle. You'd think it would mix up and turn pink, but that didn't happen. His hair had gray bits in it, and he had a small round belly that sat high up under his nipples. He could still run fast and not get out of breath.

Jay looked down. The tarmac was breaking up. There were little holes in it. It smelled like something fresh out of the oven, when it's been in there too long. Jay rattled the matches in his pocket.

The coach sighed and leaned closer to Jay. He's going to tell me a secret, thought Jay. Something he's never told before. Senhor Santos drove an expensive car, a big jeep called an UMM that looked like a posh tank. When he wasn't being a coach, he wore leather trousers in the winter and linen slacks in the summer. But everyone knew that Senhor Santos was sad because he had no children.

He was definitely going to tell Jay something, but Jay wished he would hurry up because Pedro and Fernando were heading back along the outside of the chicken-wire fence toward the village.

The coach shook his head and sighed again. He was still leaning in close to Jay, and there was nothing to do but wait.

It was worse for Senhor Santos's wife. Not having children made her crazy. She talked to imaginary people and set places for them at the table. That's what everyone said. She was called Maria Sequeira de Fátima da Gama. At the *escola primária,* they learned about her grandmother Ervanaria Guerreiro Sequeira de Fátima, who in 1936 walked on her knees all the way to the shrine at Fátima, where the Blessed Virgin Mary, Mother of God, had appeared to three shepherd children. Senhor Santos took his wife to Fátima as well, so that she could be blessed with babies, but Jay guessed it wasn't the same if you drove there in an UMM.

The coach blew on his fingers. He smelled of coffee and Trident gum. "We need a better field. You think so?"

"Maybe," said Jay. "Do you?"

"There's someone coming to Mamarrosa," said Senhor Santos. "Someone who used to live here. He's a very rich man now."

"Richer than you?"

Senhor Santos laughed. "I thought I would ask him to pay for improvements. Be a sponsor for the team."

"Yeah," said Jay. "Good idea."

"But first we need a team."

"Senhor Santos?" Jay worked the heel of his sneaker into the ground.

"Go ahead. Speak."

"Nothing. I mean . . . why . . . what . . ." Jay shook his head. "No, nothing."

O treinador set the ball down and clapped Jay on the shoulders. "Go on, then," he said. "Get lost."

★   ★   ★

The old man with one eye went past pushing a black bicycle up the road. He didn't have his patch on, and Jay got a good stare. It was cool the way there was just a hole there. The bike looked heavy, like it was made of lead. The old man kept stopping every ten steps or so. Pedro and Fernando were long gone. Jay didn't care. That Pedro was a *filho da puta* anyway.

Jay cycled out of the village. He thought about jumping off at the building site where two new houses were said to be going up, though they seemed not to be going in any direction at all. A worker in a lumberjack shirt appeared from behind a bunker of concrete bricks and wiped his brow. Jay tucked his head down and pedaled so hard his legs felt watery. At the top of the hill, he balanced in the saddle with his toes just touching the ground. Sweet. The moment before you let go was always the best.

He kicked off and let everything happen. The air flooded his nose and mouth and eyes. His T-shirt whipped up a storm. His ears sang. A stone beneath the front tire set him free, and he wheeled through the high scent of pine and the low sound in his chest and landed on his knees in the ditch.

The bike was all right. One spoke a bit bent, but that was nothing. His knees were cut. That was nothing as well. He took off his T-shirt and wiped his knees and put it back on. He wondered if he should go home. What day was it? Saturday. Dad would still be in bed, whatever day it was. When he got up, he would light a spliff, a joint, a jay. In England he used to say, "That's how come he's called it. Jay, like, know what I mean?" He might say for Jay to take the goats out. Jay didn't feel like taking the goats out. What did Mum do on a Saturday? Go to the shops, sit on the porch, drag a broom over the floor, sit on the porch, throw grain at the chickens. Same as every day, really. If he went back, she'd say, "For God's sake, Jay," or something like that.

★   ★   ★

The pickup was there on the gravel, so Jay knew Stanton was in. On the slate-topped table on the terrace was a glass half full of beer. Jay sat on the step and whistled. He shielded his eyes and saw out to the hills where they were black from the fires. They looked prickly. They made him want to scratch. He heard a hundred people died, but you can't believe everything you hear. There were only about six houses over that way. A flaming branch fell off a massive eucalyptus onto a *bombeiro,* skewered him to the ground. That's what they said. And a baby was found alive inside a ring of fire, just lying there on a white sheet that didn't have so much as a smudge. That was a great story. Jay didn't care if it was true or not. He thought the baby should have its own shrine and people should walk to Mamarrosa from all over Portugal on their knees. Stanton wasn't coming out. Jay whistled louder, giving him another chance. He went up to the terrace and touched the glass. It was cold. He held it for a moment, and it seemed to make the sweat pour out of his forehead. He put the glass to his lips and drank.

Quinta Nova da Alegria stood on the road to São Martinho, set back along a gravel drive and an avenue of palms, just like the stucco villas in the Algarve. The man who owned it lived in Lagos and came with a different woman every visit. There was a big wrought-iron gate and high walls to stop the happiness escaping. There was supposed to be a swimming pool around the back. Jay leaned his bike up against the wall and looked through the gate. No cars in the drive today.

There was a dog, though, and it began to bark in a lazy sort of way, as if Jay was hardly worth bothering about. Over to the left—Jay had not noticed it before—was a one-room *casa* with a tiny window and a splintery front door. Of course there would have to be somebody to take care of the place while the owner did whatever rich people do. Jay shook the gate to see about the dog. It snarled and took a few paces forward. It was big and sleek and black, not the usual Portuguese mutt. Now it was really barking. If it was Jay's house and Jay's dog, he wouldn't tie it up like that. "Never going to catch anyone, are you?" he said and began to climb.

The gate wobbled, his foot slipped, and he hurt his thigh against the twisted metal. It wasn't bad, but it made his heart beat faster. He sat on top of the gate and felt dizzy from the heat and the climb and the beer and that moment when he lost his balance. The dog was farther forward now, waiting to spring. Most of the guard dogs around here barked and wagged their tails at the same time. They were pretty pleased to see you, really. This one wasn't like that. It was flat-faced and hammer-headed and it didn't want to play.

Jay jumped. As he let go, he knew he had made a mistake. The dog's rope was still coiled. Jay opened his mouth to scream, but it was stuffed with fear: No sound could come out, no air could go in. He hit the ground and rolled with his hands up over his head, the dog's breath warm and meaty in his hair, the growl coming up from the ground like an earth tremor shaking his bones.

He rolled and rolled until he hit something solid and lay belly up in the gravel. Above, the palm leaves cut black slices in the sky. A tractor went along the road spreading its weary message, *off again, off again, off again*. Jay rubbed his head and looked at his hands. He smiled and turned to see the dog, straining now at its tether. "Sorry, mate, you lose."

He remembered the matches just as he was about to dive in and left them on the tiles. The sun smacked down so hard on the water it made little silver scars along the surface. A row of geraniums in earthenware pots gazed thirstily on. Jay shivered, cracked his fingers, and took a run up.

The all-and-nothingness of it.

The water closed over his head. He kept his eyes shut. Arms wrapped around his knees, hugged in close to his chest. Whatever the water did with him. The bubbles at his mouth, the cold in his ears.

It let him go, in the end, pushed him up and turned him on his side. He opened his eyes and spread his arms so he floated facedown. You only got it the first time. He knew it would be different when he jumped in again. Thin ribbons of red dust shifted over the mosaic floor. A grasshopper drifted along on its back. A leaf spun in slow motion and rested. Jay took air and swam. He did ten lengths of crawl, pulse climbing, thrill draining. He held on to the ledge and blinked away the water and panted. Then he got out and jumped in a few times. He swam another length, a good stretch of it underwater, and a blankness entered into him and flattened all desire. He got out, spread his T-shirt on the tiles, and lay down. The hot tiles bit at his elbows and feet.

The sky was so blue it hurt. He closed his eyes and watched the black strands flicker across the red. Ruby might be in São Martinho. She went in that bar near the brick-built pond with the terrapins. She said, "Miguel likes me. I'm good for business." They used to play together all the time, but one day she stopped playing. Just like that. If he found her, she might buy him a Coke. She might get Miguel to give him a Coke. She said "Just you wait" and "You've no idea, *have you?*" like something was going to happen to him, something bad. He wanted to ask her what, but there was no point, she'd never say. There was no point asking Mum either, and there was definitely no point asking Dad.

Jay thought about China falling down last night. He held his leg like he'd been shot and rolled around saying, "You're in or you're out, mate. In or fucking out."

Chrissie said, "He wets himself, he stays like that." She made herself a cup of tea. She had to step over him to get to the kitchen and again to get to her chair.

He stayed down there moaning and holding his leg. Chrissie dabbed her mouth with a handkerchief and hummed. She had that look like her eyes were open but not seeing. That used to scare Jay, so he turned her into a princess under a spell. The spell made her sleepwalk, but it didn't make her scary.

China said, "Don't talk to me about *your* percentage. You're lucky I've given you a job, you fucking piece of shit."

Ruby came in and said, "Well, I'm not clearing it up."

"Dad," said Jay, kneeling down, "it's Jay."

Ruby waved a hand in front of Chrissie's face. "Hello? I said, hello? Jesus Christ. I mean." She went out again.

"Do you want me to help you up, Dad?" Jay tried to get an arm under him. The alcohol hung like rain in the air.

"Can't say anything, mate. Lips is sealed."

China fell asleep then, or passed out. It was like he'd been tortured. There was a video they had in England, they used to put it on sometimes when they'd run out of cartoons. It was black and white, and it was about World War II and this pilot who'd been shot down over Germany and taken prisoner. He escaped and got back to England, but he kept staggering around the streets thinking everyone was an enemy and talking in this crazy way. It was because he never told any secrets, no matter what they did to him. In the end it was all right because they took him to a hospital where the nurses had squeaky shoes and stiff dresses and he looked a bit dazed but his hair was tidy and he smiled at a nurse and then the music swelled up and you could see he was going to get better. Jay started thinking of China like that. He never decided to, but it happened anyway.

He was going to try this thing. It was like a science experiment. He picked up an old newspaper on the back terrace and poked around the garden until he found a piece of glass. Back by the pool, he scrunched a few pages and laid two matches on top, head to head. Then he held the glass over the matches, making sure he got a good angle on the sun. The glass heated up all right. Jay switched hands. He moved the glass closer in to the match heads. After a while he moved it farther away and over a bit to the right.

Jay put the glass down. Dud matches. He struck one on the tiles, and it flared straight off. He tossed it on the paper and stepped back.

The paper decided to fly. It took off on flaming wings and began to drift over the edge of the pool toward the garden. Jay knew he should run after it, but the message didn't get through to his legs. Oh, he thought. And then again, Oh.

The paper went nearly the length of the pool, then did a kind of backward somersault and chose the water for a soft landing. Two black strings of soot hung in the air like exclamation marks. It was time, Jay decided, to leave.

He wasn't going to look for Ruby, though. In fact, he wasn't going to speak to Ruby anymore, not until she started being nicer to him. And he wasn't going to tell her that either. She'd have to work it out for herself.

He needed something to drink. "I've got a thirst on," Dad would say. That meant he was going to drink a lot of beer.

It was supposed to be different here. That was why they had come. "You can play outside, can't you," Chrissie kept saying. "All that space. Go on."

"Am I Portuguese now?" Jay asked once.

Chrissie didn't look sure. "Suppose so."

"Don't be bleeding soft," said China. "'Course you're bleeding not."

A car passed, hooting and swerving, though there was no need. A moped came from the other direction, and the man nodded to Jay, who tried to get the bike on its back wheel as a kind of salute. He managed it in the end, but the man and moped were gone by then.

Jay decided to go to Senhora Pinheiro's. Senhora Pinheiro's garden came down to the street with a wall only thirty centimeters high to mark it off. She had the best fruit trees in Mamarrosa, especially the peaches. Most of the peach trees in Mamarrosa were sick. If you bit into the fruit, it was always rotten in the middle. But Senhora Pinheiro's peaches were like Our Lady: beautiful on the outside, sweet perfection inside.

Pedro said that if Senhora Pinheiro caught a child stealing her peaches, she beat it with a brass poker and threw it in the nettles. He said that once, a long time ago, she beat a boy so hard his brains got shaken up, and after that he couldn't speak Portuguese, only Spanish, because that's how dumb he was. Jay knew this was a joke, but the first time Senhora Pinheiro caught him stealing he was so scared he peed—just a bit—in his pants. "I don't like dirty little boys in my garden," she said. "Come with me." Jay wouldn't, so she dragged him along by the arm and left him outside her front door. She came back with a damp rag and attacked his face and neck and made him wipe his hands. "Now sit there." She pointed to a stool. Jay thought she was going to fetch the poker, but he did what he was told. She was a very tidy-looking lady in a flowered housecoat, and her hair was scraped back with not one strand escaping. It made sense that she would want to clean him up before the beating. "Now drink this," she said and gave him some lemonade. "And take this bag of peaches. And if I catch you again, you may not be so lucky."

He had always been lucky so far, but today, the day when he was thirstiest of all, he could not get caught. He ate a peach and trod the pit right into the earth so another tree would grow. "Somebody in your garden," he sang. "There's somebody here." He walked beneath a pergola, getting closer to the house, and picked some grapes off the vine. "Look what I'm *do*-ing." Jay heard the fly curtain tinkle and turned toward the door, but only the wind had stirred it.

Screw everyone, thought Jay. Nobody wants to know. He sat down to think about what it was that nobody wanted to know, but he soon gave up. He thought about Chrissie and the way he could go and stand in front of her sometimes and not a thing in her face would change and then he'd see how she worked to make it change like she had to force each muscle to move, had to put a real hard effort into making her eyes look at his. She could fight off the spell most of the time, only sometimes she couldn't. He had this dream a long time ago where she was dressed up as a princess in a long floaty pink dress and she was running around everywhere with a big bottle of medicine that was a cure for spells and everyone who came near her begged to be given some and she just laughed and blew kisses and didn't care at all about anything. It was a dream he had just once, but he turned it into something else, a kind of daydream or fantasy he could play and rewind and repeat when things got too boring. China was in this one too, dressed in some sort of uniform the color of olive leaves. He sat in a chair with a high carved back and said, "You'll have to kill me first," and four men lifted him on the chair and carried him to Chrissie, who didn't laugh like she did when she saw the others, but stroked his hair and held his hand and said, "Who did this to you?" That's where the thing got stuck. It wasn't supposed to end there, but he didn't know how to make it go on. That black-and-white film filled up with music, and you knew from that what was going to happen. Jay thought China should get out of the chair, but he never did, not even when Jay said, practically out loud, for him to move. It showed you it wasn't all make-believe, because China really was like that. Chrissie said that he'd never done anything he was told, and she'd wasted enough breath on him to last the rest of her life.

There was nowhere to go, so he rode out toward Covo da Zora and into the woods. Some of the cork trees had been freshly harvested. They looked like old men who had rolled up their trousers, fallen asleep in the sun, and had the skin cooked right off. The numbers that the *corticeiros* painted in white stood out brightly against the dried-blood bare trunks. The numbers told you which year the cork had been cut. You counted forward nine years, and you knew when the tree would be ready again. Sometimes you got a band of the same numbers together, most often they were all mixed up. Jay played a game where you had to ride between one tree and another, counting down the numbers from nine to one. You weren't allowed to stop until you found the last number. Sometimes it took ages.

By the time he got to number one, Jay was sweating. Even his

bum was sweating. His shorts were wet, like he'd sat down in a puddle. He let the bike drop and collapsed under the tree.

China was still on the floor when Jay had gone to bed last night,
but he wasn't there this morning. There was a jug of amber liquid on
the table. Jay got rid of it so his mother wouldn't have to see. He bet
the World War II pilot never peed in a jug when he could have
walked a few yards and peed off the side of the terrace.

There was a beetle with beautiful green-black wings crawling
along a rock just next to him. Jay put out his finger and let the beetle walk over it.

China wasn't like the World War II pilot anyway. Jay never
thought he was. It was stupid.

The beetle reached the end of the rock, and Jay cupped his hand
and moved him back to the beginning.

That pilot wasn't even a hero. All he did was get captured and
then run away and go mad.

Jay sat up to get a better look at the beetle. The markings on its
back were like eyes.

Chrissie wasn't a princess. She had lines on her face. She had tea
breath. She had hair under her arms. A prince wouldn't kiss her and
wake her up.

For a brief moment the beetle whirred its wings and hovered.

Stanton came into his mind. He had not realized it before, but
Stanton had fat hips like a woman, and his lips were far too red.

Jay held his thumb over the beetle. All around, the crickets called
out and the birds answered. He brought his thumb down and
pressed until it hurt.

Where the ground turned steep, he dumped the bike and scrabbled
up the rocky slope, using his hands when his feet began to slide. He
paused and took off his T-shirt and tied it over his head to stop
the sweat dripping into his eyes. When the path leveled out a bit, he
stopped again and looked back down over the trees and the road

beyond. It wasn't a path he was on, really, it was a firebreak. You saw them on lots of the hills: parched orange streaks set into the scrub.

Jay picked up a stick and bashed at a prickly bush. Ruby used to do races with him through the *silves*. They had a big stick each. The rule was you had to go in a straight line, and if you got scratched, you had to take it like a man. If you cried out, the other person won.

He walked through the scrub, taking swipes at everything. He came up to a young pine and parried and feinted and thrust and then jumped up to knock off a cone. "Ha," he said. "Got you."

"Got you," he said louder. "Got you," he said again.

If there was a fire up here now, it wouldn't spread too far, because of the firebreak. He wondered what it would look like to see a fire spread across the hill. How high would the flames go?

He squatted down on the floor of brown pine needles. They would light pretty easy. He imagined the needles on the tree sparking up and showering down like one gigantic firework.

He would run to the nearest house—there was one down by the road where he'd come into the woods—and then he'd run back with a blanket to start beating out the flames. You'd probably see the smoke from the house.

The *bombeiros* would come, and when other people heard the siren, they would come as well. They might let him hold the hose. He'd definitely get a ride in the fire engine. His face would be black with soot and streaked with sweat. He could almost feel the hands on him, clapping his shoulders, patting the back of his neck.

Jay took the box of matches out of his pocket. There was a picture of a hedgehog on the top and its spines were all red-tipped matches. The first match was a dud. He took a second and struck it and held it up level with his eyes. The flame was weak yellow, a sickly thing. All he had to do was drop it. And stand back when the fire caught.

*   *   *

He blew out the flame and put the match carefully back in the box. He stood up and dusted off his hands on his shorts. Looking around, he calculated the shortest route back to his bike. When he got home he would feed the animals, maybe clean out the chicken shed.

Those were the things that needed doing. Somebody had to get them done.

Five

My husband has a particular way of disagreeing with me. He'll say, "Any sane person would see that's complete rubbish and utter codswallop." Sometimes he just says, "Any sane person, Eileen," and leaves it at that. Which is rich coming from a man who can't open a book without first holding it under his nose and giving it a good sniff.

He's here somewhere, marching around the town with a panama on his head and the Insight book in his hand. I'm supposed to be sitting in the café by the Galp station writing postcards. "Hot flash?" he said. I said that's what it was.

I'm walking (aimlessly, he'd say) around the main square, which is only about the size of our garden at home, though I suppose our garden is *quite* large. It's hot again today but fresh. The sky is the exact same shade as a bowl I cradled all the way back from Agadir—one of *his* holidays—only to drop it the next day on the kitchen floor.

Yesterday it rained. One of those rapid drenchings you get when everyone's just about at the point where they can't breathe anymore and then it buckets down, like God emptying His bathwater on your head. This morning I opened the window and I couldn't help it, I said, "Lots of air today." He was still in bed, fighting with the map and being cranky. "Is there really, Eileen? How much air, exactly, would you say there is today?"

It's lunchtime, but I'm not hungry. I am hot, though. I'm going to sit down for a while. There are two benches, but they're not in the shade. I'm going to sit on the grass under that big fan palm.

From down here I can see a long line of mud nests under the eaves of the municipal building across the square. House martins or swallows. A flash of red at the throat means swallow, but all I can see at the moment is a host of glossy dark backs. If I look the other way—through my eyelashes, because the sun is pretty strong—I can see the town climbing up above. All those white houses standing on each others' shoulders, and some leaning out to the sides as if they're trying to get a better view. I like the sidewalks here too. Chunky cobblestones in black and white laid into diamonds and squares and zigzags. They're very uneven, though. In England, I expect, there'd be lawsuits.

All the shops are closing for the two-hour lunch break. A cashier just came out of the Crédito Agrícola and checked her hair in the window. She was very smart. She looked like the kind of woman who would never leave her cereal bowl in the sink all day. The sound of her heels on the cobbles made me feel lazy and rather disorganized. I fussed inside my bag, but why I should pretend to be busy, goodness only knows.

Next to the bank is a motorbike repair shop on one side where the sidewalk has turned dark and oily, and a furniture shop on the other. The man in the furniture place has turned the sign and lowered the blind, but he hasn't pulled it all the way down, and I can see him taking off his shoes and lying down on a bed. He's got his knees drawn up and is kind of hugging himself like he means to settle down for a good long sleep rather than—I heard this phrase the other day—a power nap. I think they used to be called catnaps, but that's a bit lacking in executive tone.

Speaking of cats, I discovered a litter of kittens in the grounds of our *pousada,* right behind the shed where they keep the garden tools. The mother had left—just for a minute, as it turned out—and there they were, turned into this little heap of struggling flesh that gave me pins and needles in my heart. The errant mother, a tabby with a white-tipped tail, hopped back on the double when she saw me and crashed down on her side with her teats in the air. The kittens all got stuck in, and she gave me a long sideways look with her slanty golden eyes, and I thought, Don't stare at me that way, you're just a bloomin' cat.

The bank has got these browned-out shiny windows, like sunglasses, and I've taken a glance (a bit more than that, actually) at myself, which was a mistake. I look like a suet pudding in a sundress. And I deliberately didn't tuck all my hair up into the hat but left some strands coming down around my face, thinking it would be what the hairdressers call *softened*. I can't say I'm pleased with the effect. The polish on my toenails is unbelievably garish. Did I do that?

When I couldn't get into my favorite black trousers, I said to my husband that I was going low-carb. He said, "Any sane person, Eileen." Then he put his arm around me. "It's what every woman goes through." He kissed me, just missing my lips. "Frankly, I'm surprised you kept the weight off as long as you did."

I think I might be having a hot flash now.

This, as my husband keeps reminding me, is my holiday. For once it really is. I dug my heels in this time.

"But what are we going to do there?" he said.

"Break bread and drink wine."

He sniffed the Portugal guidebook. This was just before he opened it up and realized there were only nine pages devoted to our entire region. "That's what we do every day," he said. "We do that at home."

I had to get away from that window. It was like an achy tooth, I couldn't leave it be. I've walked round to the front of the municipal building, but I still don't know what it is. Law courts, perhaps. A library?

I hadn't realized how white my legs are. Practically blue.

There are pink marble steps up to the entrance and green metal fretwork doors. Left and right are big primary-color murals painted on white tiles. One is of the town, the bridge and the river and the white cube houses stacking up and up. The other shows workers—peasant women in flowered skirts and scarves, and the men all in hats and knee-high boots—gathered in the field looking over wheat and olives to a distant village.

My aunt Betsy's legs—she was my great-aunt, really—were blue. I'm talking about the last year of her life, when she went to live with Nana McGowan. She had venous ulcers and it made the skin on her legs turn all duck-egg and shiny. They'd swell something rotten, even with the bandages on most of the day. She used to say, "Never mind me, dear," and hobble about getting under everyone's feet. It's awful, but that's all I remember, an old woman with bad legs muttering "Never mind me" and getting in the way. I said so once to my mother. "Sad to think that's how she was fixed in people's minds; a whole life diminished." My mother didn't even look up from her tapestry. "Betsy," she said, "was a horrible woman."

I still don't know what it is, this place. I can't see any signs anywhere. I like that. I like it better than all those *delightful* Tuscan towns we "did" the year before last. All that history and architecture—it gives you a headache, just shuffling past on sore sightseeing feet, trying to blot out the English voices everywhere.

That was one of my holidays. So-called. He, my husband, says, "A bit of shopping, a bit of pottering, a bit of sightseeing. That's what you like." And buries the dining room table with maps and leaflets and brochures and books while he plans the invasion strategy. "May as well learn something, Eileen. If you don't, it's not sightseeing, it's gawping."

You don't see many old women here. The only reason I've noticed is because of the old men. They seem to be everywhere, and they hang out in gangs in their sweaters and old suit jackets, fanning themselves with newspapers or warming their backs in the dying sun or propping up the bars, or just walking about, spread across the road, holding up the traffic. But the women don't do any of that. If you see an elderly woman, she will be in a doorway, broom in hand. I saw one yesterday, and she swept the dirt onto the sidewalk, kissed the plaster saint in the alcove, and closed the door without looking out.

I've just passed four old men on my way up this street, Rua Souza Prado. In England only teenagers hang about like that. The post office has a red sign with a white horse and Pan-like figure flying across it; there's a Mini-Mercado grocery shop, a shop that sells clothes, another that sells shoes, and a hardware shop with a poster in the window advertising the forthcoming shows of a singer called Nelson Paulo Cavaco. Nelson has an accordion and eyebrows that could double as earmuffs and a way of gazing into the lens that tells you a lot about what he thinks of himself. My favorite shop so far (they're all closed, so I'm only looking in the windows) is Casa Rita. It sells everything. Watches, scarves, lipsticks, vases with hideous gold paint, Benfica baseball caps, penknives, antimony picture frames, Drakkar Noir aftershave, ships in bottles, necklaces, children's bikes, toy cars, and B.U. eau de toilette. If I took my husband in there, he would turn purple.

Squished between two of the shops, both of which are fresh and sparkly with new awnings, is a tumbledown house properly flayed by the sun, with blistered paint and a chewed-up old door and weeds and even what looks like a little tree growing out of the roof tiles. On one of the deep windowsills is a lilac pair of little girl's shoes with white laces, three peaches in a line, and, propped up against the shutter, an unframed painting of potted geraniums. On the ground below the window is a terra-cotta pot of the same flowers in a deeper shade of red. The way the sun spills over the street, it divides the window into two triangles, one dark, the other bright.

I stood there for quite a while, feeling, I don't know, happy. The peaches and the shoes and the flowers. I thought, There's a moment, there's a sight. Of course that spoiled it, so I started walking again, and now I'm coming up to another *praça,* another square, though there's still a distance to climb and I can see the big church up above with its two crosses, one plain, one lacy. I'm feeling a little giddy, happiness or exertion, I don't know. But I think I could be here. I could run away and be here. I could be one of those Englishwomen with fat ankles and capillaried cheeks and hair coming down from under a tattered hat who set up in places like this, to keep bees or grow runner beans or save donkeys. I could ride into town on a donkey, barefoot on a donkey with a wicker shopping basket, and everyone would know me and say in a fond sort of way, ah, there she goes, the crazy Englishwoman.

I might just do it too. Why not? I'd like to see his face.

When he catches me checking the horoscopes, he either smirks and says something like "So what's written in our stars today?" or he blinks very, very slowly and says, "Reason and rationality. Couldn't you at least give them a *try*?"

Before he gets into bed he has to tuck one slipper inside the other and place them just so beside the chair. If I walk past and knock them he gets out of bed to put them straight.

What's rational, anyway? This world we live in. Who's to say?

I read the other day in the paper about this woman, she was American, she murdered this other woman and stole her baby. The baby hadn't even been born. She killed the woman and slit her open and took the baby and kept it for eight days before she was arrested. You can't even imagine that happening, but it did. The next day there was another article and it said that there had been twelve cases just like it in America. Twelve cases!

I said to my husband, "They must have been doctors, these women, or nurses. I mean, to be able to get the baby out alive."

He said, "No, it's simple, you just cut straight down. It's simple as long as you don't have the mother's life to consider." Like he could do it easily, like it wouldn't be a problem at all.

*   *   *

For him, you see, it was something else to store, to know. These things occurred. Events took place. Facts. An accumulation of facts.

I sometimes think it all comes down to the factory. It makes cake decorations and accessories, not the ones you can eat but the ribbons and trimmings, foil boards, happy-birthday signs, candleholders, reindeer and Santa Clauses, plastic foliage, paper doilies. He inherited it from his father, and he's always hated it and never said so.

Boxers don't throw their weight around out of the ring.

My husband is always learning stuff. Serious, he'd say, but it's still just stuff. It doesn't help. His idea of a holiday is to go somewhere very far away and gorge on facts. He could tell you the exact altitude of Machu Picchu, or the number of inhabitants in the largest of the Cape Town shanties, or the price of a helicopter ride over the *favelas* in Rio, or the ethnic classification of the fourteen tribes of the Chittagong Hill Tracts. His holidays (we started "taking turns" about ten years ago) are always amazing. Knockout. Just that—I'm flattened by the time we get home, knocked right out.

We stayed three nights in a hut that belonged to a Mru king in the emerald hills close to the Burmese border. "Doesn't this feel too weird?" I said. "To be here. To *consume* this."

"It's not about consuming, Eileen," he said, "it's about understanding. You could read about these tribal people for decades without understanding, if you've never lived among them."

"For three days?" I said.

"Where's the mosquito net?" he said. "They specifically said mosquito nets provided."

"What about Richard? He's our son. You could try understanding him."

He slapped his neck and said, "There's one. Did you remember your malaria tablet this morning?"

"Go out with him," I said. "Go to his pubs and clubs. See it as a holiday. Live among them."

He said, "Any sane person, Eileen," and switched off the electric lantern.

‹‹‹‹‹‹‹‹‹‹‹‹‹‹‹

We met an English couple in a village where we stopped for coffee. I don't know how they ended up at our table. The man had no shirt, just a denim waistcoat that was as filthy as his jeans, and his eyes looked like all the blood vessels were about to burst. The woman was more presentable, but she reminded me of Buster when he's just had his tail trodden on. They'd been out here nearly five years. My husband asked what they did, for a living he meant. "Chill," said the man, "mainly, like," and my husband nodded as if he too mainly chilled.

We had coffee and chatted, like new friends at the Rotary.

My husband said, "Fascinating region, the Alentejo. Undiscovered."

And at breakfast he'd been saying there's a reason for that, Eileen, there's a reason why it's undiscovered.

The man said, "Poorest region in the poorest country in the European Union. Until all them eastern monkeys climbed on board."

My husband nodded as if he had been on the verge of saying this himself.

"Highest male suicide rate, though," said the man. "Still holds the record for that."

"Right," said my husband, storing it up.

"All these old geezers. Found another one today, they did. Gone and strung hisself up in the woods."

"Awful," said the woman. She shivered and rubbed her arms.

"Yeah," said the man. "I'd stick a gun in me mouth but never a rope round me neck."

"Now," said my husband, moving things along, "if you had to rank these villages here from one to ten, ten being a definite visit and one being give it a miss, how do you think they'd score?"

They didn't look to me like the most reliable of sources, but the man kept spurting information, and my husband kept taking it all in. At least he's enjoying himself, I thought. But we were driving out toward Aljustrel in the afternoon, and he started biting on his top lip. "Is it bad?" I said.

"I'm sorry, Eileen," he said, "but I'm turning the car around as soon as I can."

We went back to our room, and I set about drawing the curtains, but he said no, he was going to read. I knew then it wasn't a migraine, though we kept up the pretense.

He sat on the bed and didn't look at me.

"Shall I stay with you?" I said.

He turned his head so I couldn't see his expression. "You know how it is."

I didn't move right away. I gave him some time. If you can't talk on holiday, when can you?

In the end I said, "Poor you," and picked up my bag and went out.

At the beach I walked in the wet sand looking down at my feet and watching the way the indentations smoothed over almost as soon as I lifted my toes. I was thinking, I suppose, about my husband and Richard and the whole situation. Not in any proper way, though, not so as I could say what I was thinking. I was feeling it and walking it and breathing it. Perhaps I wasn't thinking at all. It's been nearly two years now. My husband has these times. Bereaved people are the same. Sometimes they buckle for no apparent reason, like some internal structure just collapsed, and they carry on with hard, bright eyes pretending to be normal, or they take themselves off and don't want to talk. They say with bereavement that after two years it begins to get better.

I felt bad for my husband. He didn't have a headache, but I could see the hurt anyway. All that tension around his mouth and his shoulders slumping like that. What I should have done is sat down next to him on the bed. And . . . what?

I can worry something to death and come up with a solution. It's got to be a small thing, though. Not that they seem small at the time. They get to be enormous and take over everything. Like Janet Larraway's cherry cake.

Janet is someone I don't see very often. We used to live down the street from them, down the cul-de-sac, actually, when we were on the estate (an executive housing estate, I must point out, not the other kind). Janet's house crowned the top of the road at right angles to the other houses, like it was presiding over the whole street, which Janet actually did. Anyway, she came to visit with a rather feeble bunch of freesias and a cherry cake. The cake was obviously shop-bought, but she'd taken off the wrapping and set it on a plate. We sat in the kitchen and Janet said, "Eileen, I'm glad to see you've *finally* got rid of those awful brown tiles round the cooker. Those new ones are interesting. Sort of Neapolitan ice cream, would you say?"

I made proper coffee, and Janet enlightened me about her new coffee grinder. I cut the cake and we each had a slice. It wasn't Mr Kipling, but it wasn't much better than that, something from a supermarket rather than a proper bakery. I said, "Delicious cake, Janet." Then I said, "You can't beat homemade." I thought perhaps her expression changed, but she didn't say anything. I started to get a bit desperate. I said, "You must give me the recipe. I'd love to have a go myself. Unless it's a family secret, of course, ha, ha." And all the time I was thinking Shut up, just *shut up*.

Janet said, "We've missed you, Eileen. We've all missed you. Sarah Baxendale says to tell you she knows she's still got your Pyrex and she's sorry but her grandson's started a worm farm in it and can she keep it a bit longer?"

I hardly slept a wink. I kept going over and over it: what I'd said, what she'd said, how much longer she'd stayed, how she looked when she left, how we had somehow omitted to kiss at the door, whether I'd waved too hard and too long as she pulled away in the Saab. The next day was the same. Family secret, of course, ha, ha. There was no obvious way out. I thought of ringing her up, but what would I say? "Just in case you thought I was being sarcastic, I wanted to say I did really like your cake, really." Or "Look, there's nothing wrong with shop-bought. I just wanted to let you know."

Oh, it was a mess. But I worked and worked on it, you know, trying different scenarios in my head, seeing how they played out, thinking through the angles, calculating the odds, weighing the pros and cons. Everything else I did that day, I did on automatic pilot. I can be very focused when I want to be.

And I don't even care about Janet Larraway, her or her stupid cake. I don't now and I didn't then. I can think of a *hundred* reasons not to care.

These things happen to me, though. I always know, as well, that in a couple of days or weeks, or however long, it will seem silly. Silly and trivial and absurd. Think about that time with Douglas Enright, I tell myself, when it turned out he hadn't even *heard* what you said in the first place. Think about all the things you've worried and fretted and schemed about that you can't even remember anymore!

Those are the small things. The ones it is possible to think about in minute detail. The big things aren't like that. They're the stuff that we breathe in and breathe out, the things that we don't solve like puzzles. They're the stuff that we walk through, denting the surface, like the sand beneath my toes.

I didn't ring Janet, I sent her a card—a note to say thank you for the flowers and the cake, just plain *cake* and *thank you,* no messing about with adjectives. What I did, I wrote that a bunch of us were hoping to start a book group and that since she was so experienced, we would be ever so grateful if she could think of coming to speak at our inaugural meeting and offering a few pointers. I had it just about right. The right mix of briskness and fealty that she'd warm to. Of course, then I had to actually start a book group, but I didn't mind. I almost convinced myself that I was going to in any case.

Right now I'm thinking about getting up and making the final ascent to the church. But it's rather a lovely spot here beneath this pergola, and the heat has been building up. It's jagged heat, sharp, like you might cut yourself if you move too quickly. This weight I'm carrying doesn't help.

Perhaps I'll take a while longer. There's an aviary here, though maybe that sounds a bit grand: There's a cage about the size of a dovecote, with a parrot, three canaries, and two tiny feathered harlots flashing around a seed tray. There's a drinking fountain, an ornamental fountain, and picnic benches. I've been watching a mother feed her baby with orange gloop. He stuck his fist in the pot and tried to suck it off while the mother tried to wipe it off with a muslin cloth. It turned into quite a battle. The baby thought it was fun at first but then got into a panic, like this was the last food he was ever going to see, right there on his fist, and his own mother was taking it away. She's young, mid-twenties, I'd say, with wavy black hair and a turquoise T-shirt that shows her tight little belly button. A few times she happened to look over and see me watching, and the first couple of times she smiled and I smiled back, but after that it got to be a bit uncomfortable and I had to turn away.

The far side of the square is formed by the walled and terraced garden of a house that must have been splendid once and is now rather dignified. There's a sweep of steps up, balustrades and verandas and balconies and what look like, from this distance, gargoyles above the entrance. The garden is overgrown but inviting; the orange trees along the perimeter have the darkest, shiniest leaves, and there is a row of sunflowers positively crowing out on the middle terrace. I've been wondering if the house belonged to Dr. Fernando dos Santos Agudo. There's a bronze bust of him here, a bald, bespectacled man in jacket and tie. He died in 1989, and though I would have said that I don't know any Portuguese, I have read on the inscription that he served four generations of the people of this town *com grande competência*.

Who gets their own bronze bust in England these days? Not doctors, I expect.

Well, I think I should stir. Pleasant as it is. My husband must be looking for me by now, and I ought to be making my way down, not up, back to the café by the Galp station.

I wish I were a bit lighter on my feet and could contemplate a dash to the church first. I was looking at this menopause website (incredible how the Internet hypnotizes you) and it had a list: menopause myth and fact. One of the myths, apparently, is that you always put on weight. A lot of women don't. Another myth is that you suffer some kind of memory loss. And another is that you lose interest in sex.

I'm afraid I must be one of those women who generate the myths in the first place.

With sex, it's not that I don't like the *idea*. I can see a young couple walking along, their hips brushing, and remember how it was. I don't mean I get nostalgic. I mean I feel it: a surge in every body cavity, a tingle in my toes.

My husband has a way of holding my hand that means *he* has the idea, though in his case he means to act on it. He holds my hand but works his index finger loose and strokes my palm, the edge of my thumb, the inside of my wrist.

He's a good man, my husband, one of the best. Ask anyone. The girls at the factory all love him. I say girls, but they're grandmothers, mostly, working for pin money, or perhaps for the rent, I don't know. He teases them ("On a go-slow today, eh, Sylvie? We'll get you embalmed one of these days, put you in a case on the landing.") and they tease him right back ("Come over here, Mr. Mowatt, June's got a twist in her stocking, and she wants you to set it straight").

He's got a robust way about him, I know. Any sane person,

Eileen. But that's just him: his energy, his life bursting out. Let's get this show on the road.

The factory's never been enough for him. Cake decorations are not enough for him. Business is business, he says, but you know he doesn't mean it. Has to be twice the man, that's what he thinks.

Hands. I used to spend a lot of time looking at hands. It was my party trick when I was young. I read people's fortunes. My husband-to-be called me Gypsy Rose Lee and studied my palm.

He said, "You're going to be proposed to by a dashing young man in possession of a Triumph Stag and a birthmark behind his right ear, and you're going to have five children and live happily ever after."

He didn't know how to read the lines. I knew we'd have only one child.

Today, in the car, waiting for a flock of sheep to cross, I said, "Isn't this more like it? More like a *holiday*?"

He said, "You know the etymology of the word, Eileen? Do you? Well, that's how I feel about *holidays*. That's what they are to me."

When did he start doing that? Using my name only when he wants to make me feel stupid.

I've got sweat patches under my arms that have spread right round to the front of my bra. Like I've been leaking milk. What a sight for sore eyes! We'll go back to the *pousada* and I'll freshen up. I fancy sardines for dinner. We'll have a bottle of Mateus rosé, I'll insist on it though he can be quite the wine snob, and I'll cut right through the sarcasm with cheeriness. You can always defeat sarcasm in the end with cheeriness. It's quite a good weapon, actually; a blunt instrument but a strong one.

It's easy to forget that sometimes. About a month after Richard first told us he was gay, I sat my husband down to talk about it. Not that he'd said he had a problem with it. He just hadn't said anything at all. So I got the coffee and biscuits ready, and I sat him down and said, "I think we ought to discuss it, you know, Richard's being gay and all that."

He said, "Right. Go on then."

I took a bourbon cream and tucked my feet up on the sofa, all casual, and said, "Well, how do you *feel* about it?"

And he said, "This isn't one of your daytime shows, Eileen." He pointed to the biscuit plate and the coffeepot and screwed up his face like he was just disgusted by it all, and then he got up and it was over and I was sitting there chewing on a bourbon cream and I think I finished the lot.

I know what he meant, though. All that pawing away at emotion. Sharing. Half the time it's only making the problem worse. Sometimes it seems like it's inventing the problem. There's this other menopause website, and on the home page it has this quotation, I don't know who said it, about menopausal women having to "mourn the loss of fertility." Have you ever heard such rot? Your childbearing years are long gone. I mean, I'm fifty-six. It's ridiculous. I got over that a long time ago.

It has occurred to me that it's not Richard he's angry with but me. You can't be angry with your son for being gay, not in this day and age, not unless you *are* one of those dads on the morning shows. Maybe he thinks I should have known. Maybe he thinks I did know, that I read it in his stars or in his palm and kept quiet about it, and that's made him really seethe inside.

Though naturally he doesn't believe in any of that nonsense, so I don't even know why these things occur to me. But you can know something's not true and still think it anyway. There's only so much you can do with reason and rationality. They don't take you all the way. Whatever my husband says. And if they do, then what's his problem? If they do, then why has he spent the last two years avoiding his own son?

He'd never admit it, though. I asked him once, "Why do you always sniff your book before you open it? What are you smelling?"

"I don't," he said. "I don't *sniff* my book."

"You just did. Just now. Right before you opened it."

He looked at me and chewed his lip like he always does when he's thinking something through, and I could see him remembering, realizing I was right. "Oh, *that,*" he said, "that is a pause, a moment of reflection to locate myself in the text, where I left off the previous night."

"Do they all smell different?" I said.

"Do you mind?" he said. "I'm trying to read."

There'll be no grandchildren, of course. I don't mind that, not really. I wouldn't have time, not with all the donkeys to take care of.

Oh, I can see him crossing the square now, heading toward me. He must have looped down another way to the Galp station and come back up again. He's seen me now; I can tell by the way he's shifted down a gear, pretending he wasn't at all worried. I hadn't realized how shabby that seersucker jacket has got. I'm going to take it down to Oxfam when we get home. It looks too big for him anyway, and his trousers are hanging off him too. A proper Jack Sprat he is!

"Eileen," he says, taking off his hat, "you're here."

"Yes," I say, "I am."

"Clearly. Well, what do you want to do?"

"It's my holiday," I say.

"Correct," he says and looks straight at me, so I look straight back and see the sun light up the stray hairs on his cheeks, the red glow behind his ears, the dark shadow of his eyes.

"And I'd like to sit here and do nothing."

He looks around him like a man who has entered a room and found he is in the wrong place. Then he sits down next to me on the bench, takes out a handkerchief, and wipes his head.

The parrot scratches its chest and, in its drag-queen voice, says,

"Obrigado. Por favor. Obrigado." The canaries glide back and forth like trapeze artists. I lean on my husband, or he leans on me. We are, in any case, girded together. I smell the jasmine now on the pergola. It is always stronger later in the day. I look out across the *praça,* at the winding street, the red roof tiles and rusting iron balconies, and watch the human traffic: a policeman kneeling to polish his shoe, a young girl in white fluttering up toward the church, housewives dipping in and out of shops and doors, the old men gathering with barely a nod on the stone bench by the fountain.

"You see," I say to my husband.

He does not answer, and we just stay like this, watching. I think, Now is the time to say something. Now is the time to talk. I don't say anything. But I feel I could. I could talk about anything: Auntie Betsy and her blue legs, the old woman sweeping and closing the door, the house martins or swallows and how I really want them to be swallows. I could say too that I've had enough of "my" holidays and "his" holidays, that from now on they'll be *our* holidays if he wants me to come. I don't say anything, though, because we're staying another week and there will be time. Maybe tonight, over the Mateus rosé. Maybe then.

He's heavy on my shoulder, and I think perhaps he's dropped off to sleep but then he stirs and says, "I do. I do see."

So we stay as we are and watch the shadows lengthen and smell the evening loaves being baked and feel the sun slipping low, blushing over our necks like the first taste of wine.

Six

The letter was in the back pocket of her jeans and if she shifted her weight, as she did now, she could hear the sigh and release of the paper. She determined not to think of the letter, but this was plain conspiracy: It would return to her mind, and she wanted the shock, the thrill of it.

Teresa glanced up at the clock, a habit she could not break though the clock had for several weeks been resting at twenty past three. She stood up, leaving the cashier's chair swiveling at the register, and patted a stack of long-life-milk cartons into symmetry on her way to the door. Taking hold of one half of the blue plastic strips that kept the flies from the shop, she stepped into the doorway and pinned them aside with her shoulder.

The square was empty save for a tan and black dog jumping up at the rubbish bins. His claws clattered along the side each time he slid down again. He looked around briefly before making his next assault, and his long muzzle parted in a sheepish grin. The dog is excited and also a little embarrassed, thought Teresa, pleased with this formulation. She twirled her ponytail and tapped her sandaled toes on the doorstep to mask a flush of pride. Today she was alive to everything.

When she came into work this morning, the letter crackling in her back pocket, she slipped on the pink-and-white-checked nylon coat, and the static along her arms ghosted around her body for minutes afterward. She unpacked a box of canned soup and marveled at her arrangement of the cans on the shelf, detecting there an industrial beauty that would otherwise go unhymned. As a matter of routine, she switched on the lights at the back of the shop but then turned them off again because the gloom over the cold counter wrapped the fat dangling hams and wrinkly smoked sausage in an inviting layer of tradition. When Senhor Mendes came in for a packet of rolling tobacco, she saw at once that the way he scratched his ear had nothing to do with an itch and everything to do with the fact that she was twenty years old and—nose aside—not bad to look at. Dona Linda came in for soap powder and Nutella and said, "What are you hiding back there? A dead body? You'll take your finger off on the meat slicer, my girl."

"Yes, Dona Linda," said Teresa.

Dona Linda leaned across the tower of wire baskets on the counter, and Teresa smelled eggs and the faint carbolic scent of freshly dyed hair. "Has he told you to keep the lights off?" she said, referring to Senhor Jaime. "Next thing, he'll start charging us to breathe the air."

"Yes, Dona Linda." Teresa rang the items up on the register and put the soap powder and the chocolate spread in a plastic bag.

The woman clucked on, her voice a scattering of affront, alarm, and inquisition, so that all by herself she managed to sound like a shed full of chickens.

"And it won't be long before you and Antonio tie the knot, I expect. Bless you, there, I've made you blush. Well, it's a sign. I'll say nothing more. My lips are sealed on the subject. This village could do with a good wedding. Look at my lips. Closed, closed, I'm saying nothing, you see."

"I see, Dona Linda," Teresa replied. "Will there be anything else?"

She jumped out of the doorway and stood with one foot up against the whitewashed wall. Summer was coming to an end, and it was possible now to be outside in the late morning without being punched by the sun. The square was a large patch of dusty gravel broken only by a gathering of hard-leaved bay trees and a couple of cars parked at careless angles.

Teresa stared across the square after the dog, who had run off seeming to think she would chase him. She looked right, toward the back wall of the Casa do Povo, and left, toward the hardware shop and butcher's. She reached up for her ponytail, which she wore high on the crown so that it spurted like a black fountain from her head. Sighing, she twisted it around her finger. It was all very well, she thought, to be alert. But what was there to see?

She often felt, and she hoped it was not conceited, that her powers of observation were somehow keener than those of other people. In the spring, when the wildflowers came, she never said in that cheap way, Oh, how pretty, to hide the fact of indifference. How many others, in all honesty, had noticed that Senhor Vasco was building a wall of fat to conceal his deep, deep sadness? It was possible that she was the only one to shiver inside when Dona Linda licked the tip of her finger and stroked her son's mustache.

It was a blessing and also a curse, and there was nothing she could do but live with it.

She wished someone would come and see her now. She took the letter out of her pocket and tapped it on her sleeve as if it were bait. Her spirits ran so high she could scarcely breathe. She wanted someone—Clara, Paula, anyone—to see her and wonder what it was that was making her glow. Of course she couldn't tell them, she couldn't say, not before breaking the news to her mother and to Antonio—oh, how would she tell Antonio?—but she needed a witness now, someone to declare that *something* was up with Teresa.

"Senhora Carmona! Good morning." Teresa sprang off the wall and stuffed the letter back in her pocket. Senhora Carmona had arrived silently, like an old black cat, whiskers twitching.

She came forward and held Teresa's wrist. Teresa felt the tremble in the old woman's hand. "My dear, my dear. But is it closed?" Her face shook with the effort of speech.

"No, no," said Teresa, guiding her inside.

Senhora Carmona stood by the counter. She was about the same size as the children in the top class of the elementary school but much less substantial. Pointing to her stomach, she said, "I need something for this. Be a good girl, Teresa, give me something."

Teresa looked at Senhora Carmona's loose black stockings and thought, Yes, you need to eat more. "You have indigestion?" she said.

The old woman adjusted her headscarf and muttered something that Teresa did not catch.

Years ago, when her husband was one of those who had gone abroad to work, Senhora Carmona did not do as the other wives and wear widow's black.

"The pharmacy, Senhora Carmona. They will have everything you need."

Senhora Carmona spoke louder, as if to answer, but the words were meant for someone else. *"Sorrowful Mother, pray for us. Sighing Mother, pray for us. Forsaken Mother . . ."*

A note of scandal crept into Teresa's mother's voice when she described how Senhora Carmona wore flowered skirts and lacy blouses while her man was as good as dead, toiling across the border. She was a racy woman, some said worse.

Teresa regarded what remained of the scandal: Senhora Carmona's childish black plimsolls, the tremor in her arms, the cataract clouding her left eye, the crabbing way her mouth bit around the words of the prayer, and wondered if she remembered those times, if she dreamed of them still.

It was a hundred years ago, anyway. Senhor Carmona was dead, really dead, before Teresa was even born.

"Desolate Mother, pray for us. Mother most sad, pray for us." Senhora Carmona had her hands in her apron pocket, turning the prayer beads.

Teresa would have to go to the pharmacy herself. She didn't mind. She didn't want Senhora Carmona wandering around and forgetting where she was going. "Wait here," she said, taking her bag down from the peg. But as she moved toward the door, the old woman's good eye met hers and she thought she saw something there, a flash of coquetry, an edge of steel, a hint of the woman that was.

As she waited to pay, Teresa became aware that Doutor Medeires, moving around in his dispensary, was keeping tabs on her between the shelves of bottles and tubes. Probably he had noticed something. She turned her face to the ground and bit her lip. Bending her knees slightly, she pushed down on her heels and straightened up. It was a wonder she didn't rise off the floor and float up to the ceiling. There was a huge hot bubble inside her and no way of letting it out. She glanced up at the pharmacist and there he was, peeping at her over the top of the cold-sore creams and aspirin.

Someone in the queue laughed, and Teresa laughed too, though she had not heard the joke, and turned around briefly to spread a little furtive radiance.

Then Doutor Medeires would say, "What has happened to you, Teresa?" and she would reply, "Oh, nothing special. Why do you ask?"

She thought of Senhora Carmona, reciting the Litany of Our Lady of the Seven Sorrows, and then adapted the words to her own. They became lodged in her brain. The phrase repeated itself over and over, *Why do you ask, why do you ask,* so that by the time she had paid and reached the cardboard cutout of the woman with cellulite-free thighs by the gleaming plate-glass window, she knew she had to let it out or die, and when she felt a hand on her shoulder, she turned and opened her mouth with the words pressed up against her teeth.

"For your *mãe,*" said the pharmacist, handing her a small paper bag. "It will save her from calling again." He nodded and patted the pockets of his white coat as though he had nothing else to say.

★ ★ ★

Teresa stood on the pavement and looked along the road. People in Mamarrosa, they did not have eyes to see. Sometimes she could scream, she really could. A truck loaded with half-sleeves of cork bark stacked like roof tiles came slow and ponderous down the road, dogged by a truck of rattling Calor gas bottles. In London, she was sure, it would be different.

A man, one of the *estrangeiros,* came toward her, ducking to clear the orange trees. The black and tan dog was with him. Would everyone in London be so tall? The man wore a filthy vest and he had not shaved. Teresa stepped back to let him pass and for a moment was covered in confusion.

She focused on Vasco, who had dipped out of his café across the road and bobbed about picking up the plastic chairs strewn around by the wind. Next door, at the cell phone shop, a sign flashed on and off: VODAFONE. At the other side was Armenio's house, a grand two stories high, tiled all over in green and white and glittering so much it was hard to look at. When she came back, she would not think it grand at all. But maybe she would love it, love all this, more. She spread her arms weakly to encompass the three more modest houses that stood alongside, the sheep in the garden, the small square with its brassy marigolds and tender amaryllis, the village trailing off, the houses spreading farther and farther apart, the lapsing into fields and woods, the hills rising up to seal away the world.

By the time she turned onto the side street that climbed to the center of the village, Teresa had forgotten the *estrangeiro*. She bounced on the balls of her feet and felt the swish of her ponytail and relished the *flack-flack* of her sandals on the road. The doors to these houses opened directly onto the street, and one flew open now. Clara folded her arms across her chest and said, "Well, it's you!" as if Teresa were the last person she was expecting to see. Teresa could hear Clara's baby brother bawling his head off and knew Clara had been at the window, looking for any excuse to step outside. She had prepared her face, anyway, one eye narrowed and a cheek pulled back to show how strange it was, almost comical, that she should find herself in a place like this.

"Got to dash," said Teresa, waving the bag with Mãe's prescription.

"Me too," called Clara. "Actually, I'm meeting someone."

At the corner Teresa risked a glance over her shoulder and was rewarded by the sight of Clara gazing after her, wondering, quite clearly wondering, what on earth was going on.

Senhora Carmona had disappeared, and Teresa's aunt Telma Ervanaria was behind the cold counter, slicing *chouriço*.

"Teresa," she cried, "it's darker than the Day of Judgment back here. Get some lights on."

Teresa hurried around saying, "Let me do it, please, you're not supposed to be on this side." But her aunt flapped her hand and shooed her away.

"Listen," said Telma Ervanaria, when she had weighed and packed her cold cuts, "I'm not saying Mamarrosa is bad, but for a girl like you, a bright girl like you . . . phut!" Holding her stout hips, she made a sound that indicated this kind of girl could simply go up in smoke.

Teresa slid a foot in and out of her sandal. Telma Ervanaria was the one who had written her reference for the au pair agency. Teresa was crazy to have trusted her. She wanted to run home right away and confess everything to Mãe.

"I was in Paris for fifteen years," said Telma Ervanaria. "Unless you saw for yourself, you wouldn't believe what it was like."

It's not on the moon, thought Teresa sourly. When she had been to London, she would not speak of it that way. She made a mental note to always speak of it casually.

Telma Ervanaria examined her hands. "It's not for everyone, of course."

Teresa heard the paper crease and tick in her back pocket. She was suddenly stricken with the thought that Telma Ervanaria would hear it too and demand to see what she was hiding.

Au pairs, the letter said, encounter a lot of new situations. Some might even experience culture shock.

"In France, I might have told you, the men don't sit in the cafés day and night. They work and then they go home to the family. Day and night, night and day," said Telma Ervanaria, whose husband had not worked since they returned from Paris. She touched her hair, which she kept short and forced with hot irons to curl around her square, pugnacious face.

You are considered, the letter went on, to be a member of the family. This is a great opportunity to make new friends.

It was a miracle that her aunt had kept her word and had not told Mãe about the application.

"Ah, Telma Ervanaria," sighed Telma Ervanaria. "Don't waste your breath. People do as they will. That Antonio, I don't know what you see in him."

Behind the counter, Teresa made fists. She dug her nails into her palms. She wanted to defend Antonio, who was sweet as could be, but she wanted also to say that *he* was not the measure of *her,* she who was going to London. Her aunt had forgotten about the au pair agency, or thought Teresa would never make the grade, and either way, honestly, it was typical of people around here.

"Antonio," said Teresa. She shrugged. She did not know what to say. Telma Ervanaria patted her on the arm and sighed again. "Teresa Maria," she said, "we are two of a kind."

At lunchtime Teresa locked the shop and went to drop off the tablets. She left the Vespa running to show she didn't have time to talk, but Senhora Carmona grabbed the bag and slammed the door, and there was no chance even to ask for the money. Teresa sounded the horn, three quick quacks, to say goodbye. She felt like making some noise.

Outside the church she saw Father Braga, walking along with his face turned down. Father Braga would keep the secret, but only if she confessed it as sin.

Driving to Senhor João's place, the scooter drilling lightly over the unmade roads, she summoned a vision of London, turning the tracks into esplanades, the cork oaks into marble pillars, the mossy well into a fountain that leaped and dazzled and reveled in its own unnecessary life.

Senhor João stood outside his one-room house with his hands at his waist, elbows held out, as if the music had just stopped.

"Good afternoon. I've brought your shopping," called Teresa. Senhor João had hurt his leg and could not walk all the way into the village.

João nodded and touched his hat. His face was as hard and brown as a nut but gentle too, tentative, as if apologizing for being so old.

Teresa walked up the path worn by João's feet and set the shopping on the backless gray bench. "Milk, bread, matches, three cans of sardine paste, strong glue, and two beers. You need something for tomorrow?"

"No, no," said João. "There's nothing." He covered one hand with the other and pushed his tongue into his cheek, which made him look toothless.

"What's that?" said Teresa. "Let me see."

João shook his head but stopped hiding the cut on his hand. It was a bad one, a deep gouge between thumb and first finger, with a mean raggedy edge. Teresa saw now the dark smear on his threadbare sweater and the spatters that led down to the earthy rings on his trousers where he had been kneeling in the dirt.

"Aiee," said Teresa. "You need a doctor." She wondered about taking João on the back of the Vespa, his tough tender face on her shoulder, but couldn't imagine what she would do if he fell off. "Do you want me to call someone?"

"Eh, eh," wheezed João, "doctor." He wiped a tear from the corner of his eye.

It rankled with Teresa that for a second she misunderstood and thought he was upset. Then she realized that laughter, for Senhor João, was so rare that the moment was a sad one after all, and the cleverness of this insight cheered her up.

"Let me see to that," she urged. Then, somewhat more uncertainly, "Do you have a bandage?"

João shuffled into the house. Teresa watched as the withered door swung on its hinges. Had it always been too small for the frame? She thought, You can't lie down twice along the length of the house. It was mildly shocking, as if she had already been away and returned with a new pair of eyes. She went around to the side of the house, where there was a decomposing saddle and a water butt skinned with flies, and measured it in a couple of strides.

"Senhora," said João. "Look, I found one." He held up a grimy strip of cloth.

Teresa didn't even want to touch it. She was ashamed and could not look at him. Instead she looked across the plot at the leashed tomato plants, the orderly potato patch, the rough-hewn poles and rope of the boundary, the hens scratching a living in the shade of the persimmon tree, the firewood collected and stored beneath a patchwork quilt of plastic bags, everything so neat and poor she could not stand it.

"Better, actually, to let the air at it," she said. And then, because it was important not to leave straightaway and ride under a cloud of accusation, "How did you do it?"

"Come," said João. He motioned with his good hand, and there was a twinkle in his eye, as though she were a child about to be surprised.

She followed him around the back and saw the pig tangled in rope and brambles beneath the massive spreading skirts of an old cork oak. The pig lifted its black face and grunted encouragingly.

"Eh, eh," João grunted back. "There she is, my beauty. Don't worry, I'll have another go. Get you free, won't we? No, no, we won't leave you like that." His voice was old and splintery and crooning with love.

He probably spends more time with the pig, thought Teresa, than he does with anyone else.

"I am much obliged to you," João was saying. He fished some coins from his pocket, and Teresa took them, though she suddenly wished not to.

"I'll do it," she said abruptly. "Give me something to cut with."

"She's such a nice pig, yes, nice pig," said João. His sentences rarely ended cleanly but seemed to dissolve into a private, murmured call-and-response. There was a penknife already in his hand, and Teresa felt set up.

When she had finished cutting the brambles and the rope, she had scratches down her arms and hands and a thorn in her heel from sliding off her sandals. She was sweating and she feared the pig would run off now that she wasn't tied to anything. João had disappeared, and out of pique, she did not call him. Let the pig run, she thought, it's not my fault.

The pig stayed where she was, then tossed her head and stuck her snout in Teresa's crotch.

"Sorrowful Mother," shouted Teresa. She threw down the pieces of rope, tried to dust off her jeans, and limped back toward the house.

On the bench, laid out on a handkerchief, were the loaf of bread, a can of sardine paste, two tomatoes, and two butter knives. Two tin plates were waiting too.

João came around from the other side carrying cups of water.

"It's ready," he said. "Let's eat."

João chewed his bread and paste with a faraway expression, as though engaging with issues both private and profound.

Teresa clattered her knife three times on her plate. Why did he force her, then, to stay? And what could he possibly have to think about, anyway?

She bit her tomato, lifted the tin cup and—remembering the flies on the water butt—put it down again. "Don't you want to check the pig? What if she wanders off?"

João seemed to ruminate on this but did not speak.

Teresa gave up. She poked at the puncture mark on her heel to provoke the peculiar satisfaction of a small, anticipated pain.

If only João had a wife, someone to darn his sweater and set a vase of flowers in the window. But his wife must have died long ago. There would be a photograph in a frame above the bed, an unsmiling mustached face that received his prayers at bedtime, impartially, perhaps indifferently, no matter how hard João prayed.

The cell phone, clipped onto her waistband, shivered and bleeped. Teresa read Antonio's text message, then slipped the phone into her bag as if to hide something indecent. João had no electricity. When the sun went down, he would go to bed. Teresa imagined herself on an airplane a mile high in the sky; she thought of herself in London, coming out of a restaurant or nightclub; she saw herself on an escalator, traveling through a department store that reached nearly as high as the plane. It was so sad. It almost made her cry, as though it were João she was leaving behind.

She stared openly at the deep lines on his face, the dirt that would never come out from under his fingernails, the untrimmed hair in his crumbling nose, the piteous absence of disguise, and sighed because she did not always want to notice everything.

João cut more bread with the penknife, resting the loaf on his knee and whittling it like a piece of wood. Teresa received a slice and touched her chest and closed and opened her eyes as though she had taken the sacrament.

Friday night. Are you excited? Antonio's message finally took hold. Until the letter arrived this morning, all she could think of was Friday night. They would meet at the house at Corte Brique and, after two years of romance and negotiation, give themselves freely, each to the other.

Teresa felt the warm breeze nibbling like an impatient lover at her ear. She flicked aside a strand of loose hair and set her plate down on the ground.

"I remember," said João, making her jump, "the first time I saw my father kill a pig. I loved that pig, oh, eh, loved her, but I stuck my hands in her belly, pulled out her guts. He said, 'A man now, you are,' like that's all there was to it, just pulling out the guts, see, with these hands." He held his hands up and gave a short laugh and wiped them on his trousers.

"Oh," said Teresa, who had been riding a wave of sexual longing and resented the way it now mingled with revulsion. She turned her head to take in the view over the red earth of the track, the archaeo logical stillness of the olive grove beyond, the interlocking slices of wooded hills, the single high-ridged blue escarpment, the cloudless cobalt sky.

When she left for London, it would be as a woman. Already the experience—though it had not happened yet—was emanating from her, oozing from every pore. She crossed her legs, folded her arms across her chest, and tucked her hands into her armpits. Antonio, sweet Antonio. How cruel it would be to leave him then. Perhaps it would be kinder not to sleep with him.

"Eh, eh," said João.

She turned her head, but all she could think of was Antonio. She was surrounded by his presence, and even the movement of her head felt strange, as though she were drifting through the sea of his being.

If she didn't sleep with him, oh, how miserable he would be, they would both be. No, they had waited long enough, and afterward, when they curled together, bathed in candlelight and sweat and love, she would whisper to him that while she was gone, she would not blame him if he did not wait for her to come home. It would be her gift to him. To make him free like that. And his love, his sweet, uncomplicated love, would grow stronger. It would be so beautiful, it seemed almost a shame that nobody else would see.

But with her next breath, she feared that they would fight, that the leave-taking would be anguished and hostile. She cast him as ungenerous, provincial, small, pinching up his mouth and blowing smoke rings as he did when he didn't want to talk, and she responded with her own bitter silence.

"Isn't it so?" said João, his voice crackling like a log on the fire.

She beamed at him suddenly as if they understood each other perfectly.

"Really and truly," she said.

It was obvious to her now that João did not need her pity. She almost envied his simple life. The headaches he had never known. The certainty of each day like the last. The protection of not wanting more.

João stood up, and she followed him around the back. The pig had wandered some distance off, rooting beneath the trees. She heard them or sensed them and looked over her shoulder and twitched her tail and came toward the house at a trot.

"My beauty, my beauty," murmured João, "she knows that it's better at home."

Francisco, as usual, had to be called three times for dinner.

"I don't understand a word of his books," said Mãe, her usual boast. She doled out the soup and, when she was seated, pressed her knuckles into her eyes as if even the thought of study was a strain.

"Books, Francisco," said Teresa. "Hear that? Books." She had finally gone into his room and grabbed the comic from his hands.

"I'm not deaf," said Francisco, smiling and feigning good humor and toleration so that Teresa wanted to pull the curls right out of his head.

"That's strange," she said. "You didn't hear Mãe calling."

Francisco tilted his face and frowned. "Well," he said, "I must have been concentrating."

"That's funny, because when I came in, all you were doing—"

"Teresa Maria, kindly use your mouth for eating."

Teresa tasted the *açorda*. Mãe always used too much salt. How many times a week did they have this, bread-and-garlic soup at dinner? She pushed the bowl aside.

"Dieting," observed Francisco gravely. He poured her soup into his bowl. If he only knew how greedy he looked!

When Pai died, five years ago now, it was assumed without question that Teresa would give up school.

Across the polished dark wood table in which the white bowls were faintly reflected, she watched Francisco eat. His hair curled gently, his green eyes were complacent, and his nose, most unfairly, was small and straight. He smiled at her, a strand of cilantro caught between his teeth. Teresa smiled back, attempting to feel a devilish contentment at her secret triumph, but realizing she was really too nervous to eat.

She fingered the crocheted place mat and sought out her father. His photograph, in a black lacquered frame, stood on top of the television. Surrounded by the skittish clouds of the photographer's backdrop, his face was somber and withholding, as though disapproving of what he saw—the heavy furniture, the needlepoint cushions, the preponderance of brass and malfunctioning lamps, the rag rugs draping the doorways.

"Working tonight?" said Francisco.

"What's it to you?" cried Teresa, insulted once again by his lack of care, his easy manner, the way he had never once said thank you.

"Are we going to sit chatting?" said Mãe, as if that were the kind of thing she would not stand for. "There's dishes to be cleared." She stacked and removed the crockery and brought in the salt cod and a plate of green beans and another of rice, moving with determined but pointless efficiency.

"So," said Francisco slyly when Mãe was in the kitchen, "lover boy this evening, then? The worm finds the hole tonight?"

Teresa gasped and blinked. Then she saw that he didn't know anything. God, how she hated him. She was damned if she was going to stay here and slave her guts out for him to go to university. Let him leave school tomorrow. She said, "What about your girlfriend? This Ruby. This nice English girl. Why don't you bring her home and let Mãe meet her?" She slapped her hands to her cheeks. "Oh, I forgot. She's not just *your* girlfriend, is she? She doesn't have time to meet *all* the mothers."

Her brother grinned as if this was just a bit of fun. "Ruby," he said, closing his eyes and groping something in midair, "she's got a great . . . attitude."

Teresa turned to her father, as though every point she had ever silently made had now been proved. She tried to think what he would say about her decision (that was what she was calling it now, leaving nothing to chance) to go to London.

She stared at the heavy brow, the tuck of his chin that warded off bullshit, the long hooked nose that she had inherited. He'd say, of course, that she should go. That she must go. She remembered riding on his shoulders, the roughness of his jacket on her bare legs, the smell of wood chips and diesel, the two of them patrolling the builders' yard and her father telling the customers, "This one up here, she's the boss, this one."

"Are you eating or not?" said Mãe. "Because I have to get on."

"Not hungry," said Teresa, miserable now with the certainty that Pai would tell her she should stay, that she should get over herself, that he hadn't brought her up to abandon her own flesh and blood.

Francisco slipped out of the house and Teresa washed the plates, looking out at the twilight-thickened sky and listening to the prattle of birdsong from the lemon trees and the swirling lament of the Brazilian soap opera that her mother was watching.

She went into the living room, drying her hands on her jeans. Mãe didn't look around. Nothing short of an earthquake would shift her now. She had her sewing in her lap but would not touch it all evening. It was her excuse, her cover story, her way of saying that she was not an idle woman. Her mouth pursed and flattened against her teeth as though she were forming opinions, but she never talked about her soap operas; they were too trivial to speak of, or too serious. On the screen, a woman in a low-cut dress pushed her fists into her chest and said, rip my heart out, why don't you, and feed it to the dogs, while a man standing behind her ran his fingertips up and down her arms.

Teresa moved closer to Mãe's chair. She saw the way her mother's hips spread across the cushion and quickly felt the girth of her own. She looked down at the soft curve of her cheek, the thick black flick of her eyelashes. Something she had not noticed before—her mother was young. Younger, possibly, than the woman on the screen, who had vertical lines running into her cleavage.

It was terrible that her mother was so young. There were perhaps forty years more of this, of endless busyness and torpor, of inadmissible defeat.

Teresa gripped the back of her mother's chair and squeezed it. Having dispensed what comfort she could, she went to her room to change.

The photograph of the children that came with the letter of invitation and the photocopied "Things to Know" sheet was tucked underneath her mattress. She pulled it out and, still kneeling, read the message on the back again. *Daniel and Katy say hi! We are looking forward to playing with you.* Daniel, who was six years old, had written his name in red felt tip, and Katy, who was three, had joined the dots to make her name as well.

The children, photographed in a garden, wore Indian headdresses and face paints and stared into the camera with unlimited expectation. "Ah, the little angels," Teresa said, stroking the glossy print. She quickly turned the photo over again as though they might see through her. It didn't matter. She would grow to love them quickly enough.

Teresa got up and looked around her room, trying to decide what she would take with her to London. She wished she could take everything: her mirror with the painted cherries and bows, her collection of miniature teddy bears, the beach-ball globe, the white melamine dressing table with scalloped edges and matching stool that she had paid for herself, the Rosanna doll on its special chair.

Pai had given her the doll for her twelfth birthday. She had a porcelain head, real human hair, porcelain feet and hands, a cloth body, and a brown velvet dress with white lace petticoats and lace-trimmed bloomers. She came with a little wicker chair and a leaflet with pictures of all the other dolls (Betty, Joséphine, Lilly, Tatiana) you could collect. For three years Mãe kept her locked away because she was too precious to play with. After Pai died, Mãe gave her back to Teresa, who was too old then for dolls but tended and rearranged her every day, thinking that Pai would be pleased.

She would have to take Rosanna.

Teresa sat down on the bed, feeling queasy. She should have eaten. The thought of Rosanna going so far from home made her feel sick.

Those children, what if they cried?

They wouldn't understand a word she said to them. Teresa rubbed her neck. She was getting confused. She would speak to them in English, not Portuguese. But perhaps they would not understand. Already she wanted to shake them. On the form she had filled out, she had checked GOOD for the standard of English. Perhaps she should have checked FAIR. The family would test her; on the day she arrived, they would test her and say she had tricked them. Her English was only fair.

"At school it was my best subject." Teresa, sitting on her hands and rocking, rehearsed the sentence a few times over.

"Ah," they would say to her, "but when did you leave school?"

The children, now that she thought about it, would probably be naughty. They looked like naughty children. And still they expected love.

"You're going to London," she told herself, and her stomach growled in reply.

Teresa jumped up and paced the room. She breathed deeply

through her mouth, blowing out hard and counting through the length of the exhalation. She rolled her shoulders and shook her arms and bounced on the spot as though limbering up for a race.

She picked up Rosanna and examined her absurd rosebud lips, the cold blue of her eyes, the nonexistent nose. Sniffing hard and blinking, Teresa lifted the doll above her head with both hands and brought her down like an ax over the melamine dressing table. She stopped just short. The doll's head rolled in the air, her hair across her face. Teresa laid her down and then flung herself on the bed.

She was only crying because she was angry. Mãe and Francisco, why couldn't they be happy for her? Why? Was it really too much to ask?

She looked around her bedroom and thought what a pity it would be to leave it, now that she had finally gotten it nice, cleared out all that old dark furniture, the creaky iron bed, and made it modern and sleek.

In London, though, she would have her own television. Her room would be modern, perhaps with built-in closets. She was to have her own bathroom. She wondered if everyone in the family had one.

Once she had told Mãe, she would feel better. Get it out in the open, get it over and done. She hugged the pillow and ran the scene. Mãe shrieking, "Santa Maria," and fainting. Mãe slapping her across the face and hissing, "Is this how you pay me back?" Mãe turning and staggering toward the door, her arm crashing across the dresser and sweeping the glasses to the floor.

In the soaps, that's what they always did. Unexpected news made them crazy and clumsy as well.

But Mãe was no soap star. She wouldn't know how to act.

Teresa turned over and stared at the bamboo on the ceiling. A spider dangled from a thread. Insects were always dropping out of there, but Mãe wouldn't let her take the bamboo down. God alone knew why.

What was Mãe watching now? *Woman of Destiny* or *Family Ties*,

Teresa thought. Or perhaps the next one was on by now. Mãe wouldn't move until they had finished, and then she would sigh and shake her head as though to say thank goodness she was free. Perhaps, deep down, she enjoyed them. Perhaps she was swelling inside, gorging on the passion and power and money, all the things she didn't have. It was hard to believe. More likely it was comforting because she could despise them, all those people with no self-control.

Teresa stirred it around, knowing she would reach no conclusion. Mãe was always a puzzle, so simple yet so hard to understand. She spent her evenings watching people talking but pretended talking was a waste of time. Once in a while she told a story, a tale about her grandfather being stung by his bees, or Senhora Carmona's wild ways; she unfolded the stories and aired them, like linen from the closet, and stowed them away again. Otherwise, she treated words like money, and money was always tight.

It was getting late. Teresa changed into a skirt and blouse and took the file and the brochures from the drawer. She remembered Mãe's prescription.

She would tell her everything. "So," Mãe would say. "London," she would say, as though this were exactly the disappointment she had steeled herself against.

"I've got your sleeping pills," said Teresa when she went through.

Mãe glanced at her and nodded, her face floating in the radiant projected light.

"See you later," said Teresa, knowing she would not.

The moon, nearly full, hung low in the velvet sky as if it had bounced off the rooftops. The air was sweet, almost cloying, with smoke from a wood-fired oven and the overripe scent of a lady of the night, the small cream flowers smothering the empty house across the way, obscuring almost entirely the handwritten for-sale sign that had been there for as long as Teresa could remember. Light spilled out from the other houses, washing the high stone curbs. Teresa set off down the crooked street.

"Good evening, Teresa," called Senhora Cabral from her usual seat in her doorway. "And where may you be going?" Her knitting needles flew. She never risked looking down at them in case she might miss something.

"Good evening, Senhora Cabral. I'm going to meet a man. A married man."

"Ah, I see you have your brochures. You're a good girl, Teresa. Always working so hard for your poor mother, for your poor little brother."

"Goodbye, Senhora Cabral. I think you've dropped a stitch."

At the corner she almost bumped into Telma Ervanaria, who could scarcely see over her load of neatly folded laundry.

"I'm just taking it around," panted Telma Ervanaria. "She's bedridden now, you know. Everyone's taking a turn."

"Yes, of course," said Teresa. She had no idea who her aunt was talking about. "Anyway, I have to go."

"Have you heard? Marco Afonso Rodrigues is coming back to Mamarrosa. You don't know who he is? He's closer to your mother's age, of course, but we knew him when we were young."

"That's good," said Teresa. She tried to step around her aunt.

"Left with a few escudos in his pocket and coming back stinking rich. Made his money in dry cleaning and laundries. Now he's richer than a king."

Teresa patted the stack of sheets and towels. "Maybe you should start charging."

"Two of a kind," chuckled Telma Ervanaria, still in love with the idea.

Senhor Marcelo Álvaro Mendes tapped his pipe along the wooden arm of his chair and shuffled his feet.

"Your *mãe* is well?" he said. "And your Francisco, he is well too?"

Teresa said that they were, very well. She rearranged the brochures on her knee and opened her file.

"And your aunt?" said Senhor Mendes. "How is she?" He stuck the pipe in his mouth and sucked and then picked a fleck of tobacco from his teeth.

His wife came in looking flushed and paused in the doorway, listening to check that the children were quiet in their beds.

"Shall we get started?" said Teresa. She uncapped her pen to signal that business was under way.

"Goodness," said Senhora Mendes, "I thought Henrique would never go down."

Teresa cocked her head and smiled. "How is he?" she was forced to say.

Senhora Mendes collapsed on the sofa, her legs splaying inelegantly wide. Teresa, striving for focus and a little necessary formality, pressed her knees tighter together.

"Teething," said Senhora Mendes. "And you know it can give them the runs. His bottom is bright, bright red."

"Well," said Teresa, "we'll start with the fact find. That's what we normally do."

"But where are our manners?" cried Senhora Mendes, struggling to her feet. "I'll go and make the tea."

Senhor Mendes knocked his pipe into the grate. He was scared to look at her, Teresa realized, when his wife was not in the room. If she got him on his own, he would buy; he would sign whenever she told him, right on the dotted line.

Senhora Mendes stuck her head through. "I'll only be a minute," she said. "Did you hear about Paula and Vicente? Yes, they got engaged today."

"Of course they did," said Teresa, capping and uncapping the pen. "They are such a perfect match." It was typical, she thought of Paula, always trying to outdo everyone. She was certainly welcome to

Vicente, who was nice enough if you liked that sort of thing, which Teresa actually didn't.

When the tea had been brought and poured and the cakes declined and reoffered and accepted, Teresa closed her file and decided to jump right in. The training (two days at a freezing air-conditioned conference center in Faro) was all very well, but those men in their pushy little suits had clearly never been to Mamarrosa. If she went by the book, it would take all night, and anyway, the fact find was pointless. How many children do you have? Teresa knew their names and ages and even the state of their bowels.

"The thing about life insurance is," she began, addressing herself to the head of the house, "that should anything happen to you"—from the corner of her eye, she saw Senhora Mendes making the sign of the cross—"then your loved ones will be protected. Fully protected," she added, as if Salvation itself were assured.

"Oh, foo," said Senhor Mendes, blowing through his teeth, "what could happen to me?" He leaned forward to reassure his wife. "I've not seen a doctor in twenty years."

Teresa stayed quiet. Senhora Mendes performed a quick checkup on herself, sliding her hands across her shoulders and down her sides to rest finally on her knees. Seeing his mistake, her husband gave a guilty smile. "I haven't needed to go," he said, feigning irritation.

On the coffee table there was a bowl of plums, freshly picked and bloomed still with dust. Senhora Mendes reached forward, her cuff dark and damp from her labors at the sink, plucked out a tiny caterpillar, and crushed it between her fingers.

Teresa considered her options. Senhor Mendes drove a cream-colored Mercedes taxi, the only one in Mamarrosa. Portugal had the highest road fatality rate in Western Europe. She kept her eyes low, watching Senhor Mendes's feet, the way he kept raising and lowering his heels, the creases across his shoes.

She wouldn't mention it. He spent more time, anyway, washing his taxi than driving it.

She wanted this sale. She needed the commission. When she left for London at the end of November, she would give Mãe an envelope stuffed with cash, a surprise, a bonus on top of what she usually handed over to supplement her mother's earnings from the cleaning jobs at the school and the doctor's surgery. And there was the flight (the word made her tie her fingers together) to pay for, and goodness knows what that would cost.

Teresa tugged at her ponytail, two hands in opposing directions, to tighten the band. The fine hair at the nape of her neck caught and pulled and brightened her eyes. "It's something we never want to think about," she said briskly. "We really don't." She dropped her voice and said, as if to herself, "Mãe never did." She smiled then and straightened her papers. "But we do all right. You know, we are getting by just fine."

"Bless us all," said Senhora Mendes, her eyes fixed on her husband. "But doesn't it make you think?"

It was the opening day of the Internet café, in the old frozen-fish shop, and at least a dozen people had turned up. Teresa looked in through the window below the lettering that still said CONGELADOS AQUÁRIOS and saw Antonio with his finger in his ear. The way he scratched, so vigorously that his body vibrated, he looked like a dog with a flea. She averted her eyes and licked her lips to make them shine. After waiting a moment or two, she stepped inside.

The walls were painted a futuristic shade of acid green, the chairs and tables had tubular metal legs, and by the back wall was a long trestle with two computers from which everyone was keeping well clear, perhaps for fear of breaking them. There was a small bar with a notice advertising beers at fifty céntimos a pop, and by the door a couple of shuddering chest freezers plastered with pictures of prawns.

Vicente was talking to Antonio. Teresa said, "Congratulations, Vicente. Have you set a date?"

Vicente stood there, lording it over them. He held his head unnaturally high and was constantly sucking and rolling his cheeks so it seemed as though he would spit on you. He slapped Antonio on the back and said, "You're looking at a condemned man, my friend."

They offered fists to each other and rubbed knuckles. Teresa crossed her legs.

"So," she said when Vicente had moved away, "what did he say to you?"

Antonio squeezed her knee under the table. "What do you mean? When?"

"The wedding. I suppose he was talking about it."

Antonio put his hands on top of the table, waiting to catch hold of hers. The palms were scrubbed pink, but his fingernails were lined with engine grease. His mother had stitched up a tear in his overalls using white thread. It looked like a scar across his chest. "No. Not really," he said. He smiled plainly at her, and she conceded a hand to his.

"Never mind," said Teresa. "Were you busy this morning?"

"Oil leak on a Peugeot 504. Broken fan belt on a Fiesta. Senhor Mendes brought the Mercedes in for a service. I said, 'Why, isn't she running right?' The inspection was only six months ago. He said—"

"Well," said Teresa, "sounds busy." She nodded toward the computers. "Shall we try it out?"

"Can't," said Antonio. "There's no connection."

"Of course not, no." She looked at Antonio's dark, accepting eyes, the slightly goofy way his hair sprang away from the part, the length of his earlobes smudged with dirt. *This is a great opportunity to make new friends.* "I love you," she whispered.

"Me too," said Antonio without urgency.

"I mean it." How fierce she sounded.

"Me too," he repeated, and she pulled away.

* * *

Paula, wearing a tight skirt that showed the line of her knickers, came to take their order.

Teresa stood up and kissed her. "I'm so happy for you, Paula. It's really wonderful."

Paula fanned the fingers of her left hand and studied the ring. "Yes," she said, "I'm a lucky girl."

Antonio was at least twice as handsome as Vicente, who had narrow shoulders and small mean eyes.

"Exactly," said Teresa, "you've done well for yourself. You couldn't do better than Vicente."

"Thank you," said Paula, a little louder than necessary. "And it's time for me, really, to *grow up*."

"Oh, yes, it's just right for you. Now you know for certain what the rest of your life will be. I wish you every happiness, Paula, now and for always."

"Me too," said Antonio.

Paula licked the end of her pencil and stabbed her order pad. "What's it to be?"

"I'm starving," said Antonio.

"We've got cheese toast, ham toast, or cheese and ham toast," said Paula. "Kitchen's not on till next week."

Teresa picked pink slivers of ham from her sandwich. The crust, toasted black, was sharp enough to cut your finger. She watched Antonio eat with his head down over the plate, the broad brown sweep of his cheeks peppered with stubble. He was nervous about tomorrow, and it was making him more tongue-tied than ever. Poor Antonio. She knew him better than he knew himself.

He lifted his face and their eyes locked. Teresa burned. The knowledge of what lay ahead welded them together. Forged in this moment was an everlasting bond. Where the minds, the souls, came together, the bodies would naturally follow.

Antonio spoiled it by chewing. She sighed and looked away but forgave him. Probably he felt too naked. He didn't understand that not a person here had eyes to see.

Clara came in, her baby brother like a storm cloud over her shoulder. "The pope is sick again," she said, sinking down at the table. "I saw it on the television." She nodded and panted, pleased to have shared the bad news.

"So much suffering," said Teresa. She stroked Hugo's head. It was huge. No wonder he never wanted to walk. He would be toppled by that head.

"Anyway," said Clara, dragging out the word, "do you want to come around tonight? I'm babysitting, but I got this braider out of the catalog; it's electric, and you put three strands in and press the button and it whizzes around and they're really, like, the best braids."

"I don't know. Maybe I have to work." Teresa stroked Hugo's cheek. Hugo knew that Clara didn't want to look after him. That's why he gave her such a hard time. "Cutie-pie," she said. "Little angel."

Hugo bit her finger.

Teresa screamed and jumped out of her seat.

Hugo thrashed and unleashed the full works. Clara tried to rock him in her arms, but it was like juggling with firecrackers. Glaring at Teresa, she pinned Hugo in a fireman's hoist and said, "Oh, brilliant."

"He bit me," Teresa hissed. "My God."

Clara was leaving. "He's two years old," she called back. "He doesn't like to be fussed with," she added, as though Teresa knew nothing about children.

Antonio ordered ice cream, and Paula brought two little plastic cartons of something pink and wavy from one of the chest freezers. Teresa took a sniff. "Smells of fish. Probably they didn't clean out the freezers."

Antonio got that look, a kid in class with his hand up, bursting with the answer. "Prawn ice cream," he said, tapping with his spoon. "It's prawn ice cream."

Teresa laughed politely. It wasn't his fault she was always one step ahead. "What about that Hugo, though? He bit me."

Antonio shrugged. "Someone wants to give him a good slap."

Teresa thought so too. "I would never slap a child," she said.

"Why not?"

"Physical punishment of a child is never acceptable," said Teresa, translating from the au pair information sheet.

"Why not?" said Antonio, clearly puzzled.

"Stop doing that," she barked.

"Doing what?"

"*That.* Just don't . . . Oh, never mind."

They sat in silence. A fly crawled across Antonio's forehead and disappeared into his hair.

"Want a beer?" he said.

"I've got to get back to work."

"There's half an hour yet."

They had a beer. Paula swayed by on her heels. She always wore heels because of her short legs. Teresa wasn't being bitchy, but it only made things worse.

"Are you going there in the morning?" Teresa knew he was, but she wanted to talk about it.

"Yes."

"And your mother won't . . . You know, she won't come looking for you, later on."

"No."

"You'll get everything ready?"

Antonio, she could see, did not know what she meant by this. "Yes," he said, to please her.

She did not know what she meant either. What would he get ready? What preparations would he make?

The house at Corte Brique was owned by a couple from Lisbon.

It was their holiday house. Antonio's mother looked after it. She was going to give him the keys tomorrow because there were two drains that needed unblocking, a dripping tap, and a broken toilet flush. Antonio was good with his hands.

"What's it like, the house? Is it nice?"

"It's nice," said Antonio decisively. "There's a swimming pool."

She knew there was a swimming pool. It was the only thing he had told her, and she had imagined the rest.

"But what would you say it's like? How would you describe it?"

Antonio took a deep breath. "I'd say . . . that it's nice. Very nice."

"I've seen her on television, the wife, the reporter. You can tell it's not fake jewelry she's wearing."

"That's right," said Antonio, clearly hoping that settled things.

Teresa wet her lips. "I just want everything to be perfect."

"Me too," said Antonio, squeezing her knee too hard.

A butterfly, powder blue, lit briefly on the neck of her bottle, on the tabletop, on the back of a chair, tilting and turning like a heroine making a dizzy escape. Teresa watched it dip and flutter across the room to the bar, where it wheeled away from the line of old bent backs and shaved necks and dropped suddenly to the floor.

Listen, Teresa addressed it silently, I know how you feel.

The café had been open three hours, and already it felt like it had been there forever. Although the door and one window stood open, the air was thick as paste and compromised by fish. The walls were a valiant shade of green, but on them hung last year's calendar and a stupid painting of a bullfight. It was an Internet café without the Internet, and nobody expected any better. People took up their places, the old ones at the bar, the younger ones at the tables, as if no other course were possible, and this sense, this weary inevitability, pressed down on her and made her yawn.

She stretched and looked behind her and saw the Englishman writer seated close to the chest freezers. His lips were red and full, the blood too close to the surface. He had a notebook open but stared into the middle distance as though he were having a vision. In a way he was handsome, with his blond hair and bloody lips, but he made her skin crawl. Clara said he was banging the other Englishman's wife. Was it true? It made a kind of sense. Better that they keep to their own.

The writer looked at her then. He seemed to know she had been staring. Damn him, she thought, turning. What does he want here, anyway? Suddenly she was filled with rage. She drained the last of her beer. Don't be so stupid, she told herself. You are going to London and he has come here. What is wrong with that?

She gazed in desperation around the room, certain that if she left, everything would change. Didn't she want that? Didn't she?

She thought about the other Englishman, who never washed his clothes. How annoying it was. It made a mockery of her going all the way there, with him wandering around here like that. When she was in London, she didn't want people to look at him and think of her. It was so unfair. And really and honestly, even if the wife was sleeping with the writer, the least she could do was wash her husband's clothes.

"I've got to go," Teresa said and picked up her purse.

Antonio had that look again. He whispered, "I *am* prepared, you know, for tomorrow."

"Okay," she said. "What do you mean?" Maybe he meant candles. She had bought some already, but that didn't matter.

"I've got some, *you know,* of those things that we'll need."

"What things?"

Antonio blushed, but he looked almost angry. *"You know, when we . . ."*

A stomach interjected itself across her line of sight. A high-pitched voice said, "Internet café, yes? Internet café?"

Antonio leaned back, lit a cigarette, and blew smoke rings. There he was. The trainee mechanic of a village garage.

"Senhor Vasco," said Teresa, "I'm afraid the connection isn't working yet."

Vasco made some reply but at a frequency unintelligible to the human ear.

"Ah, yes," she said vaguely, gazing up the undulating slope. From this angle, his head appeared several sizes too small. It was tiring, almost dizzying, to keep noticing the way all these bodies failed to fit properly together.

"Tell me," said Vasco, fingering his suspenders, "is my life worth something?"

"My life won't be," said Teresa, smiling. She stood up. "If I don't get back to the shop on time."

"Senhora Mendes explained everything to me. She said, 'Now I can sleep soundly, with a price on my husband's head.' She said, 'Teresa will come to see you too. She won't forget about you.'"

Teresa looked at Antonio, but he was no help at all. There was nothing to do but surrender. "When would you like me to come?"

"When I was a young man," said Vasco, "I worked abroad, in Provincetown, Cape Cod, the United States of America . . ."

Teresa took a step backward.

". . . and there was a notice that hung in the kitchens . . ."

Though she did not see his feet move, the great bulk of him drew nearer.

". . . it was placed there by my manager, a very conscientious man, and it said . . ."

His face looked like the bread dough that Mãe rested on a marble slab.

". . . do not put off until tomorrow that which can be done today . . ."

He rubbed his hands together, which surely signaled the end.

". . . and so I propose to you that we set the appointment, without delay, for this very evening. I shall expect to see you then."

Sometimes she felt like a social worker. Teresa set her brochures out on the cracked Formica bar and pulled up a stool. Vasco's café was empty. He was wiping the tables with a damp rag and humming. Every time he moved past, he caught a chair or a table leg and set the flimsy plastic vibrating. She watched him in the cloudy mirror. The last of the evening sun wound gold around the liquor bottles and licked up the mirror's edge. The wooden legs of the stool were warm as sleeping kittens, and she wrapped her own around them.

"All done," cried Vasco, hurrying to the other side of the bar. He flicked the rag over his shoulder. One end wrapped around his neck, but he did not notice or mind. "This business," he said, "is a constant war on germs. Now, I am all ears"—he located the relevant items—"you see, all ears."

"Good," she said. "Well. What I'm here to talk about, of course—"

"I'll tell you one thing," said Vasco, "that so-called Internet café will never last. Even when—even *if*—they get their little gimmick working, that will not save their skins."

"Very true," said Teresa. If she could get started straightaway, there was a chance, if not to make a sale, then at least to get out of here before dark. "Could I ask you first to take a look at this?" She turned a brochure toward him and tapped it smartly with her pen.

Vasco picked up the brochure without a glance. "Always read the small print," he advised. "When you go into business without knowing the small print, you are in deep, deep trouble. Let me say just this . . ."

This meant he was going to talk for a long time. She cast about for a way to head him off.

". . . if Eduardo had come to me, openly and honestly, and said, 'My son, Armenio, wants to open up a café, what advice do you have for him?' If he had come and spoken to me this way, I would have revealed to him the small print. This business is about details. I learned that many years ago. It was a long apprenticeship, many years in the United States of America, and I was trained by some of the best. Some people think there is nothing to it, just put out the tables and chairs and people will flock and throng, but I didn't achieve this"—he waved the brochure at the empty seats—"all this, without paying attention to detail." Vasco pulled the gray cloth from around his neck and assaulted the Formica.

"If you turn to page four," said Teresa, "the main points are clearly laid out."

"Yes, yes, I know," said Vasco, as though he had been studying it closely. "Cheap beer, I have to tell you, is not enough. Tonight they will go. Everyone is there for the cheap beer, but how long before they come back?"

Teresa shrugged. Why had she thought he was sad? Vasco was fat because Vasco was greedy. Greedy people thought only about themselves. If Vasco weren't so selfish, he would let her go.

Vasco rolled the brochure, and it sprang apart in his hands. "They are fools," he said, wheezing. "Eduardo and Armenio are fools. They are slitting my throat and also slitting their own with this cheap beer."

She was here just to keep him company. A single customer was better than none. "Super Bock, please, and a small plate of olives."

Vasco shifted her papers, performed a quick swab, and set up drinks for them both. He relaxed and let his weight rest against the counter. It was fascinating the way the flesh piled up on the surface, colliding roll upon roll beneath the stretched Aertex top.

When she had left the Internet café, Ruby was going in. They looked at each other in a way that acknowledged they might have plenty to say if they spoke. Teresa wouldn't mind telling her a thing or two, only for her own good. Save yourself, she would say. These boys, you don't know what they're like. They *want* you to make them wait.

"This should be straight and simple," said Vasco. "You tell me what you're selling, and I'll tell you if I'll buy. I've known you since you were a little bald baby. No need for fancy talk here." He topped up her glass. "And another thing I'll say is that not only have they no grasp of detail, they have no grasp even of the principles. What kind of fool spends money on computers without first purchasing a stove? Cheese toast, ham toast, cheese and ham toast!" The words bubbled from his mouth coated in spit and scorn.

Teresa sucked on an olive. How long had Francisco been sleeping with Ruby? Did they talk to each other afterward? Did they grasp even the principle of love?

"Internet café," squeaked Vasco. "They think they are so clever, they think it is the future, but what do they understand?"

Mãe didn't understand about Francisco. Her own son and she didn't know him at all.

"Do you know what is the future of this place, Teresa? It is not cork and olives. Do you know what it is?"

What if Ruby got pregnant? What would Mãe think then?

Vasco mopped his brow with the all-purpose cloth. "You only have to look south, Teresa. Think, think! When the tourists come, who will be prepared?"

The olive pit had dried her tongue. She took a sip of beer and let it sit in her mouth. The sour warmth of it made her vicious. She wished Ruby were pregnant. Let Francisco leave school and marry her. See how Mãe liked that.

Vasco's breath was jagged. The words squeezed through where they could. "Internet they get anywhere. Internet they have at home. Tourists want something different, you see, they don't want what they already have."

Francisco would say it wasn't his baby. He got away with everything. Teresa forgot there was no baby and feasted on the unfairness of it all.

"Old-world charm," said Vasco, heaving himself off the counter. "Armenio can't buy that. Oh, I'm streets ahead of that boy, and he doesn't even know it. I have traveled, you see, and I understand the modern mentality. In America, if a thing is a hundred years old, it is worshipped. I know why the tourists will come."

Teresa nodded, not knowing what he had said. Antonio's words at lunchtime undressed right there and then, their meaning all too clear. I *am* prepared, you know. She kept her face turned downward. Sorrowful Mother, the dirty mechanics of it all!

"Some old-fashioned dishes," said Vasco and kissed his fingertips.

"That will bring them flocking. Do you know what I made today? A salad of pig's ears and tail, just like my mother used to do, with a little raw onion, garlic, cilantro, olive oil, and vinegar. So tasty I don't even want to sell. I tried it and I said, 'Now, Vasco, is it fair? Is it fair to attack young Armenio with a secret weapon such as this?'" He laughed and coughed and held his chest as though it might fly apart.

Would she confess to Father Braga, this sin she was about to commit? She would not. She would say, Bless me, Father, I have argued with my brother, Francisco, and I was rude as well to Mãe.

Vasco made a recovery. He said, "This businessman who is coming, you have heard of him, Marco Afonso Rodrigues, he is Eduardo's cousin, so Eduardo thinks he can do what he likes."

She went to church just like the next person, but she wasn't going to tell him *that*. Father Braga was old, anyway, and always said, "Well, well, well, isn't it so on God's great earth?" He kept on reading the same sermons, and Teresa knew better than to bother him with a sin he would rather not hear.

"He was in the tourist trade," said Vasco. "Like myself."

"Oh," said Teresa. "Right." She sat up tall and disentangled her legs from the stool. "Shall I just leave that with you, Senhor Vasco?" she said, touching the brochure. "It has everything you need to know."

"Yes, yes," gasped Vasco. "No, no." He gripped the edge of the counter now. "I have been thinking it over. There's no sense in it at all. The money comes only when I'm dead, isn't that right? What good is it then to me?"

"Ah," said Teresa, adopting the hushed tone that was advised, "should anything unfortunate happen to you, you have the comfort of knowing that your loved ones will have everything they need."

It was getting dark, and Vasco turned away and fiddled with the light switches. He reached then under the counter, brought up a box of potato chips, and began to replenish the basket that stood by the register. "Of course," he said, "my loved ones. Leave the brochure here."

Teresa slid off the stool and looked out of the window at the doz-ing street. She said, "Good night, Senhor Vasco. If you have any more questions let me know."

The high, airless voice followed her to the door. "Teresa," it said, "when I die, I will leave this place. My nephews will come from Porto and Lisbon to sell it, and they will not remember my mother's salad, the right proportion of ear and tail and a little dash of red wine vinegar. But maybe you will tell them, maybe you will say, 'Oh, Sen-hor Vasco, he had such plans.'"

She dreamed of the house at Corte Brique. She walked through white-carpeted rooms filled with sunlight, a breeze lifting the white muslin curtains that fell to the floor. She walked through the kitchen, all silver and white, and she almost had to close her eyes. There were doors that slid open—they seemed to dissolve—at the approach of her bare feet, and rooms without function or form save that of their beauty and size. In a room without beginning and end, she lay down on a couch with carved black legs, upholstered in raw white silk. She discovered she was naked as the couch stroked her legs, her back, her neck, and she turned belly down and began to moan. She moved her hips and parted her thighs and rubbed her hot face into the silk that lapped all around. There were hands on her now, all over her, and a voice that was calling her name. "Who is it?" she said without looking around. "Who is it?" The hands rubbed every thought from her mind. She turned over again and lifted her hips and opened her lips, and her eyes she kept tightly closed.

In the morning she put on mascara and a dab of red at each cheek. She winked at the mirror and blew a kiss at the cherries and bows. From a certain angle, her nose was straight and proud, and she prac-ticed a little, looking up and to the side.

"You had the face paints out?" said Francisco. He tried to give her a hug. He was always like that, pretending he was nice all the time he was being vile. It worked on Mãe, no problem.

Teresa pinched his cheek and said, "I love you, little brother," and that shut him up, all right.

Leaving the house, she paused in the doorway and stretched up to touch the beam. When she came back through the door, she would not be the same. And also, she would tell Mãe about London. Perhaps Antonio would be there, and Mãe would see that they both had to let her go.

She wore her black slingbacks and a white cotton dress with blue flowers that matched the paint that framed the door. Alentejo blue. There she was, in a picture, in a moment, setting out for the rest of her life.

The clock said twenty past three. If she looked at it again, she would take it down and smash it. She stood up because her dress was getting crumpled. She sat down because it was too late anyway, and when she rode to Corte Brique on the Vespa, it would only get creased again. She should have brought it in a bag and changed at the house.

After lunch there had been a rush, but now there was nothing to do. Teresa kicked the floor, and the cashier's chair spun around. This morning Senhor Jaime put rat poison in the storeroom. That was the highlight of the day.

Teresa looked at the shelves: the cereal boxes and packets of biscuits, the disposable diapers and toilet paper. It was a crime that she was locked up in here. No one could expect her to stay. Antonio would understand. Perhaps not at first. But when he got over the shock, he would kiss her and say, "I'll be waiting for you, my love."

She tried to get the evening organized. She knew how she wanted it to go. First they would drink wine in the kitchen and only their fingertips would touch. Antonio would be so nervous he would say hardly a word. There would be music, because he was taking a portable stereo and she was bringing some CDs, sweet sad fado that would fill the air with tender longing.

Next they would move to the sitting room and lie side by side on the rug. She imagined a white rug, but really, the color should not matter. She would lie on her front and cross her ankles in the air; her dress would fall loosely on her thighs. An orange rug, for instance, would clash with her dress. Please, she thought, let it be white.

Teresa stood up and walked along the aisles, past jars of jam and pickled onions. It was getting out of hand. The rug, she told herself, is neither here nor there. The point was they would lie side by side, shoulders in line, and talk of everything intimately and kiss and rub noses and maybe nibble an ear. After a while she would encourage him, let his hand travel further than it had gone before. The kitchen would be amazing. She wondered if they would go back in there. And what about a tour of the house? Perhaps they should start off with that.

I have something to tell you. I'm going away. I have something to tell you. I need to go away for a while. I need to tell you something. Antonio, please don't cry.

They would set candles around the rug.

London wasn't the end of the world. Perhaps he would come and see her there.

Go to London? Why? She saw his broad blank face as he said it, the pale line of his scalp where his hair parted and sprang to the side.

It wasn't the end of the world, for goodness' sake. People traveled all the time. Even Vasco, and look at him! Waiting with his pigs' ears and tails for the world to arrive at his door. When the tourists came— but would they?—that is what they'd want. A dish of ears and tails. She giggled and put her hand to her mouth. A gust of laughter blew it away. She howled and bent over and held her knees. Oh, oh, oh, they'd be lining up for that!

She would have to tell Clara about it. Clara was good for a laugh. When she got to London, she'd tell them too. It would be a good story to tell. First, she'd have to explain about Vasco, tell them what he was like. And also Mamarrosa; you couldn't understand unless you knew about this place. It would be quite difficult, actually. She straightened up, still giggling, the laughter out of control and empty and heaving dryly out of her mouth. It slowed down and came in shudders, came fainter and finally silently, shaking her shoulders and pricking her eyes, and by the time it came to a standstill, she scarcely knew if she had laughed or cried.

When Paula stopped by for some milk, Teresa had, thankfully, retouched her makeup and recovered her usual poise.

"Who's going to make your dress?" said Teresa, being friendly.

Paula stood with a hand on her hip and one foot turned out like she was at a photo shoot. "I'm going to Lisbon for it. You don't think I'd trust anyone around here."

The way she said *Lisbon,* it was as if she thought it was special, like going to London, and it was not.

"Fantastic," said Teresa. "You'll get something really beautiful, I bet."

"Mmm," said Paula. She spread her hand across her bosom, just to show off her ring. The blond streaks she had put in her hair were turning orange, tracks left by a leaky tap. She had a pretty face, like a girl in a catalog, but she thought she was beautiful, like a girl in a magazine. Her body was long and her legs were short and she wore bras that pushed up her breasts. She had seaweed eyes and red-brown hair that fell past her shoulders and she sort of looked like a mermaid, but not nearly as beautiful, of course.

"So," said Paula, "I've been talking to my fiancé." She looked at Teresa as though this deserved a response.

Teresa just looked at her back.

"And," said Paula in the tone people use when they have some news to tell, "we have discussed *everything.*"

Three cheers for you, Teresa wanted to say.

"And," said Paula, who really was being quite annoying, "he has told me a little something about you."

In school, all the way to junior high, Paula was a nobody. To get attention, she started eating insects. She'd eat a line of ants and everyone would cheer. She ate a spider the size of her hand and got very sick. After that she ate no more insects, but she still had a lot of friends, and that just went to show.

"Right," said Teresa in a flat voice.

"And," said Paula, "I just wanted you to know that I'm really okay with it. I mean"—she hoisted a buttock onto the cash desk—"I always thought you liked him. I just never knew you'd fooled around."

Teresa opened her mouth. She didn't know where to begin. Liked him! My God, she . . . she *hated* him. She'd rather eat a spider than touch him. They were, like, fifteen when it happened, and it was only the one revolting kiss. A kiss and—okay—a squeeze; he grabbed her breast so hard that it hurt.

Paula framed her face, pointing out her smile. "Anyway, look, I'm only saying. Better that we clear the air."

Teresa wanted to get out of there. She looked at the clock and then jumped up and grabbed it.

"What are you doing with that?"

"Bloody thing," said Teresa, setting it down on the floor. Vicente always looked at her, so cocky, jutting his chin. It was like he thought that she fancied him, and if anyone was doing the fancying, it was him.

"A husband and wife," said Paula, speaking with authority, "should always tell each other everything. That way a marriage can't fail."

But you're blind, screamed Teresa inside. If there was ever a man not to be trusted, it was the one she was about to wed. "I wish you all the luck," said Teresa, and in truth she felt sorry for Paula, because Paula did not know.

"Thanks. I'll need it." Paula laughed, meaning she would not. "You've heard, I guess, about this Ruby."

Teresa clicked her tongue. "What now?"

"Everyone's talking about it." Her eyes were dull green, like seaweed dried in the sun. "She's, you know, she's . . . whatsit." She pointed to her stomach and pulled a face.

Teresa grabbed at her ponytail. "Oh, right," she said. "Oh, right."

"Isn't it awful? Such a shame."

"Yes, really," said Teresa. She felt sick; there was bile in her mouth.

"Francisco, he's friends with her, isn't he? Did he say anything to you?"

"No, nothing. He's not friends with her, anyway. He was, but a long time ago."

Paula slid off the cash desk. She straightened her skirt and turned out a toe. "Mmm," she said. "Yeah. I thought I saw it in her face. Her stomach's not showing, but you can read a lot from a face."

Teresa nodded; she tried to smile, but it made her gag, and she covered her mouth with her hands. If Francisco didn't finish school, she would kill him. Mãe would go out of her mind.

"See you later," said Paula. "We'll have fun." She swayed out of the shop, and Teresa turned to the wastebin and spat.

A couple of miles outside Mamarrosa, on the road to Ourique where the ocher fields rose and fell gentle as a lullaby, Teresa slowed the scooter as the man stepped out of the low cistus hedge. He held a long stick to which he had tied a red cloth, and when he raised it, she stopped. The cows pushed into one another at the roadside, heads resting on bony backs. She watched the stragglers; the lazy march across the dormant land, the little circus of dust at their hooves. They were cream and fawn and brown and glorious in the rich evening light. The man shouted and waved his stick, and they began to cross the road.

Teresa turned off the engine. She observed, without even trying, the particular way that they walked. Heads high, ears twitching, legs that looked set to buckle, joints that rolled deep in their shoulders in that loose, dislocated way. In London, she thought, it would finally be fruitful, this gift or this burden she had.

She set off again with her skirt whipping fancifully at her thighs. London would be big, dark, and dirty. She knew it wasn't the place that she let herself dream. Whatever it was she was ready for it. If she could she would drive there right now.

Francisco was on his own, that was it; he could mess up his life but not hers. If she stayed, she could just imagine it: Oh, Teresa will look after the child.

The silly, silly boy.

Jesus, Francisco. Maybe it's not even yours.

The road curved up and the land to her right dropped away. She glimpsed a stream, a string of diamonds thrown across the earth. The road wound around a wall of red clay and boulders cut into the side of the hill. A eucalyptus plantation ran alongside, the young trees recently thinned, and the felled trunks lay crisscrossed through the wood like giant matches dropped from a box.

At the steepest bend, the Vespa strained hard. Teresa squeezed it with her thighs. "Come on," she said, and they came up to the flat and at the crossroads turned left and let fly.

Beyond a hamlet of ten houses there was a sign. THANK YOU FOR VISITING, it said. "You're welcome," said Teresa, *"tchau."* There were a couple more kilometers to go. She got stuck behind a tractor, bouncing and swinging along. On a wide verge, a picnic bench of whitewashed concrete with a man on top, asleep. His bike rested in the shade. She came to an avenue of umbrella pines that knitted a green roof in the sky. It was the next track that she took, or the one after that. She had to look out for the cork oak with the trunk that split in two.

It looked like any other farmhouse. But there were encouraging signs. Plumbago and bougainvillea covered the outhouse, and an iron stork sat on the terrace. Antonio must have parked around the side, because she could not see his car, but Teresa left the scooter at the front and walked to the farthest door, the one that stood ajar.

Antonio was playing rock music, Guns N' Roses, she thought.

He leaped on her as she entered, catching her around the waist. His mouth, too much saliva, beery, sloshed around her face. "Darling," she said, "Antonio." He was reaching beneath her dress. "Antonio! Get off!"

"I love you," said Antonio. His face looked squishy.

She honestly felt like wiping her cheeks. How did he get them so wet?

"I've got beer," he said and went to the fridge.

"Wine for me, please." She had to shout to be heard. "And turn that music down." She picked up a tea towel and dabbed delicately at her chin.

The room was not what she had expected. There were no cabinets at all. The countertops were local marble, and they were nice enough, but just the usual plastered pillars and open shelves held them up. There was a stone sink, a tile backsplash in the old blue and white style, and the fireplace was open and large enough to smoke an entire pig.

Antonio held out a beer. He was wearing his favorite shirt. It had big Chinese letters, or Japanese, down the front. She had only told him she liked it so that she didn't hurt his feelings, and now he had it on, and that was what she got for being so bloody nice.

She ignored his outstretched hand. "Wine or gin and tonic," she said. The portable stereo was on the windowsill, and she went and turned it off.

"Relax," said Antonio, "have a beer. That's all I've got."

Teresa rolled her shoulders. She laughed. "Okay, okay. I'm sorry." How silly she was being.

She took a CD from her bag, and Antonio looked at it and groaned. "Mariza? You're kidding. That's what we'll play when we break up."

"Fine," she said brightly, "let's have nothing at all."

They sat at the pockmarked oak table that smelled of linseed and wheat. Cradling a beer apiece, their fingertips finally touched. Antonio set his beer down. He put his elbow on the table and rested his heavy chin on his hand. His eyes were black as licorice and spoke for him very well.

"Toilet's still knackered," he said. "You'll have to go outside."

She reached over quickly and kissed him. It was better if they didn't talk.

"The bedroom," he mumbled, with his lips still on hers.

They stood up with their mouths locked.

She broke away. "Let's not rush. Darling? Would you give me a tour of the house?"

"What's this room?" inquired Teresa politely as they stepped into what seemed to be a courtyard, enclosed and roofed in as well.

Antonio shrugged, his hands in his pockets. She hoped he wasn't going to sulk.

There was a cobbled floor and a stone trough along the back wall and a wooden chest with a pile of books and a vase of dried poppies. "Well, they haven't finished it yet." She pressed on, lifting the rug that hung in the doorway, just like the ones at home.

This room was big, bright and airy, like three rooms knocked into one. The walls were white and the windows large, but there was no carpet, not even a rug. And the furniture looked ancient. Even Mãe had newer stuff than that.

Antonio was breathing right on her neck. She stepped smartly away and sat down.

"It's nice," he said, "isn't it?" He stuck his finger inside his ear.

Teresa knew she should look away but didn't. It seemed like his entire body vibrated while his finger stayed stock-still.

"You know," she said, "when you have an idea of something and then you have to let go of the idea?"

"What idea?"

"Any idea. If you've really been looking forward to something."

"What something?"

She tucked her feet up on the couch. The fabric was hard and hairy. She arranged her skirt like a deflated parachute. There was a huge painting over the fireplace, daubs of violet, purple, and maroon. It was modern art, of course.

"Kiss me," she said. "Antonio." In her stomach, where butterflies should have been, there was only a cold, empty space.

She looked over her shoulder to watch him come near. He was tall and wide-shouldered and handsome and he loved her oh so much. There was a picture behind him on the wall by the woodstove and she realized now what it was. A section of whitewash and plaster peeled away to reveal the old mud bricks underneath. The clay and the mud and the straw. This is what they had framed.

He knelt in front of her and she closed her eyes. The secret now was not to think at all. It was easy too, now that she'd stopped trying. She would relax and go with the flow. She ran her tongue around his front teeth and undid two buttons on his shirt. His hands ran down her back and up to her shoulders, up and down again, once more and then over the top, and massaged inquiringly at her breast. Now, she thought, now or never, and began tugging at his belt. He lifted her skirt and drew circles on the insides of her thighs. She sucked on his tongue so madly, like she would never, ever stop. His hands burned on every inch of her, and she heard someone calling her name.

"Who's that? Who's that?" she hissed, jerking free, but she knew. It was the voice that had called in her dream.

Antonio's face was in front of her, so close it was more of a blur. She looked up and glared at Vicente. "What are you doing here?"

"Relax," said Vicente, curling his bare toes on the red flagstones. Why was everyone telling her that?

"What's this?" she snarled at Antonio. "A party?"

"Babe, I was going to tell you. You never gave me a chance."

Vicente sniggered. She wanted to smack the smile right off his face. He was watching her with his small mean eyes as if he could see through every stitch of her clothes.

Antonio got up and sat on the couch, draped an arm across her neck. "I was telling Vicente we had the house. We thought it would be nice, you know. Sociable, you know."

Vicente looked on, chewing on his damn cheeks, making his cheekbones stand out. She wasn't going to give him a show. She patted Antonio's leg. "That's nice, darling. Perhaps we could play cards."

Paula appeared, shoeless, in what seemed to be a nightdress or slip. "Hi! Teresa!" she shrieked, as if they were long-lost best friends.

See you later, she'd said in the shop. We'll have fun, she'd said. What a cow. Teresa had been thinking of Francisco. Or she would have put a stop to this.

Paula slid up to Vicente and tucked herself under his arm. Her hair was mussed up, there was mascara on her cheek, and she thought she was a woman now.

"Paula," said Teresa warmly, "who else is coming tonight?"

"Just us," said Paula in a sicky-sweet voice.

Teresa looked up at Vicente and wished it were just her with him. A spasm ran through her body, and for a moment she wished she were dead.

The swimming pool was burnished like a giant smoked-glass table-top. Teresa dipped a toe in. It was colder than it looked. A swift came down and skimmed the water, and then another and another. They came and they kept coming and the air was pierced through; they fell like arrows but vaulted right up, black darts in the twilight sky.

Antonio came out clinking beer bottles, and the swifts dispersed. He stood a little away from her. "Are you coming in?"

She shook her head. "No. Not yet."

He said fine and went, leaving one beer on the tiles.

Teresa stood on the top step of the pool. She dropped another step down. She went down again and held up her dress, but still she got it wet.

A cuckoo called, a dog barked, and its solitary friends made their pointless replies.

Paula ran from the house in a silver bikini. She shrieked as she jumped in the pool. "It's lovely. Thanks, Teresa, lovely. You should get changed and come for a swim." She lay on her back and flapped her arms, and her breasts and her hips glinted beneath the surface like fish.

Vicente was stripped to his boxer shorts. He had a tattoo of a lizard on his back. His body was hard and wiry. Teresa looked right at him to show him she didn't care.

"Hold this," he said. "I'm getting in."

Teresa held the home-rolled cigarette. She knew what was in it. She took a puff.

She carried the beer and the spliff into a bedroom and sat down on the bed. It was a high iron-framed single, like the one she had thrown away. She sucked on the spliff, and an ember fell onto her dress. The dress was wet enough to put it out.

Her limbs were heavy, aching, as though she had caught a cold. She thought she would leave now but then thought she would not. She really wanted to sleep.

If the house had been different, she thought. How very silly she was.

She toked again and sipped her beer and tested her tongue on her teeth.

Anyway, she was going to London. Nobody could spoil that. She flicked her head from side to side to make her ponytail jump.

What was the point, though, really? Why was she going there? Those children with their Indian headdresses and their thoughtless expectation of love. Who would she be in London, and who would be there to see? She would be there and the writer would be here, and the tourists would come or they wouldn't, Marco Afonso Rodrigues went and was coming back, and Telma Ervanaria was in Paris and Vasco was in Provincetown, and Mãe was lost in Brazil and everyone was going around and around and it didn't make one bit of difference, as far as she could understand. They come here and I go there. Around and around. This bed, that bed, new bed, old bed. If the room would just hold still!

"I knew it," she said to Vicente's legs, the dark hair plastered to his shins.

He lifted her face and took the spliff, which was lifeless, and put a finger to his lips.

"Go on, then," she said, and he kissed her, and it was he who made it stop.

He licked her ear and winked at her. She watched the lizard dance away.

It was a second, an hour, a second, before Antonio came. He took off his shirt and closed the door. "If you don't want to anymore," he said.

If she could, she would take off her dress. There were thousands and thousands of things to say. Or maybe, in fact, there weren't.

She grabbed her hair band and tugged it out. So much freer now, she was.

Antonio, sweet Antonio, sat on the bed, and she pulled him down with her.

She kept her eyes open the whole time, watching the bamboo ceiling and counting the insects that fell.

Seven

China kicked me out. When I say *kicked,* I mean it. Strange, this, but when I'm sitting, I can't feel it. It's when I walk around that it hurts.

I wasn't arguing. When you've been caught out telling lies, you take what's coming. Thing is, he was happy when he walked through that door thinking he was going to be a grandfather. I didn't see that. He was shouting, where's my pregnant daughter? Ruby was right there in front of him. Bet it was Bruno did the gassing. Might have been Vasco. He's always had it in for Ruby. Who's to say? The whole damn village knew. Even the father, I guess. I ain't pregnant, Ruby said. He kept going on and on and she kept saying no I ain't and then I said she definitely ain't and China said how do you know and Ruby said I ain't *anymore,* like that, and then it all came out.

I'm in Michelle's caravan. She wouldn't mind. She's back in England doing two months in a factory, packing lightbulbs. I've never had a job. When I was at primary school, I was top of the class up until Miss Macleary's. *Something's gone wrong with you, Christine.* She kept a pair of glasses balanced on the end of her nose and looked at you over the top of them. *Do you want to tell me what it is?* Did I hell.

No, I've never had a job. Michelle is probably hating hers right now. It's no place for an eco-warrior, is it, a factory? She built a compost toilet all on her own. It's a bit too close to the well.

She's left some clothes in the caravan, underneath the seats, and we're more or less the same size.

When I was growing up, I knew what I wanted to be. What I wanted to be was small. I had a book about these tiny people who lived under the floorboards. They used matchboxes for storage and postage stamps for paintings. For dinner they ate half a pea.

It was called *The Borrowers*. I also had *Anne of Green Gables* and *Ballet Shoes*. I kept them in a box under my bed, with my charm bracelet and a photo of my father. There were five other books in our house. A Bible, which we weren't allowed to read because we'd only spoil it; a car manual that we stood muddy boots on next to the back door; and an ancient book about guinea pigs called *Shaggy Shelties and Waxy Rexes: A Complete Guide to the Care, Maintenance, and Breeding of Guinea Pigs*. We never had a pet. Mum had a cookery book on the kitchen windowsill. She didn't need it for what she made. The last book was the *Collins Concise*. The corner of the cover was chewed right off. Mum said I did it when I was teething. I used to take it up to my bedroom. **a** 1. the first letter and vowel of the English alphabet. 2. any of several speech sounds represented by this letter, as in take, bag, or calm. 3. also called: alpha. the first in a series, esp the highest mark. 4. from A to Z. from start to finish. Eating the dictionary again? Harry never asked if I liked books. People think they know so much about you, and they haven't got a clue. To be honest, I don't like books much. I only like words when they float about on their own.

Ishmael's a good word, don't you think? I've always liked epiphany too.

The hospital is over at Beja. A hundred and thirty kilometers there, a hundred and thirty back, and we must have managed six sentences between us. Ruby took the blanket off her bed and sat pulling fluff off it. Sometimes she put it over her head. It never heats up in the car. She never said thank you, but I don't expect that anyway. The doctor looked like a goat. I swear his eyes were yellow. I remember his shoes. They were black with brown laces, and they were built up very high, like you see if someone's got one leg shorter than the other, only both of his were like that. I bet he's got hooves in there. Dr. da Silva speaks good English. He said, "Simply rotten weather today." And he said, "It's rotten luck." Have you noticed how some words, if you say them over a few times, go silly on you? Rotten is definitely one of them.

He said, "It is a complicated situation, Senhora Potts, but I will help your daughter. It is fortunate that I am the one who took your call."

They took Ruby off on a trolley. She was making eyes at the orderly. Honest to God.

There's a Dutch ship anchored somewhere off the Algarve. Michelle had hers done there a couple of years ago. If you go to the floating hospital, it's not illegal because you're not actually in Portugal. How do you find it, though? Start swimming and hope they throw you a line.

Ruby bled on the seat on the way back. I cleaned it up. No point asking her to do it. Well, if there's one thing I know about, it's getting out bloodstains.

Jay came to see me yesterday. He brought my scraps and my wool and my needles and the eight peg dolls I did last week. There was nothing else left to sell. You know what, they look a bit miserable. They shouldn't, because I drew smiley faces on them. Jay forgot to bring more pegs. He was cross with himself about that, but I said let me see if anyone buys these first. No point working for nothing. The car boot sale's only a couple of days off. I'm making coconut ice and no cakes because there's only a fridge here and no oven. I don't know how much to charge for the dolls. They took hours and hours, putting all that detail on, but I don't think anyone will want them. Jay said I'll help you, Mum, with the sewing and that. He blushes just with his ears. That sweater with the train on the front is a bit baby-ish, but it's stretched over the years, sort of grown with him. I thought I was going to cry, so I said, if you keep wagging off school you'll be a moron just like your mother, now go on and try to fill that space between those ears, and don't keep popping up round here when you know you're not supposed to.

I could have kept him here with me.

The rain's coming down, day after day. You hear it, then you stop hearing it, then you know it's there but you're still not really hearing it, then you start listening and in the end that's all you can do, listen to the rain and think, oh, it's got a bit lighter now, no, it's slow now but heavy, and then you imagine there's a tune in the raindrops and you try to follow it and it really pisses you off because you can't because it's just rain for God's sake, just bloody rain on a bloody tin roof.

I've always liked this word: dogged. Don't know why. Dogged is the opposite of me. Sum yourself up in three words. What would you say? I could give you a list of the things that I'm not.

As soon as Jay left, I wanted him to come back. I ran through the mud in my socks, Michelle's socks, but I couldn't make him hear me. Sometimes I think I can't really exist. I dig my nails into my skin to see if I'm really there, I'm doing it now, and it's good when the blood comes because that proves something, and you can't just believe, you have to have proof.

It's warmer outside than in tonight, and I'm sat out under the stars. I can see a few house lights. They look so far away, like you could walk all night and never reach them. Every now and then a little dot of silver slides across the black and disappears. It's a car going over the hill and down toward the sea. There are shooting stars as well. I've seen one tonight already. You never see them in England, hardly, because of all the light pollution. Some things you only see clearly in the dark.

It was the car boot sale today. I sold all the dolls for two euros each, so that was sixteen euros, and all the coconut ice and chocolate crispies went in about an hour. Nearly forty euros altogether, which is not bad. I gave Ruby and Jay ten each. Ruby will have spent hers by now.

The Portuguese loved my peg dolls. *Bonita,* they said. *Que beleza! Requintada!* I almost started thinking, Yes, aren't they? Aren't they beautiful, my dolls? But they're the same with anything small, the Portuguese. Any little child, they stop and tickle it on the chin and pat its head and pull its cheeks and say, *Que coisa fofinha, que graçinha.* It might be cross-eyed and dribbling and stink of shit, but if it's small, it's gorgeous, end of story.

She was wearing my clothes, but I didn't say anything about that. They were too tight for her. Ruby's always been bigger than me. I thought she was smiling when she started across. There was a dog in one of the gardens that backs onto the square, chained up like they always are. It went mad when it saw Ruby. I thought it was going to die right then and there, just strangle itself to death.

She wasn't smiling by the time she got to me. I said how's your dad, and she said he's all right, and I said is that all you can say, and she said well what do you want me to say, and then we were both quiet for a bit. When she was a baby, she used to stare at me all the time, follow me around with her eyes, head wobbling all over. If I left the room, she screamed. She's always driven me crazy, one way or another. I said your eyebrows look nice. They didn't. She's plucked them so there's just a thin line like a child would draw.

"He's furious," she said, "about what you did. He ain't never going to speak to you again."

Someone came up and bought one of the dolls. My hands were shaking.

"Good job," Ruby said, "good job he's got me to look after him."

The worst thing is, while she was saying it, I was listening to the words falling out of her mouth and landing on their heads, and I was thinking, You might be young, but you're not so pretty it cancels out that voice. How do you like me as a mother? I said Ruby, it was your decision too. She said have you got any money so I gave her ten and she walked off shaking her hips like she's Marilyn Monroe and I think she's split the seam in my good velvet skirt.

You know what, the day when we got back from Beja, she went out that same evening. I was getting a hot-water bottle ready, but no, she had to go out. What did she think she was going to do with a baby? Like I want another to look after. Like I did such a good job with my own.

China was in Mamarrosa today. I saw his motorbike outside Vasco's. He'll come over when he's ready, never mind what Ruby says. God knows I've tried enough times to leave. He fetches me back in the end. There's never going to be anyone else. No one else would be so stupid.

The sky isn't really black, you know, not even out here. When your eyes adjust, it's more purple. That's a word I love. Purple. It sounds like what it's saying, like thud and crack and patter, only you don't expect it with a color. There's quite a lot of purple in churches, the Catholic ones. It must be a religious color. I went into the church, the *igreja,* today after the fair wound down. No service on, but there were three women inside, two down on their knees with their eyes closed and the other lighting a candle up near the front and looking very stern, like she was really going to hold it against Him if she'd just wasted her fifty céntimos. Another woman came out of the confessional box. She was about a hundred years old, dressed all in black like they do, legs like two black bananas and a white lace apron over her dress. What did she have to confess? Forgive me, Father, for today I have not done the dusting. She crossed herself and said something to the woman with the candle, and they both had a bit of a laugh. If I've ever hated anyone, I hated those women then. I mean, they have it so easy, don't they: Press your hands together, light a candle, ask to be forgiven.

To be honest, I didn't hate them, but I wanted to. I'm not even capable of that. I like to look at the stars and think my own thoughts.

This man I read about once said he had an out-of-body experience on the operating table. His body was being cut open, but he just drifted off and up and away. I was so excited, because that's what I have sometimes, but I never knew it had a name. *Out-of-body experiences*. I've had them most of my life, ever since I was in Miss Macleary's class.

I bought some more pegs and I've made three more dolls. They're a family. I'm working on the mum. She's got yellow wool for hair and black beads for eyes. The dress is blue stripes, out of an old pair of Jay's underpants, and the apron I made from a bit of old bandage. It looks a lot better than it sounds, but the eyes keep falling off. I'm wondering if anyone remembers to feed the chickens. They'll be cross with me when I go back, the chickens. They'll try to peck my toes, just letting me know they missed me. This caravan is a bit of a dump. There's moss growing along the inside edges of the windows. Michelle's supposed to be building herself a log cabin. You don't need planning permission if you build with wood. She's been here three years. I guess you get used to anything in the end. When Harry said he wanted to stop seeing me, I felt awful for about a minute, and then I got used to it. When Ruby told me they'd been together, I didn't believe her at first. I thought she was saying it because I made her do the dishes and sweep the floor. Then I did believe her because she told China, but I wasn't really sure, not until Harry came round, and then I knew it was true because I saw his face go dead and that was the proof of everything. I got used to that too.

   That's what all this is about, though. Harry bloody Stanton. I mean, it can't be about the baby. All that anger. He's got a talent for it. I'll give him that. My husband is good at being angry, and it made him good at his job. It's not much use to him out here. He's got a chance now, I suppose, so he's making the most. Bet he doesn't even think about the baby. I do. If you're Catholic, you believe a new life is created the moment the sperm enters the egg. That's another soul being born. And then you've got to believe that when the body dies, the soul carries on. The soul doesn't die. You've got a soul but no body. I can't say that sounds so bad to me.

⚯

This happened.

I was at the well, getting water to boil up the sheets. The sun was shining, and it was raining that needle kind of rain. It looked like someone had thrown a striped sock across the sky. The rainbow was that bright. There was a woodpecker in the cork oak that spreads across the toilet hut; a nuthatch flew into the mimosa and an eagle, no less, fussing about over the pines. Sometimes it hits you like that. All this nature.

I'd got two buckets up, and I was going to go back when I heard the car. In this place, when you hear a car, you always wait to see who it is. Imagine doing that in Yarmouth. The two men got out first. They looked like locals but with suits and ties, which was confusing. Then China got out. Then Jay.

He said, "Mum," and gave me a hug and backed away, all without looking at me.

I said, "Your hair's getting long, almost an inch now." There was a hole in the top of his sneakers, and I thought, Not another pair.

I don't know who spoke next, and I can't remember who said what as we went up to the caravan. When we sat down, everyone's knees were almost touching, like we were about to play patty-cake. The man with the blue tie and the fat neck was Senhor Luis Costa, and the one with the green tie and the high forehead was Senhor Helder Pedro Something Something de Araujo. They were policemen, and they had come down from Lisbon.

After that they switched to Portuguese because, please forgive them, their English was not too good, and Senhor de Araujo said that Jay was going to translate for everyone.

"What's she gone and done now?" I was prepared for anything.

My husband rubbed his palms on his knees. I thought, There's hair growing out of his ears, like an old man's. I'd never noticed that before. I felt sorry for him then, if you can believe that.

"She's done nothing," China said. "If," he said, "you don't count opening her legs to every Tom, Dick, and Harry."

When we were courting, I used to look into his eyes, and they were such a soft, soft blue. I thought that meant something. The blue's turned watery now, if you see it at all beneath the red. But we had some wonderful times. Our parties were the best, nobody would say different, China holding court in that smelly afghan he used to wear, my savior. I was saved for a while. I was.

Senhor de Araujo said something to Jay. *"Diga a ela,"* he said. Tell her.

Jay wrapped his arms across his chest like he was cold, though it was getting quite hot in the caravan, with all of us steaming it up. "He says they've come here to talk about something serious. He says that he wants you to help him and not to hide anything. He says that they are going to interview you and he wants your full . . ."

Jay didn't know the word. My husband leaned forward, and he smelled of the goats. "Cooperation."

"Ah, yes, cooperation," Senhor de Araujo said. If you're a policeman, perhaps you know that word in many languages. His forehead looked like an eggshell, the exact same shade I get from my best layer. His friend had taken a little spiral-bound notebook out of his jacket. The end of his pen was chewed. Senhor de Araujo spoke some more.

"He wants your name and address," said Jay.

I didn't say anything.

"Get on with it," my husband said. "You know who she fucking is."

Senhor de Araujo and Senhor Costa looked at each other. You could tell what they were thinking.

Senhor de Araujo talked at Jay, who twitched and fidgeted and drummed his feet on the floor until I almost gave him a slap. I thought, When Michelle gets back and hears that my husband tried to have me arrested for breaking into her property, she's going to wet herself. I smiled at the one with the fat neck, Senhor Costa, but he just stared at me like I was going to break down and confess because of how powerful he was. I smiled at my husband as well, because he of all people should know that I have never, not ever, told the police a single thing. Eggy Head had hold of Jay's elbow. He lifted it up and down. Policemen always come in pairs like that, the one who talks and the one who doesn't. The stringy ones usually do the talking.

"Come on, Jay," I said. "Get it over with. Nothing to worry about."

He turned his face away from me. His ear was like one of those sunsets you get sometimes at the end of a long summer's day, all red and swollen and throbbing.

He started talking then. I wasn't listening properly, I was thinking about when you see the Asian kids translate for their mums. The mums wear saris or baggy colored pajamas or sometimes a big black bag that covers everything except their eyes, so you don't really expect them to understand anything much. I was thinking, I'm like that now. I'm the bloody foreigner.

"He says if they find out all of these things that have been said about you are true"—speaking fast, gabbling—"then you will be arrested, and the charge will be"—Jay looked at me then, and I knew just before he said it what he was going to say—"and the charge will be murder."

Now, that is such an ordinary word. No music to it at all. We use it all the time. It was murder at the shops today. I'll murder you if you don't stop that right now. I could murder a cup of tea. See. It doesn't set you off. It's not what I call a special word.

I had one of those things last night. An out-of-body experience. I must have lifted that tin roof right off, because I was up high, higher than the trees, the pylons, the hills, and it was dark but I could see everything and I saw a woman, I knew it was me, and she was lying in the caravan where the seats push together to make a bed and she had a knife in her hand, she was drawing it very carefully across her forearm, writing a message, perhaps, concentrating hard and bleeding softly on the sheets.

I left the car in Mamarrosa and walked to the house right through the woods. The ground was crispy underfoot, a bit of frost in the early morning, though you could still feel how soft it was below that top layer. I saw a nightjar, three bee-eaters, and I lost count of the hawfinches. Before I met Michelle, I never knew what any of the birds were called, apart from the obvious ones, the owls or the eagles or the storks and herons down along the lagoons. If you can't name something, it's hard to be interested. You go, There's a little bird, big deal. So I saw all these birds, and I was that busy looking at them, I forgot to look where I was going and got a bit lost. But I was still there early, the last of the mist drifting off the branches, and I had a long wait behind that big old tree on the slope where Jay used to have a rope swing. They came out about eleven o'clock and got on the Honda. How many times have I told China to make Jay wear a helmet? I knew he wouldn't be going to school, not without me there.

It makes a hell of a noise, that bike. The chickens started up like the sky was about to fall, and I calmed them and fed them before I went to the house.

Ruby was laid out on the big chair with her legs over one side and her head lolled back. I watched for a while through the window. She was winding a piece of string around two fingers, unwinding it and winding it around again. I thought, God help us. She sat up when she saw me, though, which was a good sign.

I said, "Looks nice in here." She'd put a cloth on the table and some of those long grasses with pods in a vase.

"Did he see you?"

I shook my head. She let the string fall on the floor. She had her nightie on and a cardigan and a pair of boots. I said, "I've come to get some things."

"Sit down," she said. "Would you care for a drink?" Honest to God.

She made peppermint tea because that's all there was, and we drank it, and I thought, This is so stupid.

"Ruby, you know what's happened."

She fiddled with her hearing aid, turning it up and down so it whined and wailed. When she washes her hair and does it nicely, you can't see it, but most of the time she lets her hair get ratty and there's no way of hiding it then. In the end she said, "Who'da thunk it?"

I said, "Can you believe it? On a murder charge. Me."

"Ridiculous," she said. Every now and again, a word pops out perfectly formed. It made her sound really and truly shocked.

"Do I look like a murderer?"

"Nutso," she said. "Crazy." She's got my eyes, Ruby. You have these moments when you see how totally your child is your own.

"I mean, Chris the Ripper."

"Yeah," she said, laughing. "Chris the Killer."

"A dangerous woman."

She was laughing hard now, honking, really. I caught it off her, and it was funny, I swear. Just then it was bloody hilarious.

"Wooo," she said, holding her knees. "Lock her up quick."

"Throw away the bloody key."

She was fairly choking by now. "The Murdering Mummy and Dr. Death. Lock them up together."

I was getting a stitch. There's muscles you use to laugh that don't get used very often. "So he's been charged as well?"

"Yeah, they've hauled up Dr. Death."

"How does he plead?"

"Ooh! Plead! Plead!" She was hiccuping now, and that was making her laugh even more. "Plead let me go! He says—ha, ha—he says the notes are all lost. Hospital can't find them."

Well, I laughed at that. "What about you? Been arrested yet?"

There was the time lag then that you get when someone hears something they're not expecting to hear. Her face changed a few beats before she stopped laughing. "What do you mean?"

"I was just asking, what's happened? Have you been inter-
viewed?"

She chewed her lip and pulled her nightie over her knees.

I said, "If we get our stories straight, they won't be able to
touch us."

"Us?" she said. "I'm a minor. That's the law. In case you didn't
know."

"Ruby," I said. "Ruby. This is not what you want."

Her eyes went cloudy, out of focus. I wonder if mine do that. She
shrugged and said, "Ain't up to me. As per usual."

When I went into the shop, everyone stopped talking. I said *bom dia*
all light and airy, singing, practically, and people mumbled it back
and turned away. Doesn't take long. Not around here. If someone
in the next village farts, everyone knows by lunchtime. So, you can
imagine.

I was going to get some bits and pieces, a tomato, a piece of
cheese, a banana, a yogurt, a slice of ham, make them last a couple of
days. China's given me no money, so what do you expect? But I
wasn't going to do that now, not with everyone watching. She bought
one tomato. Did you see? One banana. I'm not giving them the satisfaction. I bought some ham, the best stuff, and held my breath
while Gonzalo weighed it.

You know how in England everyone always says, Oh, there's no
community anymore? Well, here's a community for you.

They do things together. Like the women who look after the
orange trees along the road. They dig tiny ditches around the trunks
to keep the water in better, always bent from the waist, though it's
bad for your back. They pick the oranges together every winter, and
every summer they put flowers in the concrete beds around the
square. Spring and summer they have these festivals where they link
arms and walk along the streets singing traditional songs, men and
women both but separately, of course. It's mainly the old ones,

though. In England the council looks after the trees. It might get like that here.

I know what they think of us. I know what they think of me. And I don't blame them.

There's only one thing upsets me. The first year we were here, I had a birthday party for Jay. He was six. I made all these invitations and stuck on little silver stars and drew clowns' heads and balloons, and I gave them out to all the mums of the kids in his class. I baked a cake and I made streamers, you can't buy them, and I got three presents wrapped for pass the parcel, and Jay and even Ruby were so excited they kept running up to the top of the track to look out for cars. They kept running up and running down and Ruby said the kids stay up that much later here, they'll be coming later, and Jay kept checking the parcels and saying how many layers, Mum? I'm going to get one of them prizes, just see. Nobody came. Not a soul. We didn't have the pigs then, so a lot of the food went to waste. I said Jay, I expect they were busy, and he said that's right, Mum, I expect so.

I told Michelle about it the year after, and she said they don't have birthday parties here, they just have the family over, it's a different tradition. It certainly bloody is.

I found some coins in a little tin with a picture of Harry Potter on the side. Michelle's got all the books, though it's not what you'd expect her to read. Even eco-warriors can have too much of this world. I've borrowed the money, and I'm treating myself to a cup of tea and a *pastel de nata* still warm from the oven. I've driven over to Lindoso, which is an escape of sorts. From the café I can see the iron tree in the middle of the roundabout. It's all scraps of junk welded together, and it looks just like the kind of tree you'd have in a fairy tale where the children get lost in the woods. I'm making the tea last, even though nobody cares. There's a Brazilian soap opera on the television. All the women in it have that shuddery way of talking, like they're about to have an orgasm. I think the heroine's husband has caught her cheating, though it could be the other way round, everyone seems equally worked up.

What I'm thinking now is that I should plead guilty. In England you get life for a murder. A life for a life. But they let you out before you die, there's no symmetry, which, by the way, is a word that I like. You know what, it doesn't scare me anymore. I think I'd like it. All this business of what to do next, how to do it, when to do it, why you're doing it. Well, they take that off you, don't they? You don't get to be small and live under the floorboards, not in the real world, but this is as close as damn it. You don't have to pretend anymore about pushing on, going somewhere. You just have to serve your time. Isn't that what we're doing anyway? And there is this as well: I am guilty. How easy that is to forget.

I'd make some Portuguese friends. Isn't that a laugh? I like that idea. I like everything about this now. Give in and make it easier. Might as well make it easy on yourself.

Today I went to Beja to see my lawyer. All these phrases kept popping into my head. How do you plead? Guilty, m'Lud. Take her down. I couldn't get there fast enough. I was practically holding my arms out to be handcuffed by the time I walked into the office. Silly, I know. He's supposed to be on my side.

He said, "Senhora Potts, allow me a moment to refresh my memory." And he started reading through the papers on his desk, like I'd just happened to barge in and he wasn't expecting me at all. I thought I could save him the bother by saying I was changing my plea, but when you're in front of a man like that, you don't interrupt. He's called Senhor Soares de Macedo, he has a brass plaque outside his office, a receptionist with acrylic nails, and a crystal decanter on a mahogany sideboard. He looks like a little bird in a suit, all puffed-up chest and tiny bones.

"Ah, yes, yes." He said it a few times.

He has a really big chair, and I glanced down to see if his feet touched the ground, but the desk panel came too low. I've been to the office before, but last time I was in such a daze, I didn't take anything in. This time I was calm, only a little impatient to get on with things.

Finally he stopped shuffling the papers. He put his elbows on the desk and pressed the tips of his fingers together. "Senhora Potts." It sounded like Pootz. "Senhora Potts, you are a lucky woman." He didn't go on; he stopped and smiled at me as if that was all he was going to say. I knew he'd have to say something else if I kept quiet, but I guess I'm just too polite, or too weak.

I said, "What do you mean?"

"Ah," he said, "the lost hospital notes." I thought, This could take a long time, and all for nothing. Did I tell you he has orangey hair? That's not normal for a Portuguese.

"They have been found, Senhora Potts. Do you wish to know what they say?"

I didn't, not really, because it wouldn't make any difference. I said, "Yes, please," like a schoolgirl.

He bent his head to read, and the sun caught across his hair, and I could see for the first time how thin it was, how it must really be white with a terrible dye on top. I could see then how old he was, how frail. He looked up again and said, "Yes, that's right. They *have* been found, and they say that the baby, this baby, died in the womb."

The first thing I thought was: How terribly afraid of forgetting he is that he must keep checking and checking again. The second thing I thought was: This is not fair.

"That can't be right," I said.

Senhor de Macedo stared at me for a few moments, and I stopped digging at my arm. I saw the confusion come over his face. He bent so quickly to his papers it was funny, like he'd dropped off to sleep. Then he did the position again with his fingertips pressing together. It seemed to give him confidence. "'She can't believe her luck.' I saw that once on an advertising poster in the London Underground. I was there in the year of nineteen hundred and seventy-six." He made it sound like the Middle Ages. "It was promoting a—I think you have the same word like us—perfume."

"Same word," I said. "So what do we do?"

"Give thanks," said my lawyer, tipping back in his big chair and looking up, as if to some Just and Almighty Power.

On the drive back, I thought about my hens. I thought about a lot of things. I thought about good luck and rotten luck. And I thought about yellow eyes.

I knew he would come and get me. He said, "It's finished now," and I got my things and didn't say a word. He carried me inside ("Over the threshold, darlin'") and sat me in the high-backed leather chair. I held the back of his neck and remembered how much his skin feels like scars, even where no scars have ever been. He rolled a joint and said, "Suppose we're sort of celebrating."

I said, "I suppose we sort of are."

Eight

Outside Beja, they stopped for petrol. Huw went to pay and saw the bar and laughed out loud. Drink and drive. You have to. Dancing around the puddles, he returned to the car and rapped on the window. Sophie looked at him but didn't do anything, so he shouted through the glass: "Pull over."

When she got out, she held her hands over her head, trying to stop the rain. "What's the matter?"

"One for the road," he said and pointed to the right of the cashier's booth at the liquor bottles dangling upside down along the back wall.

She sprinted across the forecourt, gaining dark wet tracks up the back of her jeans.

He ordered two large whiskeys, and they stood at the bar. "It's three o'clock," she said, shaking her head.

"When in Rome."

"You're such an idiot," she said, banging her hip into his.

"That's why you're marrying me."

"Only out of pity," she said.

He slid his hand, briefly, over her backside. "I love it when you talk dirty."

"Shut up," she said, laughing. "Let's drink."

"Remember that guy," he said, "in our village?"

"'If the fool would persist in his folly, he would become wise.'"

"Quoting himself, maybe. Said he was a writer."

"Yeah, right," said Sophie, digging a band out of her pocket and pulling back her hair. "Writing his own excuses."

"Well, he wouldn't have a problem with three o'clock."

"And that's good, is it?"

In the village where they had rented a house for the week, they went to a café at lunchtime. The man was there. Drunk but contained, slurring a bit, perhaps, but rising above it with an elegant kind of self-loathing. It's only the happy drunks you have to avoid. Huw could imagine, back in Mamarrosa, a late-night session, getting down to brass tacks.

"Don't beat me up," he said. "I'm still sore from last night."

In the car she said, "Where are all these damn birds, anyway?"

He fiddled with the binoculars, the road going in and out of focus. "You know, playing Scrabble. They'll be out when the rain stops."

They had taken a circuitous route, on small roads in the region of Castro Verde, traversing the grassy steppe and fallow fields, encountering few houses, and most of these lay fallow too. He had seen, he thought, a lesser kestrel and a great bustard, but at such a distance that he could not be sure. Now they were moving slowly, behind a truck, across the rolling plains of wheat north of Beja, and if the sun came out, he'd ask her to stop and take a walk and hope for some luck: black-bellied sandgrouse, hen harriers, a red kite.

"I'm sorry about the weather," he said. "November can be lovely. It just happens not to be."

She took her hand off the gearshift and laid it on his thigh. "I've got all the sunshine I need. Right here with me."

"What are you doing?" he said, watching her jerk her shoulders and screw up her nose.

"Twitching," she said. "Just twitching."

"You'll pay for this," he said. "Hey, look. Look at these."

"Oh my God. *What?* Dodos!"

They looked up at the nests, vast, untidy edifices crowning dozens of telegraph poles. The storks fussed around the neighborhood, seeking verification of something or other. Huw could almost hear the clatter of long red bills.

"You're learning fast," he said.

"Shall we stop?"

"No," said Huw. "Let's just get there."

They were heading to Évora, an ancient town replete with city walls and Roman ruins. They were splashing out—he was splashing out—on a night in a *pousada,* a state-run top-of-the-line hotel.

He looked at Sophie, leaning in to the wheel as she watched for a chance to pass: the fine line of her nose, the permanent, promising hunger of her mouth. He breathed deeply, and the interior of the rental car smelled of plastic and deodorizers, of cheap and illicit exchange.

If you went to a real down-and-dirty fleabag, that was the exception that proved the flashy-hotel-equals-hot-sex rule. In Calcutta once he rutted with a girl, a fellow backpacker, in a brown-stained room where water and cockroaches trickled down the walls, and attained not only orgasm but Enlightenment that lasted as long as the night. But as a rule, sex adhered to star ratings: one star, perfunctory; two stars, businesslike; three stars, comfortable; and four stars—depending on setting and style—lavish, experimental, or baroque.

"You realize," he said, "that when we're married, we can only have sex twice a week."

"As often as that?" she said.

The rain let up, and the sun came through a nauseating kind of yellow. In the distance, roiling black clouds smothered the sky and the fields like a chemical explosion.

"Look what's waiting for us," said Sophie.

"I love this kind of landscape," said Huw.

The plains spread out on either side. Here and there a cork oak stood grieving. The land rose and fell in modest dimensions. Now and again a gleam of machinery, glittering drops of water on an acacia, a giant eucalyptus shedding its splintery scrolls. Field upon field upon field, wheat and grass and fallow, on and on and on, and in this flat composition there was a depth, both sadness and tremulous joy.

Huw rolled the window down. "Lapwings," he said. "Up there."

"Get the map. Let's find the main road," said Sophie without looking.

Just before the turn was a house with ocher-framed doors and windows, a pigsty fashioned from branches, rough as a stork's nest, a small stone well, and a striated vegetable plot. Planted in the thin soil, an old couple leaned on their hoes and waited for the car to pass, as if this would be the day's main event. Huw, leaning through the open window, raised his hand. The old man pushed his hat up an inch. His wife bowed her back and attended to the earth.

"In the north of Portugal, it's all small farms like that," said Huw. "Here it's big landowners."

"Come the revolution . . ." said Sophie.

"It came," said Huw. "Collectivization. And it went."

"What?" she cried. "When?"

"Seventies. Didn't work out. The old landowners started buying their land back on the cheap."

"Crafty sods. Why couldn't the workers just get their own bit each?"

"Because," said Huw. "I don't know. The peasants didn't have any money, probably, to buy a share. And besides, there's nothing more conservative than a landowning peasant, in case you didn't know."

"Yes, there is," said Sophie, "there's you."

"Thanks. But it's over now anyway, this life. How many men does it take to drive that tractor? How many young people have you seen? How many empty houses?" ·

"And it makes you happy, I suppose, that a way of life is dying."

"Not at all," said Huw. He reached across and massaged the back of her neck. It would be raining in Évora. They'd have to stay in and make the most of the room. "Peasants are so picturesque."

She put the radio on and scanned through the stations playing American soft rock until she hit on a mournful Portuguese song and turned it up. Huw stared at Sophie's face, the small scar at the temple, the artful lift of her eyebrows. He thought about the old couple at the side of the road and how their expressions had not changed, unaltered, it seemed, through the centuries. In their sturdy boots and frayed sweaters, they worked side by side, and he imagined the understanding between them ran deeper than the well. He tried to swap places with them, he and Sophie forever in the field and the others passing through, but he could not. He thought about growing old with Sophie, about being old with Sophie, and that was real, and he thought, Yes, we are not so far apart, we are not always passing through, and he felt something for the old couple, gratitude, love, that made him cough and begin to sing tunelessly along with the unknown song.

Sophie taught English at a large public high school. Her friends were teachers or social workers or had jobs in local government.

"Have they excommunicated you yet?" he asked.

"No," she said. "They haven't. But they want me to go into therapy."

The way they looked at her, he could tell that all the men fancied her. They bought him pints and ribbed him and said, "How much, then? How many millions today?" but he could see that they were bitter too, that they thought how unfair it was, how typical, that the pretty one would jump ship like that.

They began sentences with "If you believe." "If you believe in social justice . . ." "If you believe in participatory democracy . . ." "If you believe in civil liberties . . ." Huw found it interesting. It was like a church. He wondered what beliefs he had and decided he didn't have any. He knew some things were right and he knew some things were wrong. Or he didn't care either way.

Sophie, he had learned, would always take the side of the under-dog. She had a big heart, his Sophie. And she liked to argue a lot.

On the main road, they were going a hundred and ten. They came up to a village and Sophie slowed the car right down. Whitewashed houses ran alongside the road, with barely a scraping of shoulder in between. A mother carried a small child out of one house and into another. White smoke rose from the chimney. There was a wind chime in the doorway.

A car, a big black BMW, overtook them at such speed that it left in its wake little ripples of anger, a swell of outrage.

Outside the village, Sophie hunched in to the steering wheel.

"What are you doing?" said Huw.

A humming vibration started up in the door panel. Huw won-dered if the door was properly closed.

"You're not trying to catch him?" he said.

The tendons in her hands stood out. Huw couldn't see the speedometer.

"He was an arsehole," he said, "but honestly, some of the drivers here . . ."

The BMW came into view.

"Sophie," he said. "Sophie. My door. I think it's not properly shut."

Her hands looked totally alien. He had never seen anger in a pair of hands before.

They gained on the BMW. They were too close now, the rear bumper high in the frame. Huw held on to the door handle. "It's not funny," he shouted. "Sophie."

She swung the car out, and Huw saw the yellow bus—a school bus, it had to be—coming at them. He let go of the door handle and grabbed her hand and turned the wheel so that they veered off again to the right, slicing in front of the car and then skidding left, and sliding a couple more times across the road and back before straightening up finally with him in charge of the wheel and Sophie pressing hard on the horn.

The BMW dropped far behind, though they were not going fast now.

"So that was fun," said Sophie.

Huw couldn't speak. His heart wasn't in his mouth. It seemed to be in his throat, beating violently and blocking his airway.

"Did you think you were going to die?" asked Sophie.

Huw put his head back and closed his eyes. Adrenaline, he told himself, you're not having a heart attack.

"I did," said Sophie. "I thought I was going to die."

Another twenty minutes and they'd be there. Huw made himself busy looking up the directions to the *pousada*. They'd driven into the clouds now, and the rain bounced hard off the hood and turned the windshield into a vertical lake, the wipers swimming through.

They passed a power plant, commandingly ugly, painted on the gray canvas of the sky: high wire fences and great metal vats and spiny towers that flashed in the milky light of the storm.

"What's this?" said Sophie as they drove past the plant. "What are we driving through now?" She sounded upset.

He didn't know at first. He peered through the window at the dark rows of claw-ended posts and the long lines of wizened black stumps and had this wild thought, that this was where they grew the power plants, out of the ground, in nursery beds of coal.

"It's a vineyard," he said finally. "Scenic."

"God," said Sophie, "they look like severed arms. Charred-up severed arms."

The wedding, he thought, was getting her down. They had taken it over. They were turning it into a charade.

It was easy at first to laugh about it. A church wedding. For the sake of Sophie's parents, who had her baptized, who had her confirmed, who sent her to Sunday school, who would weep discreetly at the exchanging of the vows.

Sophie and Huw had to see the vicar every time they went down to Devon to visit Sophie's parents. "I don't need to tell you," the vicar said, "that marriage is a serious business." He seemed embarrassed. He fiddled with the biscuits on the plate. "I have to ask you," he said, as though if it were up to him he would not, "how you, ah, perceive—I say *perceive,* I mean *feel*—that your faith in the Lord will reflect upon your relationship in the . . . er . . . married state, as it were, as it will be."

He had a strawberry birthmark over his right eye that, Huw fancied, was in the shape of a cloven hoof, and the tips of two of his fingers were missing.

"He used to be a carpenter," Sophie said later.

"No," said Huw. "No. And born in a manger as well?"

She punched him softly in the stomach, and they collapsed on the bed, their legs in a tangle. "Do you mind?" she asked. "Do you mind doing all this?"

He blew in her ear and said, "None of the silly stuff matters." But now, he thought, it was getting too much. Before they came away, there was tension. Sniping and snapping over every little thing. Her saying what hymns shall we have and him saying "Away in a Manger" and her walking out and slamming the door.

They agreed not to mention the wedding on holiday. "Let's have a break from it," she said.

"Let's just take a Bible with us," he said, "in case it rains."

It wasn't only the church stuff. Everything else was spiraling out of control too. The guest lists and seating plans, the caterers and flowers and cake and dresses and car rental and wedding list and God knows what. None of it for their sakes.

"Apparently," said Sophie, "I've got to have four bridesmaids and two page boys."

"Why?" said Huw. "Who?"

"Marsha and Tatiana," said Sophie, naming her nieces, "and the rest are just kids in Mum and Dad's village."

"Great. Why don't we adopt them as well?"

They hadn't mentioned the wedding. Three days now. But maybe it was making her crazy.

Over dinner tonight. That would be a good time to discuss it. Not now, not while she was driving.

"Sophie," he said, "I think you should put the headlights on."

"Oh, Jesus," she said. "Stop fussing."

"Shall we talk about the wedding?" he said. "Shall we just bloody well talk about it?"

"Please! What are you doing? Why are you saying that? I don't want to talk about the bloody wedding, and neither do you. We're having a break, remember, a holiday."

"I know. I thought. I thought maybe it would be better . . ."

"We'll only end up arguing."

"And you hate that, don't you? You really hate to argue."

She set her mouth and didn't answer.

"In fact," he said, "I know you'll do anything to avoid an argument."

She tried to keep her cross face, but he could see that she was cracking.

"In a Christian marriage," he said and rested a hand on her knee, "I think that is usually the wife's burden."

She smiled tenderly. "Fuckwit," she said.

In the altar room of the Capela dos Ossos, abutting the Igreja de São Francisco, a woman dropped to her knees and prayed, hands either side of her face, palms facing forward to the life-size purple-robed statue of Christ kneeling under a cross.

Underneath the window were two giant electric candlesticks and between them a wooden box of small red lights. Sophie dropped a one-euro coin in the slot.

"What does that buy you?" said Huw, though he could see that four of the candles had lit up. "A place in heaven?"

Sophie put a finger to her lips.

The woman was still praying. Huw put his hands in his pockets. This, he thought, is where the veneer comes off. To kneel before an effigy like that.

Sophie had moved through to the next antechamber. She was buying tickets for the chapel and a guidebook in Portuguese, French, and English. "Hey," she said when he joined her at the desk, "if I faint, will you carry me out?"

"You?" he said. "What about me?"

Yesterday's mood had passed. When they got to the hotel, they had gone up to the room, and she turned on the television and watched two hours of CNN. The hotel was a converted monastery and the rooms were monks' cells, tiny with high vaulted ceilings, dark wood furniture, and elderly drawings framed in faded and padded silk, of Senhor Jesus dos Passos on his way to the crucifixion. After dinner, in the cloisters, they took their books to the lounge and read until someone came to turn off the lights.

Nos ossos que aqui estamos pelos vossos esperamos.

At the entrance, they paused while Sophie looked up the translation. She had her hair up today, showing her long neck. The teenage boys in her class . . . God, she probably had no idea what went through the mind of a fourteen-year-old boy.

"'We bones that are here, for yours we are waiting.'"

"Good gag," said Huw. He looked through into the chapel and whistled softly. They went a few paces in. "It's like drystone walling. Not what I was expecting."

The room was about the size of the church hall where their wedding reception would be. It was divided into three aisles, marked out by rows of pillars on which the ribbed and vaulted ceiling rested. The floor was tiled, cream and red, and there were *azulejos*—glazed hand-painted tiles in blue and yellow and white—forming a low skirting to the walls. At the far end of the room were a golden altar and crucifix, lit by two small windows, and the rest of the room, cast in electric light and shadow, was made out of human remains.

Sophie had her hand over her nose and mouth. "I don't want to smell it," she said, muffled.

Huw put his nose up to a skull, right into the eye socket. "Come on," he said, "there's no smell. They've been here five hundred years."

She took her hand away and sniffed the air. "You can smell *something,* can't you?"

"Devotion?" said Huw. "Fanaticism?"

"Look how tiny these skulls are."

"Kids."

"No, they're all monks."

"Why did they do it?"

Sophie walked up to a pillar and stared at the neat arrangement of tibiae and vertebrae and skulls. "Here," she said, "you can see the cement or stone or whatever underneath. They're just kind of set in here."

"But here," said Huw, over to the side, where the rounded tips of the bones were packed tightly together, "it looks like they *are* the wall, bones instead of bricks."

They walked to the far end of the chapel. Another couple entered—Scandinavian, thought Huw—and giggled and whispered together as if they had caught the priest with his pants down.

"Good acoustics in here," said Huw, louder than he meant to.

"What?" said Sophie. "Is it giving you the creeps?"

Huw started singing. "'The knee bone's connected to the thighbone. The thighbone's connected to the hip bone. The hip bone's connected to the . . .'"

"That's not how it goes."

"Them bones, them bones, them—thighbones!"

"Shush," said Sophie. "I'm reading." She stalked off, holding up the guidebook.

Huw looked up at the ceiling. Angels and weeping angels. A crown of thorns, a crude tree and castle. A black cross, more angels, a rope. Whoever painted this stuff wasn't very good.

Huw moved across to a side aisle. Two butterflies heading for a candle. *Mors in Luce,* it said. Death in light.

There was a landscape of sorts here, an awkward assembly of parts: a building with a round dome, a floating skull, a bird—not in flight but with wings spread, and on a boulder, a pelican feeding its chicks. Huw examined the unidentified bird. What was that supposed to be?

Sophie used to ask him, "What do you like about bird-watching?"

"Everything," he'd say.

One time, she persisted. "But what?"

"The birds," he said. "I like the birds."

She stroked the back of his neck and said, "Tell me." She meant it. He could see she meant it, as if she thought that was a key with which she would unlock the secret part of him.

"Seeing them, you know, just as they are." There wasn't much else, anyway.

"Go on," she said.

He folded his arms. "A boy has to preserve *some* mystery. It's part of our allure."

He had a crick in his neck. He twisted his head from side to side and went to look out the window. There was nothing to see but a blank wall. The Scandinavian couple passed him arm in arm, as though on a school outing. They wore white sneakers and waterproof jackets, hers red, his green. Well, thought Huw, well.

He put his hand on a skull at the edge of the window. He looked quickly around the chapel. How many skulls here? Hundreds. How many bones from how many people? What a sick joke it was. The Catholic Church at its best. Doing what it did best. What a brilliant way to shock and awe.

This is what you are and you are nothing.

To the glory, not of God, surely, but of the Institution. Built from these bones. Yes, indeed.

The skull was smooth beneath his fingers. This, he thought, was a man. He took his fingers away.

Yes, indeed, the Institution.

He thought about the bank, to which he would return in five days, the vaulted atrium and marble-floored reception. Built from our bones, more or less, too. At least they didn't ask for your soul.

Though in a way they did, they did. And who struck the best bargain? Eternal salvation or a 100K bonus. Which was the better deal?

Huw closed his eyes and pressed his little fingers against his eyeballs, noticing how loose, how thin, the skin was. He opened his eyes and scratched his ear, his nose, his scalp. Where was Sophie? There was nothing else to see.

The 100K is better, because that is all there is.

Five hundred years holding up a wall. It's a long time, he thought stupidly. He had not slept well, on that high, narrow bed with the carved wood headboard. Where was she?

All you know, really, is that you are going to die. It's the only thing you know and the only thing you don't think about.

Well, he thought, shit. So what?

The Scandinavian couple came around for a second lap. Huw noticed the engagement ring on her finger. He was furious, truly furious, about the wedding. If he saw the vicar now, he'd knock him down. He'd like to stamp all over that kindly face. For a few moments he fought it, trying to push the thought aside, then hatred, released, coursed warmly through his body and made him calm again.

It wasn't too late. That was the thing. He would speak to Sophie after the holiday, and she would be relieved. They'd take the wedding back into their own hands, where it belonged.

There she was. Over by that tomb, that sepulchre, whatever it was. Standing on one leg with her other foot pressed flat on the side of her standing leg, and it was a wonder how she stood like that and didn't fall over. She saw him looking and kind of waved. "It makes you think, doesn't it?" she said when he went across.

"Certainly," he said, "it does."

Huw went to pay for the petrol, and Sophie sat in the car staring at the dashboard. The rain came in shudders, harder now then softer, unable to get a grip. An engine started up and a car pulled out and another took its place. She listened to the executive click of the door and the bellyaching pump, and then the fumes rolled in and caught in the back of her throat.

Petrol smelled like remorse. Tasted like it too. It wasn't usually as easy as this.

Huw banged on the window and put his face to the glass. His thick dark hair was plastered across his forehead, and the rain ran off his nose. "Pull over," he shouted, and she turned the key and watched the needles float over the dials.

At the bar she swirled the whiskey in the low glass tumbler. Huw wiped his face on the back of his hand. She stood close to him and felt drawn to him, the matter of him, as if what she had previously only imagined had suddenly taken physical form. He wore a navy blue polo shirt that was soaked along the shoulders and down the front and a thin steam began to rise from his chest.

"Let's drink," she said and raised her glass. The whiskey smelled like nostalgia, or perhaps it was more like regret. Maybe a mix of the two.

"That guy in our village," said Huw. "Remember him? The sad case in the café."

They joked around and sipped their drinks, and Sophie thought about the writer. He was the kind of person you felt sorry for but went out of your way to avoid. He was patronizing and probably a misogynist, and his mouth was unnaturally moist.

What you wondered, always, about expats was not why did you come here but why did you have to leave?

She wanted to ask Huw what the whiskey smelled like but didn't. It was a game that she used to play with Oliver when he was the one she took to bed.

Huw laced his fingers through hers. "Shall we go?" he murmured into her hairline. "I'm sorry about the weather. It's not what I asked for when I booked."

"You don't get out of it that easily," said Sophie. "You've got a lot more groveling to do."

There was nothing much to look at. The pale green fields yawning up ahead and on either side. A hundred or so svelte black pigs on a black mudflat. More fields. A plane tree heavy with seed balls. The fields going on, unadorned. Sometimes a cork oak. Wild rosemary straggling along. A field and then another. They were taking the scenic route.

Sophie switched the windshield wipers off. At last the rain had stopped. She sighed and settled back in her seat and tried to think of something to say.

"Yes?" said Huw. "What?"

Dampness was settling around her, and she tried to shake it off.

"Mmm?" said Huw.

"Afternoon drinking," said Sophie. "Feeling a bit sluggish, that's all."

"Want me to drive?"

"No," she said, because she had that at least to do. When they got there, she'd feel better. Have a bath, put on a fluffy dressing gown, use all the lotions and creams.

"I love this kind of landscape," said Huw.

He was joking, but she didn't make the effort to laugh.

"Get the map. Let's find the main road."

They went past a long low cottage with a roof that sagged in the middle. An old couple stood in between lines of cabbages and watched them driving by. In a while Sophie turned on to the main road and changed gears. The traffic went at a pace unconnected to the land, moving in a different time, a different place. Huw started up an argument about peasants. She argued back, but she was too tired, really, worn out. Do we have to? she thought. Will we always? Better that than be bored, she told herself, and squeezed her buttocks together to stop them from going numb in the seat.

She thought about the old couple in the vegetable patch. The woman's cheeks were apple red; her mouth looked like it never opened, like she'd said all she would ever have to say. Sophie chewed the flesh beneath her bottom lip. There was a hollow cave in her stomach. She wanted to curl around a pillow and never get out of bed.

It will pass, she told herself.

"What will pass?" said Huw.

"Oh, nothing," said Sophie. "Or everything. Depending on your point of view."

"Oh, yes, wise guru," he said. "And tell me, what is the meaning of life?"

She pinched his knee and felt better and sailed along on this thought: We fit just right together, and that's all I need to know.

It was Jonnie Singh who started it. One of her Year 9s. "Dunno, miss," he said to her. "Dunno what else to write."

She'd assigned an essay on *Lord of the Flies*. Examine Jack and Ralph's relationship. What happens to turn them into mortal enemies?

Jonnie handed in half a page. *Jack and Ralph could have liked each other but they don't. It wasn't the way it turned out. It's all about fires and hunting. Piggy is the one that gets it in the end. There's no reason why it should turn out like that. It could go one way or the other. This way makes a better story. Jack and Ralph hate each other and that's why they are mortal enemies.*

"What are we going to do with you?" she said.

Jonnie Singh stood in front of her desk with his hands in his pockets. He had ketchup down his shirt and his tie flicked over his shoulder. "Dunno, miss," he said again.

He was a bright boy and no troublemaker, but she couldn't do anything with him.

"It says in the question that they're enemies, but you haven't explained why. That's what I wanted you to do. Explore what happens in the story and write down the reasons why."

Jonnie shrugged and looked down at the floor. "That's how people are, miss. Dunno why."

"I agree with you, Jonnie," she said. "That's what makes it a good book. I just wanted you to . . ." She stopped because all of a sudden she felt ridiculous. What was the point of it all? She thought of the lessons she would give that afternoon and the things she'd say and the hands that would be raised and the answers she would hear and the praise she'd give and the prompts and the chiding and the ring of the bell and none of it, none of it, held any meaning. That's how people are. She stared at the page in her hands, the scrawly, childish writing and the blank lines beneath, and froze.

She'd go home tonight and eat and talk some more and lie down and close her eyes and get up again and eat and then talk and then walk down the corridor and enter the classroom and everything would begin again. It's not *my* life, she thought, it's just *living*. There's nothing you can do about that.

"Miss," said Jonnie. "Miss."

"Sorry, what?"

Jonnie looked at the door. "Please, miss," he said, "can I go?"

* * *

When she was twenty-one, after she had graduated, she spent some time in the hospital. There was no reason for it. It was just a chemical imbalance. Nothing happened to make her depressed, no crises apart from the inability to get out of bed.

She spent a lot of time crying. She didn't even feel sad. But crying was something to do, a kind of achievement, and she noticed her mother preferred it to when she sat and stared into space.

She came out of the hospital in time to start the teacher training college. She took the pills. After a couple of years she stopped taking them, and the doctor said that was fine. When she told Huw about it, he said "It can happen to anyone" and "It's just an illness" and all the other things you're meant to say. It still felt like she was hiding something, but only because it was impossible to explain.

They were away now for the half-term holiday, and she had thought that she would shake it. It was beginning to be a concern.

There was a village, cleaved in two by the road, and Sophie slowed the car. "There's a boy in my Year Nine class," she said.

"You've got to have the patience of a saint."

"No," she said, "not really."

"Okay. Go on."

"He wrote this essay. It was only ten lines long."

"How old is he? Fourteen? Must make you wonder why you bother."

"No," she said. "Listen. Never mind." It wasn't his fault, anyway. A fourteen-year-old boy made you afraid?

A car overtook them, going so fast it sent a reverberation down the roof of their rental car.

Pulling past the village, Sophie pressed down on the accelerator. These fields are a deeper green, she thought, it must rain here all the time. The small of her back pressed against the upholstery. Faster, she wanted to go faster. Down her spine there was a draining sensation, and her mind now was marvelously clear. She felt all the power of the engine. It connected directly with her pelvis. Her leg was the conduit. The power was in her. She stepped down harder.

Huw was saying something, but she wasn't distracted. She needed to get up more speed. How liberating it was to focus. She would take up meditation. That was it.

Whiskey, she knew what it smelled like. Not a pure emotion, not a real one. There was something synthetic about it. Sentimentality. Yes. Something old, something new, something borrowed, something blue.

A car in the way now, but that was no problem; she would just swing out to the left.

Huw offered again to drive, but she needed to hold on to the wheel. When she saw the bus, she thought that was it, over, and her life did not flash before her eyes. She had one thought. One clear thought. She would miss the fitting next Thursday. The fitting for the dress.

After church, when she was small, she used to play with Alicia in the graveyard while their parents chatted on the porch with the Whitmores and the Clarkes and the Woods. "Find the oldest dead person," said Alicia. They went running around the tombs. "Find the youngest one." They found four babies. "Let's put flowers on," said Alicia, and they picked daisies. "Now we've got to say which ones went to hell."

"This one," said Alicia. "He definitely went to hell."

Sophie stood next to her sister and waited for her to explain.

Alicia put her foot on the granite slab. "See, it's all black. And there's no poem. Nobody cared about him."

"Why was he buried by the church, then?" said Sophie. Alicia thought she knew everything.

"You're a stupid baby," said her sister. "I'm not playing with you anymore."

Jasper died the next week. Daddy left him at the vet's. At the church she hung back with her parents. The vicar came out after a while. "You want to speak to me?" he said to Sophie. "Let's go inside and take a pew."

Sophie followed the black cassock, trembling, because she thought she was going to speak to God. For those few minutes she was confused, because he had known what she was thinking and because she always imagined God looking like him, anyway, except with a fluffy beard.

"Do animals go to heaven?" she asked when she found her voice.

He thought about it long and hard with his hands planted on his knees. That vicar was old and unmarried. He went into a home in the end.

"It's hard to say for certain. But I think they probably don't."

"Oh," said Sophie, blinking. "Is it only for people?"

He smiled and held her shoulder. "Well, we won't know until we get there ourselves. But if an animal doesn't have a soul, then the soul can't be saved."

"Don't you know?" blurted Sophie. She crossed her ankles and swung her feet and hoped her mother hadn't heard.

The vicar didn't seem cross. "I don't know," he said gently. "I believe. That's what we call faith."

She carried on believing into her early teens. She didn't even notice when she stopped. One day, during prayers, she opened her eyes and knew that she hadn't believed for a long time. It was surprising, as though somebody else had done it, walked into her bedroom and taken something away.

I meant to ask him where animals go, thought Sophie. I never asked him that.

They were driving through a storm and there was thunder but it was bright outside, a whitish light. At the outskirts of the town now, the houses beginning to build up. A construction site at a standstill, an office block, and a fan of parked cars.

What did I believe, though? What did I believe?

She was getting married in that church.

Alicia went to a registry office.

The bus. There were children on board. It could go one way or the other.

She died and her last thought was the dress.

You didn't die. You didn't.

What did I believe?

"Sophie," said Huw. "I think you should put the headlights on."

"Oh, Jesus," she said. "Stop fussing."

In the morning they stood in the little marble-clad bathroom and looked at themselves in the mirror. Huw stuck out his hand. "Hi, I'm Huw Ridley. And this is my wife, Sophie. Sophie, say hello to these nice folks here."

She crossed her eyes and stuck out her tongue.

He put his arm around her shoulders. "How do we look together?"

She leaned in to him. "I think we look just fine."

He turned on the tap and picked up his toothbrush.

"Sorry," she said, "about yesterday."

"Forget it." He applied the toothpaste. "Feeling better today?"

"Much better. Thanks. I'm going to get dressed."

"You realize," he called out to the bedroom, "that you'll have to mend your lippy ways. Because when I'm your husband, I'll want a lot more respect out of you."

"Come here and say that, pussycat."

Huw appeared in the doorway. He struck a bodybuilder's pose.

"Idiot," she said. "Come here."

"I said that when I'm your husband, I'll want a lot more respect out of you." He was close enough now for her to pull off his towel, so she did. "What's this?" she said. "What's this?"

*   *   *

In the Capela dos Ossos, Sophie left Huw by the altar and went back to the entrance, wanting to read the guidebook as she walked around. She began instead to read the graffiti on the skulls to the right of the gate. Nuno, Gary, Lena, Justin B, Pinto, Paulo, Marie Rosta, Susana Alforas. All had signed their names. *Kiss me,* it said on one skull. *I'm hungry,* on another, in pink felt tip.

She opened the book.

An anthology could be compiled on the subject of the Insight of Death, the perception of which has preoccupied Mankind from time Immemorial.

There indeed should be no great need for the Church to remind us every year on the first day of Lent that thou art dust and to dust shall thou revert, this being as it is probably the foremost of eternal verities . . .

She paused and looked around and tried to imagine the monks who had built this place, fitting the bones together, choosing from a pile, sizing and stacking and balancing. Did they shiver? Did they sing? Did they work in silence?

Taking a deep breath and rolling back her shoulders, she tried to assess how she was feeling today. It was hard to tell. Am I feeling normal? A little heavy, perhaps. Everyone feels low sometimes. Especially in a place like this.

She pressed her teeth together. If you think about how you feel, then you inevitably start to feel bad. Forget it, please, stop fretting. Do you want to make yourself ill?

Flicking forward a couple of pages, she began to read from the tombstone inscriptions.

> *This is a tomb*
> *and beneath this slab*
> *lies Antonio de Macedo*
> *reduced to dust and dark ashes*
> *he was a very noble gentleman*
> *abundantly rich of worldly wealth*

in the end he took nothing with him
and here he lies in complete destitution
Died in the year 1565

At St. Dominic's Monastery in Lisbon:

I was a renowned learned man
and I read most every book
but to sum up I came to die
like any brainless fool does.

She looked up at Huw, who was studying the ceiling. She wanted to laugh. She wanted him to come and read over her shoulder and say something to make her laugh. He had his hands on his hips and his head tipped back, and she thought he looked very fine.

She didn't know what to think about this place. Huw would know what he thought, he always did, and later she would argue with him until she became clear about what it was that she felt. She liked the way that worked.

Only, with the wedding, it was different. All the church stuff, he hated it. To him it was just telling lies. She couldn't argue with that, but she wanted to; she realized now that she wanted to. How do you know? she wanted to say.

She looked at him: his brown suede shoes rimmed with tide marks from yesterday's rain, his dark jeans and tan belt and the blue checked shirt he hadn't bothered to iron. Huw moved and she looked away, guilty, as though she had been spying on him.

Father Antonio Vieira, S.J., wrote a masterly definition of the boundary between the living and the dead:

"The living are dust that stands and the dead are fallen dust. The living are no more than dust that walks as the dead are dust that lies.

"In Summertime the squares in town are full of dust as dry as powder; there

blows a puff of wind, the dust is raised in the air and what does it then do?
What the living, and very alive for that matter, do, for the dust will not settle
down nor can it stay still. It walks, runs, flies . . . The living are dust that is
blown and therefore inflated with conceit; the dead are windless dust, there is
no vanity left in them."

Sophie closed the book. She was thirsty, really thirsty. Her lips, her mouth, were dry. The old couple in their vegetable patch came into her head and made her want to cry. Oh, God, she thought, it's coming again. Her mind began to race, it wanted to get away. A hand with fingertips missing, her mother peeling potatoes, Jonnie Singh saying, "Miss, please, miss, can I go?," Huw pushing back his fringe. If she had a glass of water. If there were somewhere to sit down. Something old, something new. Her mother had given her a brooch. She would wear it in her hair. Huw in his suit and tie, coming through the door. An eagle, they'd seen an eagle. If she slept with another man, she'd know. Up the aisle and through the door and over the rainbow. Christ, it was and it wasn't. That's just how people are.

"Excuse me," someone was saying. "Are you okay?" It was the young woman in the red jacket, her boyfriend standing behind.

"Yes," said Sophie. "Thanks. I was just . . . a little dizzy. Now I'm okay."

The woman paused, then turned away. "It's kind of spooky, yes?" she said over her shoulder.

"It's not," said Sophie quickly. It sounded rude, and she wanted to say something else, to be nice, but the couple had carried on walking, and now she had missed her chance.

She went slowly along the line of the tiles as if treading a tightrope and stood by the Founder's tomb. There was nothingnothing wrong. There was a cast of sunlight on the floor, shrugged off by the window, and Sophie stared at it and sank.

"God always welcomes us back," Reverend Chambers had said.

He never took a biscuit, but he touched every one on the plate. "I mean, if we've been away. He understands."

Huw had said something sarcastic. He barely covered it up.

Please, she thought, and raised one foot to rest against her knee, please, I would like to know. I don't want everything to be nothing. What's the point? If I open myself, will you let me in? If I open my eyes, will you let me see? I am trying. I'm helping myself now, but I need . . . I need . . . What I'm asking for, I don't think it's too much, I'm asking you to see me.

She stood for a while and was calm. Her lips no longer felt dry. She looked at the walls of yellowing bones and thought, It's been a long time since I prayed.

Huw walked across, scratching his head. "It makes you think," she said to him.

He took her arm. It was time to leave. "It certainly does," he said.

They walked through a tangle of Moorish alleys to the Praça do Giraldo and went into a *pastelaria* for a late lunch.

"Do you want to do more churches after?" said Huw.

Sophie shook her head.

"We've done quite a few, I suppose." He bit into his toasted sandwich and burned the roof of his mouth.

He took a napkin from the plastic dispenser on the table and wiped away a string of cheese. The napkin was thin and slippery, like cheap toilet paper. The coffee machine clattered and hissed. A man in white overalls delivered boxes of cakes stacked on a forklift. A waitress bent over to inspect them, and Huw stared at her varicose veins. They should have found somewhere proper to eat.

"Not the most glamorous, is it?" he said to Sophie.

She picked out a toothpick and snapped it in two and looked away.

Her sister had gotten married in a registry office. That didn't kill her parents. Sophie built things up into problems. He would just have to be firm.

"Do you want coffee?" he said.

"Okay," she said, "if you want to."

"God," he said, "don't let me force you."

"I'll have one, I said."

He pulled out his wallet. "No. Let's not. I want to go."

On the way back to pick up the car, they looked in some tourist shops. They were all the same: hand-painted earthenware, ceramic cockerel fridge magnets, tiles saying PORTUGAL, crocheted place mats, leather belts, and novelty items made out of cork.

"Do we need a cork cruet set?" said Huw. "How about a cork hat?"

Sophie picked up a cork wine cooler and put it down. "I'm not in the mood for shopping," she said.

Back on the street, he tripped over a basket of white plaster churches. "Why don't they keep the goods inside the damn shop?"

She strode on ahead. Huw tried to catch up, but his foot was hurting, and he was forced to stop again and take the weight off it for a while. The street, which had been quiet, suddenly filled with young people carrying books and files. If Sophie looked back now, she wouldn't see him. All these students hogging the road. It was her fault, anyway, for walking off like that. He was going to take his time.

He sat down on the curb and eased off his shoe.

I'm not going to spend the rest of my life at the bank, he thought. I'm not going to be a lifer.

Some of them—most of them—they can't see beyond. Not me, he thought, not me.

The students flowed around him. They talked loud and fast, as though they were about to be kidnapped and this was their last chance to speak. A bag knocked into his head. *"Desculpe,"* said a girl, bending down to him. "Don't worry," he said, "I needed a new one, in any case." She shrugged and walked quickly away.

Huw rubbed his foot. If it swells up, he thought, how am I going to get it back in my shoe? He shivered; it was far too cold to be going about in a shirt. All the students had sweaters or jackets. They hadn't been fooled by the sun.

It occurred to him that Sophie would have to drive again. He sighed and tested some weight on his foot.

The street had cleared again, and Huw looked up to the far end where it began to rise steeply and then curved away under an arch. Sophie had not waited. He picked up his shoe and began to ease the lacing wide apart.

Huw was dawdling, and that was all right with Sophie. He didn't need to hurry up, and she didn't need to wait. She wasn't quite sure which turn to take, but then she saw the Misericordia and got her bearings again. They had looked around the church in the morning. "What do you call this style?" Huw had asked. "Don't know," said Sophie. "Baroque?" Huw looked in the booklet they'd gotten from the *tourismo*. "Mannerist," he said, "apparently, but it seems more like High Kitsch to me."

She thought about the way he had said that, with a smile on his face, as if gold leaf and carvings proved everything, as if that settled it all.

At the cathedral she paused and looked up at the odd mix of Gothic arches and Romanesque battlements and watched a middle-aged man come out and cross himself beneath a photograph of the pope; he lit a cigarette as he stepped off the porch.

She had decided to wait until they got home before she told Huw. He might think she was breaking off the engagement.

Perhaps she was breaking off the engagement.

She edged along the square, past the side of the monastery-turned-hotel where they had stayed, the pillars of the Roman temple coming into view.

A bellboy ran out to an arriving car, chased by a phalanx of fallen leaves. Sophie stood on the corner outside the hotel, one arm in the shade and the other in the sun.

What she was going to suggest was a postponement. She couldn't just rush ahead and get married when it would mean something different to each of them. When she didn't even know what it meant.

It seemed suddenly ridiculous that they so lightly, so casually, had agreed to be bound together for life.

They had left the bag in the car when they checked out, so they went straight to the parking lot. There were citrus trees set in the gravel, and Huw picked a couple of oranges.

"Don't," said Sophie.

"What?" said Huw. "Don't be so uptight."

"You would be. If someone took something of yours."

Huw bent and set the oranges beneath a tree. He held up his hands. "All right. I've put them back. Now let's be nice."

"You started it," said Sophie.

Huw took both her hands. "Sophie. Have you been spending too long in the playground?"

She smiled but pulled away. "Probably." She walked back to the tree and picked up the oranges. "May as well have them now. They'll only rot on the ground."

"Whatever."

"If my kids say that, I tell them off."

Huw zipped his finger across his mouth.

"So what happened to your foot?"

"Tripped," said Huw. "You'll have to drive."

"I don't mind."

He was about to throw the keys over but changed his mind and walked around. He hugged her into his chest and said, "Next holiday we're going to Vegas."

"How about Ibiza? Hit the clubs?"

She looked up and it seemed that they might kiss but they did not.

"Huw," she said.

"Hang on," said Huw, "I can hear a pipit."

"_____"

"I can't see one, though. No, no, no. It's . . . what is it . . . can you hear how he keeps changing the call? He's whistling . . . now he's buzzing . . . listen to that clear note now, completely different tone."

"It's all different birds," said Sophie.

"It's not. It's the same one. It's a lark. He's having fun. Calandra lark, maybe. If I could see him, then I'd know."

"Shall we get in the car?" She opened the door and threw the oranges on the backseat. Then she closed the door again. "Or do you want to look for him?"

"Hey," he said, "*we* are going to have some fun here, you know. I like our little village, don't you?"

"I do, actually. It's lovely. I might just potter around tomorrow if you drive out to the lagoon."

He rubbed her shoulders. "Okay," he said, "okay. And we'll go out for a few drinks in the evening. Observe the locals. That writer guy might be there. Bet he's got a few stories to tell."

Sophie wrinkled her nose. "Best avoided."

"Well, if he's there, he's there."

"But not with us."

"Not *with* us, no."

"I mean," said Sophie, "that I didn't like him."

Huw stopped massaging. He passed a hand over his face. "Right. I should have known."

"What does that mean?" cried Sophie. "You mean you should have known that I'd be so *uptight*."

"All I said is we might have a drink with someone, and you get fucking hysterical. Some people might call that a little uptight."

Sophie held her throat. "Oh, oh, if a woman makes a strong statement, she's hysterical. That's right! And why would I want to have a drink with that awful, fat-lipped, drunken old cynic? Why would you even suggest that, why?"

Huw stared at her. He backed away slightly and put more weight on his bad foot than he had intended. He winced and drew breath and looked around and kneaded his thigh. He laced his fingers together at the back of his neck and pulled his head forward. Then he looked up and opened his mouth and closed it again.

Sophie's lip trembled as she started to speak. "You don't even know . . ." she said.

Huw thumped the car hood. "What do *you* know about him?" he shouted. The sound of his own voice appalled him. He wanted it to stop. But it went on. "What's so special about you?"

"I'm not going near that man," she screamed, though she could barely remember him now. "He was horrible. I hate him. And . . . and . . . I don't want you to talk to him at all."

Two kitchen boys came out of a service entrance for a cigarette break. Huw looked at them, and they studied their toes.

"You're crazy." He almost whispered it, hobbling around to the passenger seat.

She looked at him over the gleaming red roof of the rental car. Her eyes were full of reflected light. "That's just it," she said softly. "I am."

A window on the second floor opened, and a maid shook a duster outside. The kitchen boys squatted with their backs to the wall, blowing smoke from the sides of their mouths.

Huw sniffed and cleared his throat. "I want to make you happy, you know."

"I know," said Sophie. She stood on tiptoe and reached her arms across the roof.

Huw stretched out and held her wrists, and she grabbed his as though they were drowning there in the parking lot, clinging on to this bright red raft.

Nine

The station at Garvão was three winding kilometers from the village, where it could sleep in peace, and it was a hall of dreams: a yellow-stone fantasy of fin de siècle Paris, broached through a Manueline porch, heightened with Italianate finials, and crowned with a Moorish cupola. The cupola, though it often leaked, had been greatly admired through the generations by a colony of mouse-eared bats.

At seven-fifteen on the twelfth day of October, a ferret, looking sensibly left and right, crossed the tracks. A minute later the wind woke a bunch of leaves and dust and chivvied them across the platform and beneath a bench, where they settled down again. At seven-seventeen a voice clanged down a distant metal nose and through the loudspeaker to announce that the arrival of the seven twenty-one was delayed by six minutes exactly. The message was delivered in a peremptory manner, as though nobody, in any case, would hear.

When the train pulled in, two people got off, a man and a woman from separate cars. The woman wheeled her case straight off the platform, through the hall, and into the parking lot, but the man set down his bag.

He looked up at the dreaming edifice, the powdery sheen of the stones, and down at the new-laid double-gauge tracks that the train was leaving behind. For a few moments he held still, as though there was something he was trying to hear or smell or recall.

The man was neither young nor old. His head, which was shaved, was dependable and smooth except for the two creases where it joined the back of his neck. His eyes were dark and wide-set, sloping gently back and up. He wore black jeans, scuffed black shoes, a blue shirt, and a black cape, fastened with a gold chain and clasp.

He hoisted his bag and in long, even strides dispensed with the station, emerging just as the woman drove away. The car disappeared around a bend, and the man stared down the empty road.

In a few minutes he would go home for a nap, but first, as was his custom at the end of every morning shift, the baker took a bread roll and a *bica* and sat out on the sidewalk in the broken-backed chair.

He sat with his legs splayed, leaning forward, his hands planted high up his thighs, thumbs hooked back and fingers curled so that he looked like a boxer waiting to go back in the ring. Baking, he thought, is tough and nobody knows it. The weight you lift, the heat you take, the hours you work, the time all spent on your feet.

He knocked back his coffee like a shot of medicine.

He was a small man, dark and hard, like a loaf left in too long.

Women, he thought, have never been bakers. Now, that—now, *that*—was a fact.

The man walked up the middle of the road, a holdall slung over his shoulder. "Oh, senhor," he said, "I need a taxi."

The baker nodded. "You've walked from the station."

The man said nothing.

"You're not from here?" the baker asked, but the man gave no reply. The baker cracked his knuckles. He changed his mind. He thought he knew this man. "You've been away?" he said.

The man looked at him evenly and smiled. "I'm looking for a taxi, please."

The baker brushed flour from his knees. "Be lucky, you would. If Silvio's up before noon, I'm a cat's arse. On the drink last night."

"Which house?" said the man. "If you would be so kind as to direct me."

What the hell, thought the baker. Let him wake the lazy bastard up. Some people were up before dawn. "Second turn on the right, third house on the left." But he was sure he knew this man.

"Thank you. You are very kind indeed."

"Oi!" called the baker as the man walked away. "I've seen you. On the television. What show? What show are you on?"

The man turned, smiled, shook his head, and continued up the street.

The baker tried to crack his knuckles, but none of them obliged. Big shot, he thought. Arsehole. Stuck up. If you would be so kind.

Silvio opened the door in a rage and his underpants. "Somebody better be dead. Can't a man sleep? Is somebody dead, or have you woken me up to tell me . . . What? What? What is it?"

The stranger with the strong, shaved head looked him straight in the eye.

Silvio's anger receded, and he was filled with a sudden dread. For a moment he was certain that he was about to be called to account. I've always done my best, he argued. What else is a man supposed to do?

"You are Silvio?" said the man.

Silvio plucked at his underpants. "So what if I am?" He was still half asleep and very hungover. Whose heart wouldn't race a little when they got pounded awake like that?

"This is your taxi?"

The man had a way of looking at you. Like he knew everything already and had never been surprised in his life.

"Okay, okay, I'll take you," said Silvio. He tried to sound angry to cover his relief. He dressed quickly, brushed his teeth, and spat, and though his head was still foggy, there was light in his heart, as if he had been given a second chance.

Silvio wore his sunglasses. It was a preemptive move. The sun was not yet out.

"You came in on the early train, huh? From Lisbon. Or it's the Portimão train gets in first?" He glanced in the rearview mirror and nodded to the passenger, who was looking back at him. "I'm usually there," he said. "I try to be there, pick up whoever, you know. Nine times out of ten."

"Nine out of ten," said the man. "Top marks, more or less." There was something about his voice, something peaceful or sooth- ing, the way it flowed. When you fell asleep by a river, it made you feel the same way.

"Ha!" said Silvio. "Try telling my wife." He let the window down. "You want a cigarette? No? That's another thing. The cigarettes. She gets these ideas. Me—I'm a smoker. So what?

"You had a good journey? From Portimão, you said? Well, it's fast now, isn't it? Too fast. Wham, bam, you're here. Right in the middle of nowhere. All that E.U. money, they spent it, all right. New tracks, new trains. You can really get nowhere fast."

Silvo tossed his butt out the window. "Too breezy for you in the back?"

The man didn't say anything.

A lot of fares today, Silvio thought. He could feel it in his bones. "Want me to raise the window?"

"Up or down. Doesn't matter," said the man. "It's all good to me."

"Wish some people had your attitude." Silvio slowed the car so he could spit without getting it on the door. "The way some people go on."

"Some things are important," said the man. "Most things aren't."

"Every little thing! My God! As though it's the end of the world."

Silvio nodded and kept on nodding. He thought he didn't feel too bad, considering. But tonight he would not drink. Give it a rest for a while.

"So you're not from around here? Knew it from your accent. Not from around here myself." He checked on his passenger, who was obviously listening; most people looked out at the grass. "The wife's family, you see, Alentejanos. That's how come we're here. Up in

Porto the first few years. Well, you know that's where life gets lived. Had my own business, everything sweet, all the extras, but the minute things get a little bit complicated, she's screaming because she wants to come back. Business, you know, it's complicated, but she just wants to run away."

"Natural instinct," said the man, and Silvio could tell that though he understood, that did not mean he approved.

"You a . . . what? . . . psychologist or something?" It was the cape that gave it away. "Anyway, so we're here, but that's not good enough either. I drive this taxi ten, twelve hours a day, and all her family expect rides for free, and I'm telling you there are a lot of members of that family, lot of free riders all around. Most times, like I was saying, up at daybreak, at the station, nine times out of ten. At least. And she's still going on. 'Silvio, we've got to do something. Silvio, what about that mess we left behind? Silvio, you've got to stop wasting money.' I'm a very patient man, you see. Very, very patient." Silvio breathed through his mouth. There was a pain in his stomach, a stitch, as if he'd run all the way up a hill. He put a hand beneath his T-shirt and massaged the soft, furry flesh.

"Yes," said the man.

"Extremely patient," said Silvio. "I keep telling her, 'We left our troubles behind. It's what you wanted, isn't it? Don't push me too far, Jacinta.' Every man has his limit, you know."

"It's been proven many times."

"Hey, you speak like a professor. We don't get a load of those around here." Silvio laughed. He saw his brown teeth in the mirror and the blackheads dotting his nose. They annoyed him, but he looked forward to squeezing them later, when he got home. If Jacinta was still out, he'd sneak back to bed, just until his head cleared. It wasn't professional to drive with a hangover. Except in emergency cases like this.

"You heard the one about the Alentejano," said Silvio, "he has a race with a snail?" He bashed the horn to let a car know he was passing and was rewarded by the sight of it swerving. Must have made him jump. "Who wins? You're thinking the snail, right? Has to be.

No, the Alentejano wins. The snail is disqualified after two false starts." He laughed and turned around. "Ha, ha, ahaa. . . You've heard it before, I guess."

The way the man looked at him, it was like he'd heard *everything* before. Not hostile or bored or anything. Just prepared. For whatever it was.

Silvio scratched his head. "Listen, Professor, tell me the truth. What's the point, coming to a place like this and then always be nagging your husband to do something? It doesn't make any sense. If you were me, would you open a business? I mean, what would you try to do?"

"The only advice I give is 'Never give advice.'"

"Right," said Silvio warmly. "Wish other folks felt the same way." He chewed it over for a couple of kilometers. "Yes, I really do." After another few minutes he said, "I got the feeling I saw you already, once before, maybe. Is it Porto you said you're from? No? Well, I don't know. You probably just got that kind of face. I bet people say that all the time."

The sign on the window read CONGELADOS AQUARIOS, but the fascia declared INTERNET CAFÉ. At a hole-in-the-wall place next door, a donkey was being shod. The man paused for a moment and went inside.

"Marco?" said Eduardo, squinting. "Marco! I'll kiss you. You've come. Is it you? Marco! Of course it is."

"It's good to be back," said Marco. "I'll give you a kiss, here, like this."

"Everybody! It's Marco. My cousin has arrived. We didn't know when you were coming, but everything is ready. Will you be staying long? Sit down, sit down. He just this second walked in the door. Armenio, get some coffee. You remember Armenio, Marco? He was only a little kid when you left. Big kid now, he is!"

"I remember like it was yesterday," said Marco.

Eduardo looked around the room. He clapped his hands together. "Hear that? Like it was yesterday. He remembers us so well."

On her way to do the shopping, Telma Ervanaria stopped off for a pastry and a cup of apple tea. Dona Linda was there, sitting at a computer and pulling her bottom lip inside out.

"What is that you're looking at, Dona Linda?"

"It's a bench on the main street of a village called Little Rock in Canada."

Telma Ervanaria looked closer at the dark, grainy blur. "I can't see anything at all."

Dona Linda sighed. "That's because it's the middle of the night."

The woman was obviously crazy. "Wake up, Dona Linda. It's ten in the morning." Telma Ervanaria grabbed her arm and gave it a little shake.

"There," said Dona Linda. "It's the middle of the night there."

"It's a photograph?" said Telma Ervanaria, pulling up a chair.

Dona Linda shook her head. "It's a film. There's a camera fixed to a tree or a lamppost or something, and it films everything that goes on. And it all gets sent through the air or the wires or something to every single computer in the world. Armenio explained how it works."

Telma Ervanaria put her nose up to the screen and snorted. "But there is nothing going on. Oh! Little Rock, that's where your daughter is."

"Little River. But I thought maybe they were close together. I mean, what if I see her walking down that street? She might sit on that bench."

"In the middle of the night?"

"Telma Ervanaria, how do you think I raised my daughter? Of course not the middle of the night."

Telma Ervanaria took a bite of her pastry. She thought, day or night, she would not care to travel all the way across the world just to sit on a bench like that, which, even in the dark, any fool could tell was no better than the very worst bench in Mamarrosa.

"If you press on this bit here," said Dona Linda, "it tells you the temperature. The actual temperature it is right now."

"So cold!" said Telma Ervanaria. In Paris sometimes it was bitter, but it was never as cold as that.

"Ladies, may I remind you," said Eduardo, coming across with arms raised as though to chase ducks from the porch, "eating is not permitted at the computer stations."

Telma Ervanaria took another bite. "It's a café, isn't it?" she said.

"No, it's not," said Eduardo, who would tell you that black was white, "it's an Internet café. Is a table just a table?"

Telma Ervanaria stared at him. She didn't like the way hair grew out of his nose, in curls. "Yes," she said. "It is."

"That's where you go wrong. A table over there," he said, pointing, "is a table. A table in a school is a desk. A table beside the pulpit is an altar, and this table here is a computer station. No eating allowed."

Telma Ervanaria swallowed the rest of the pastry. "No eating, okay, I get it. But in the future, if you want an argument, go and find Vasco. I won't argue with you, Eduardo. I've got better things to do."

"May I turn to marble," said Eduardo. He said any old thing to try and sound clever.

"What?" said Dona Linda. "What did he say?"

"Doesn't matter," said Telma Ervanaria. You were never sure if you'd heard him right; sucking in his words like that instead of spitting them out like an honest man. She stretched her stout legs and crossed her ankles. "Now tell us about Marco. He's settling in? Told you all his plans?"

There was a crafty look on Eduardo's narrow face, like that of a child with a slice of cake behind his back. "He's come home. That's all we care about—those in his family, I mean."

She looked him over like a piece of gristle on the side of her plate, searching for some meat to extract. "He's at Armenio's house, I hear. Has he found a place to buy?"

"He'll live in his hotel, I expect," said Dona Linda. "No sense buying a house as well."

Dona Linda reckoned she was common sense incarnate, but she never thought things through. She cut her own hair because it was only common sense, but look what she did to her fringe. "The hotel," said Telma Ervanaria patiently, "is going to be at Porto Covo or Praia de Malhau. You think there's going to be a four-hundred-bed hotel right here in Mamarrosa? No, it is certain he'll buy his own place here. Or maybe he'll build something new."

Dona Linda licked the tip of her finger. She had no idea how crazy she looked. "Four hundred beds? No, no. It's not going to be that kind of hotel."

The less people know, thought Telma Ervanaria, the more they talk.

Sure enough, Dona Linda went on, "It's a rural tourism thing. Horse riding and looking at birds and going for walks through the hills. My son told me. Why not Mamarrosa? Mamarrosa is as good as anywhere. A lot, a lot, a lot of new jobs. Maybe your husband could have one. Put in a word, Eduardo. Poor Telma Ervanaria is at her wits' end."

Telma Ervanaria set her not inconsiderable jaw. "So much more convenient not to have wits at all."

"Ladies," said Eduardo. He undid and then did up again two buttons on his waistcoat. "Ladies, when the kestrel lands on the roof, the sparrows are all in a spin."

"What?" said Dona Linda.

"He says we are sparrows." Telma Ervanaria watched Eduardo, still fiddling with his buttons. The fabric around each buttonhole was shiny with misuse.

"Hark at him."

Eduardo snatched up Telma Ervanaria's plate and also her cup, though she had not quite finished. "All I am saying is—patience. You'll see soon enough what he plans."

Telma Ervanaria lowered her voice when Eduardo had moved away. "Marco hasn't told him anything. I can see it in his eyes."

"Two weeks he's been here now," whispered Dona Linda. "His own flesh and blood, but he doesn't say a thing."

"Eduardo's a slathering idiot. With a man like Marco behind him, Armenio could take over more businesses. I mean, Marco could really shake up this place." She would make Bruno go and see Marco and ask him straight out for a job. Ask him straight out, she would tell him. Don't be a sparrow like everyone else.

"Electrical appliances," said Dona Linda. "That's how he first got rich."

"Dry cleaning," said Telma Ervanaria. "Maybe electrical appliances after that." Bruno had worked in Paris as an electrician. Somehow it augured well.

Dona Linda pulled her bottom lip and let it go with a plop. "He doesn't look like a rich man, does he?"

Telma Ervanaria laughed. "What does a rich man look like? Those who have don't flash it around."

"I heard he chopped logs for Senhora Carmona, all into tiny pieces for that itty-bitty stove of hers."

"He was at Nelson's calving on Tuesday. Heard he stayed all night."

They stared at the screen, at Little Rock, Canada, their heads together, tight and low. "There's something strange about him, though," said Dona Linda. "I don't know what it is."

"That cape he goes about in? Everything is strange about him. We're not used to people like that."

"I know. But I mean something else. Look. What's that on the screen? Something's happening now."

"Snow," said Telma Ervanaria. She'd have to force herself to get up or she'd sit here all day, staring at a bench. "It looks like they've got snow."

"I know what it is," said Dona Linda, her voice rising in excitement. "I've just realized what it is. I've sat and watched him at least three times, and he never, ever blinks."

*   *   *

Antonio drove off the track and into the woods. They were way out past Covo da Zora. Mud splattered up to the windshield, the brakes squealed, and Teresa gritted her teeth.

He got out and opened the back door and let her climb in first.

"Let's talk for a while, okay?"

"Talk to me, then," he said.

She cupped his chin, blue with stubble, in her hand and turned his face to hers. In three days she would be going away. Every minute had to count. "I love you."

"Teresa," said Antonio, kissing her hand. "Can we talk about something else?"

"Fine. We'll talk about something more important. Head gaskets or exhaust pipes or something interesting like that."

Antonio lifted his knees against the back of the driver's seat and slumped down, his sweater riding up in a hideous hunchback around his neck. "Go on, make fun. That's it. I'm not good enough for you anymore."

Teresa sat forward. "I was just saying that I love you, you . . . you . . ." She smoothed her skirt and pulled her ponytail. "You silly thing."

She put her hand on his knee, but he didn't respond. Thank God she was going soon. It was all too painful now.

With a sharp intake of breath, she said, "I've got to tell you something. That Marco is a son of a bitch."

"Cars aren't boring," said Antonio. "If you knew anything about them, you'd know."

"He's going to buy up thousands of acres. He's going to kick everyone off. People who built their own houses when they were working on the land." A picture came to her mind of João, walking across the field with his pig. "It's terrible. Just terrible. There should be a law against that."

"There is a law," said Antonio. "He'll have to wait until they die." He put a finger in his ear but caught her eye and took it out again. "He's going to make a nature reserve and breed Iberian lynxes. They're an endangered species. He's into the environment, all that."

"João is an endangered species," she shouted. Tears pricked at her eyes.

Antonio went fiercely at his ear. "What are you talking about?" he said.

She looked out the window at the cork oaks, the acorns littering the ground. They were all taken in by Marco. Marco with his sand-and-sea voice. "He can't just come here and change things. What gives him the right?"

Antonio got out of the car and slammed the door. He walked away, straight through the mud. He walked back and yelled through the window. "What do you care, anyway? I thought you were leaving us all."

"Brown Eyed Girl" came on the jukebox for the third time. Stanton looked around to mark the culprit. Senhora Carmona was over there, shuffling and trembling, studying the floor with her cloudy eyes as though it might give way.

"Surely not you too, Senhora," said Stanton, turning back to the pinball. Another ball loaded and Stanton squared his hips. This time, he said to himself. This time. He pulled back the lever and released it with a smack. The ball flew up, hit a bell, and danced around the machine like a firecracker. Save it, thought Stanton. Wait. Now. He slapped both the buttons at once, and the ball bounced off a dragon's head and ricocheted into a spaceship. A light flashed, something buzzed, and the ball vibrated on an indent before crashing down and out of the game.

Stanton checked his score. He loaded in more coins. Every day for the last two weeks, he had woken up and thought about standing here. He wanted his name on the high scorers' screen.

He downed his brandy and nodded to Vasco. The funny thing about Vasco was he was fat but he didn't look heavy. He walked around on his tiptoes like he might at any moment float away. It was his voice as well. It made you think of helium balloons.

Stanton was finally in the zone. Burning up. These few months he had been wading through the writing, but now he was truly ready. That's why he couldn't leave, not yet.

You can try and take it with you, he thought, but it might not want to come.

The ball slammed around the machine, setting off alarms. Right hand, left hand, thought Stanton. Not both at once. The ball skidded across toward the dragon's mouth. Stanton slapped both buttons. *"Filho da puta,"* he said. "Fuck."

Vasco put down a drink. "What has that pinball done to you?"

"Not now," said Stanton, "not now." Instinct, not reason, he said to himself, narrowing his eyes. Go, go, go. The ball flew and kept on flying. Whatever, whatever, whatever. That's what made it work.

To Mercy, Pity, Peace, and Love, all pray in their distress, to Mercy, Pity, Peace, and Love, all pray in their distress . . . The words chased around and around his head, creating the chasm he desired.

Two months to finish a second draft. Once he got started, it was going to roll.

Now he'd lost the knack. He fired another ball. The lever was sticky in his hand. Everything in this whole place stuck to you. Made you feel like Vasco's cloth had rubbed over every bit of your skin. The rain had started up again too, after a few days' truce. It got so that you never felt entirely dry. Even the bed felt damp.

Stanton swallowed his drink. He thought he would play just one more game. It was another reason not to leave. He wasn't leaving until he beat this bloody thing.

He smiled, because he was only joking, and loaded up the coins.

Marco came in, his head shining wet. Stanton raised his hand, and Marco acknowledged him in some way, though Stanton couldn't tell what that was. It was as if he had spoken without even opening his mouth.

I must be drunk, thought Stanton. Don't let me drink any more.

*　*　*

"I'll buy you a drink," said Stanton, sitting down. "Vasco, two beers for us."

"I don't drink," said Marco. "I'll have a glass of milk."

Stanton met Marco's gaze and decided he would not be the first to look away. The people who made a virtue of looking at you frankly were the ones with something to hide. There was a shaving nick on Marco's head, a tiny scab that would fall off soon. His eyes, which turned up at the sides, were placid brown but full of misplaced confidence, as if they could not possibly be deceived.

"When did you give it up?" said Stanton, smelling the sanctified air of a reformed alcoholic. It explained a lot of things.

"I never started," said Marco, smiling.

Stanton looked down at his beer. "Everyone's talking about you. As if you didn't know."

"They'll stop soon enough."

Marco had that stupid cape on. Didn't he ever take it off? "Where did you get that cape from? What's the story with that?"

"On my travels," said Marco in his damnably calm way.

"Where did you get to, Marco? I hear Macau's where you made it big."

"I'm no bigger than the next man," said Marco. He took a sip of his milk.

Stanton bounced his leg under the table and spilled a bit of his beer. The one man here he might actually be able to talk to, but he was on some spiritual, holier-than-thou, reformed-substance-abuser fucking high. "What's the big secret?" said Stanton, shredding a napkin. He resented the way Marco sat so still. It was a performance, that's what it was. "Look," he said, "you know and I know that the only reason they talk about you is because you don't speak. If you want them to stop, all you've got to do is talk."

"It doesn't bother me."

Stanton wanted to snap his fingers in front of Marco's face. Make him blink for once. "You really think it's some big deal."

The bird-watcher and his *fiancée* (saying the word to himself made Stanton's lip curl) more or less fell through the door, flicking water out of their eyes.

"Brought the weather with us," said the bird-watcher. Stanton recalled he was companionably dumb.

"Take a pew," said Stanton. "Have a drink. Allow me to introduce you to Mamarrosa's most famous inmate. Stephanie and, er . . . ?"

"Huw," said the dumbbell, "and Sophie." She had something sharp stuck up her arse.

"I want you to meet Marco. Marco was just telling me about his time with the French Foreign Legion."

Marco and Huw laughed politely. Sophie condescended to smile.

Stanton wasn't interested anyway. "Vasco! Three brandies and a glass of milk, at your leisure, *se faz favor*."

He stared at a trail of red mud from the doorway and thought, That is why I can't go. It's the earth, that's what it is. The garden this morning was magnificently morbid, seen through a glaze of rain. Suffer and the land suffers with you. Those are the ties that bind.

The others were locked in conversation. You take it in turns to say something, thought Stanton, and you learn nothing at all.

Vasco was watching Marco from behind the counter. He thought Marco would make him rich. He didn't dare approach him directly, though. Out of respect for his wealth.

"I had this feeling," the fiancée was saying, "when we were in the Chapel of Bones. Like there was this part of me opening up, and I did and I didn't want that, and it's been opening and closing ever since."

"That's good," said Marco, in a tone he must have learned at the drying-out clinic, "just to recognize it."

She thinks he's a guru, thought Stanton. Setting her on the redemptive path. However blind you made a character, they were never blind enough.

He laughed inwardly and turned away. The Pottses, all four of them, were at a table by the cigarette machine. Now, that was new.

That they could come quietly into the room. The Pottses behaving themselves, being a family, mum and dad, two kids.

They sat at the table as if they were having a séance, messages from the dead more likely than messages among those four. All of them wearing clean clothes and best faces. It was touching, it really was. What a reformation. Though reformations never last.

Not so long ago there had been rumors. Wild ones, even for this place.

But China had a job now, with a builder in São Martinho. Chrissie was helping out at the Casa do Povo, volunteer work fit for a nun. The boy, Jay, was going to school every day, and Stanton was pleased, really pleased. Ruby—he'd heard nothing of Ruby, and that meant something, of course.

Happy families, thought Stanton. Why shouldn't they play too? Play it well or badly, it was always only a game.

He looked at the back of Jay's head, and something welled inside. For a moment he thought he would cry.

He looked instead at China, the one who had claimed he was rising above, or diving below. But here he was, buying in to it. Morality, someone said, is the herd instinct operating in the masses. Nietzsche, wasn't it? Fucking right.

Chrissie looked over and caught him staring. He took refuge in his glass. It was only a social convention, for him to look away. If he'd felt guilty once, he didn't any longer. They ignored him, but that was their problem. In fact, it made it easier for him.

Conscience is but a word cowards use to keep the strong in awe.

Someone said that.

Someone or other.

Someone with a brain.

If you looked at a bald head long enough, you wanted to touch it. That was a fact of life. If you needed some added charisma, which Marco obviously did, you could do worse than shave your pate.

"I feel like I'm finally beginning to understand," the fiancée was burbling, "the need in life to make space for things that, you know, might come from . . ."

She was cute, actually. He wouldn't mind. Any port in a storm. But she was dreaming, and she thought she was just waking up.

"The search itself," Marco was saying, "is what prevents us from finding our true being."

One thing he was glad about now, he'd left his illusions behind. Disillusioned, was it called? Oh well, it fitted nicely on the page, and that was all that mattered to him. He looked at the girl and at Vasco and the *tableau vivant* of the Pottses. Dreaming, they were all dreaming. Marco was dreaming too.

Marco said, "In order to attain Awareness, the mind simply has to make way."

Stanton knew what Marco was. Some old hippie, fresh from an ashram where they chanted and indulged in free love. He got up to leave and, steadying himself with a hand on the table, whispered in Sophie's ear. "Don't listen to him, for God's sake. If you end up like him, you won't have a single thought to call your own."

The Mamarrosa *festa* late in November was second only to the April 25 celebrations, but its provenance was unclear. It fell on one of the few days that, as far as anyone knew, was not a saint's day. It was named simply for itself. Festa da Mamarrosa. In the afternoon there was a procession, with a line of little girls carrying cakes baked in the shape of houses and decorated with miniature Portuguese flags. Bruno said it was to give thanks that the village had escaped unharmed in the Great Earthquake of 1755, but nobody listened to him. Others said it had begun as a birthday celebration of Manuel II, the Unfortunate, but most said it went further, much further, back. A few reckoned it marked the deposing of the duchess of Mantua in 1640 and the restoration of Portuguese rule. They were listened to with respect, but as that occasion was on the first of December, it made the position hard to defend. Vasco's theory had something to do with Henry the Navigator and also Vasco da Gama, but hardly a single villager was equal to the task of listening to what the theory was.

In the evening there was a party with music and dancing held at the Casa do Povo. People had been known to leave their sickbeds, and on at least one occasion, deathbed, to attend. Last year the Junta da Freguesia exceled itself by hiring a fire-eater and also an a capella group, As Camponesas de Castro Verde, though some said it was hardly necessary to bring talent in from so far when so much of it lived beneath their collective nose. Some minor complaints notwithstanding, it was generally agreed to be the best *festa* ever, something that was agreed every year.

After the procession, and as the day darkened, men prepared with tetchy heroism to shave for the second time, and even Teresa's mother, Cristina, switched off the television set.

The Casa do Povo was a building without pretension except for the pair of sickly magnolias by the entrance and a—to use the term somewhat loosely—copy of Gonçalves' masterpiece, *Panéis de São Vicente,* which hogged the back wall of the main hall, framed in an explosion of gold. The room had been decorated for the event with bunting sewn by the primary school children and the crochet work of older hands. A stage erected from pieces of scaffolding stood beneath the duke of Bragança and his supplicants, supporting two loudspeakers, a mike, and a stool.

At the far end, arraigned at a trestle table, João and his friends began with beer.

Manuel, wiping his mustache, said, "I drink to Rui."

"Rui," they said as one, and drank.

"I drink to Carlos," said Manuel, "a true friend for forty years."

"Carlos," the old men said and raised bottles to their colorless lips.

"I drink to José," declared Manuel, warming to his theme.

"Drink all you like," said José, poking him in the chest, "but don't go blaming me."

"João," said Manuel, "do you remember when they put this building up?"

João chewed his tongue for a while. "No, I don't remember."

"Phut! That's right. You got lost for all that time." Manuel pulled a tobacco pouch from his pocket and inserted a wad of brown leaf into his mouth. "You want? No, okay, so chew your tongue. Someone came from Lindoso, gave a big speech like he was Salazar himself."

Carlos said, "Manuel, who will you drink to next?"

Manuel banged the table. "Yes, yes, it was all to be so brilliant. The Casa do Povo would look after us all. And when I was out of work, what help did I get? None."

João looked across at the painting, at the knight and the beggar and the priest. Everything keeps changing, but still it remains the same.

"It was a long time ago. Why complain?" said José. "You do well enough from it now. I hear you've been coming to play cards with the Englishwoman."

"We never talk about anything," grumbled Manuel. "If what is gone is gone, then what is there left to say?"

João rubbed his bad knee. He looked down at his hand and wondered when the knuckles had grown so big.

"Cards on top of the table, footsie down below." José poked Manuel again.

Manuel grabbed José's finger. "I'll break it," he said, "next time."

Carlos raised his arms heavenward, as far as his arthritis allowed. "Soft in the head, the two of you. Any more and I'll throw you out."

"Like to see you try," said Manuel, twisting his mustache.

"Pansy like you," said José, poking Carlos, "wouldn't get very far."

"I drink to Rui," said João.

"Rui," they said and drank.

★   ★   ★

Quite a few couples were dancing in the area that had been kept clear next to the stage. Teresa stood by the wall, pointing her toes and pursing her lips. Nelson wasn't half as good as he thought he was, and who liked the accordion anyway? Girls in ribboned dresses and boys with newly shorn heads buzzed like flies around the dance floor, chasing or being chased. The women who weren't dancing grouped around the tables, setting out plates and glasses and forks. They wore sleeveless tops and gold necklaces, arms and cheeks still pink from the shower. The men stood and fingered their collars and joined in sudden bursts of laughter sealed with a clearing of throats. Nelson's son, Fernando, sat on the edge of the stage. Pedro and Francisco took turns offering their bums to be kicked. Such a child, Francisco, playing with the kids. Thank God he wasn't going to be a father. That was a pack of lies. Clara said Ruby got rid of the baby. She said a lot of other stuff as well, but Teresa wasn't listening to any more of her lies.

Telma Ervanaria and Bruno were dancing, holding on to each other's shoulders and the place where their waists ought to be. Telma Ervanaria wore a crocheted brown top. You could see her bra through it. Her sturdy thighs strained a straight beige skirt, and her feet, in brown heeled pumps, shifted side, side, backward in protesting little steps. Bruno stared somberly over her shoulder, breathing through his mouth as though fixed on a difficult but achievable goal, like shunting a filing cabinet across the room.

Clara and Paula were gossiping and sticking out their chests. They were looking at the writer and giggling and probably giving him ideas. The writer sat on a chair backward, his chin propped on his hands. His cheeks were red as well, but Teresa doubted a shower was the cause.

This evening Mãe looked magnificent, her hair done up in a French twist. Her dress, pale lilac and 60 percent silk, cinched her tidy waist and skimmed just right off the hips. She wore her peacock brooch and two gold bangles and tortoiseshell combs in her hair. She was carrying plates from the kitchen, holding them well out in front as though they might dirty her dress. Marco stood up as she approached and took them from her and across to the table. He turned back to her and gave a kind of bow.

Teresa tapped her toes and crossed her arms. What if Mãe got married again? People did sometimes, why shouldn't she? The way that Marco looked at her, surely there was something in that. Of course they used to know each other before Marco went away. Probably Marco was in love with her then but lost out to Pai and couldn't bear to stay around anymore.

She looked at Marco and she looked at Mãe. They would make a handsome pair.

In London she would say, "Oh, my family owns a lot of land in Portugal. If you ever want to come and stay."

But Marco, she remembered, was planning to do terrible things. If Mãe married him, it would be awful. She hugged her arms in despair.

"This next one is a love song," said Nelson, hitching his accordion. The loudspeakers wailed when he leaned in so close. "If there is someone in the room that you love"—he paused and forced his eyebrows a little higher—"stand up now and take her arm."

He pumped at the suffocating instrument, and the notes scattered out everywhere.

> *"When I heard the lark singing in the garden,*
> *I rose from my troubled bed and sang for him . . ."*

She scanned the room for Antonio and saw him sitting on the edge of the stage with Fernando and Francisco, smoking a cigarette. In any case, she was going to help with the tables. She unfolded her arms and pushed back her shoulders and jumped when someone touched her hand.

Spinning around, she saw Vicente fixing her with a look and cocking his head toward the side door.

★   ★   ★

They walked down to the small square and sat by the edge of the thick green pond. Vicente sparked the spliff and handed it over. "So you're leaving tomorrow," he said.

"I'm so excited." She took a hit.

Vicente laughed. "Don't sound so miserable, then."

A car passed and lit their faces. In the bushes a cat was being sick.

She shivered and Vicente moved closer. "Here. Let me warm you up."

It was exactly as she had imagined it. Eileen sat on the raffia-bottomed chair and sipped a pineapple Sumol. Next year she would be part of it too.

"Have you actually found a house?" said Sophie.

"Dear me, no," said Eileen, rubbing her chest, "I've only just started to look."

"Good place to retire to," said Huw. Eileen thought he seemed ever so nice. The type you'd want for a son-in-law, if you had a daughter, she meant.

"Not retiring yet," explained Eileen. "Well, I've never worked, but my husband, you know."

"Holiday home," said Sophie. She seemed ever so nice as well, but Eileen wished she'd sit back in her seat. She was perched right on the edge of it, and Eileen kept on thinking she was about to fall off.

"More than that," said Eileen. "For me, anyway." She was feeling rather gassy. No more fizzy drinks today.

"My parents are divorced," said Huw.

"Huw," said Sophie. "Please."

"Oh, I see. Yes, it must have sounded . . . No, we're still soldiering on. Death us do part, the old-fashioned way. Why people bother getting divorced at our age beats me, though apparently a lot of people do. Not that we're unhappy. I didn't mean to say that."

"Of course not," said Sophie, leaning dangerously forward to pat her hand.

I must look, thought Eileen, like the kind of woman who needs a pat now and then. If it were Janet Larraway sitting here, it wouldn't cross anyone's mind.

"I *love* this singer," said Eileen. "Saw a poster for one of his concerts in the summer. I think he's a bit of a star."

"Definitely." Huw rested his hand on the back of Sophie's swan neck. "Back to work tomorrow, work and wedding plans."

"Many, many congratulations," cried Eileen. "I must say, I've been admiring your ring."

"Thank you," said Sophie, curling her fingers.

Eileen shifted in her seat. Bits of raffia were sticking through her dress and into her bottom. But if she sat on the edge, like Sophie, she was bound to crash to the floor.

"Have you set a date?"

"Yes," they said at once and exchanged a look.

"Lovely, lovely," said Eileen with far more emphasis than necessary, as though possession of a date were a triumph to be praised up to the skies. "Where's it going to be?"

"Devon," said Huw, with his eyes still on Sophie. "It's where her parents live."

"Church or registry?" said Eileen. He looked a solid sort, proper haircut, the type who'd stick around. She realized she might have a son-in-law, sort of, one day.

Sophie twisted her ring around her finger. She mumbled something that might have been *church*.

Huw looked at Eileen as if to say sorry. "You see, we agreed we wouldn't discuss the wedding on holiday. The planning gets quite stressful. Worse for her, of course."

"Quite understand," cried Eileeen. "Goodness, yes, I do! You want to relax on your holiday. We'll talk about something else. I'll tell you about this place that I saw, a ruin, but it had the most marvelous view . . ." She carried on talking to smooth things over, and then just because there seemed no natural place to stop. All the while she was thinking how high-strung the girl was, nice but high-strung, and how—though it seemed a little harsh to even think it—maybe Huw was making a mistake, and also a thought pushing in there about how brilliantly Huw would get on with Richard, she was sure they would get on, and she had this daft, this wild idea that the two of them could be an item, Huw and Richard, and she was stupid, really stupid, and having a hot flash as well.

Vasco rolled over, fanning his face with a napkin, saying, "Yes, yes, too hot in here. Too hot for the dancing. It would be my pleasure to sit with you."

Eileen turned to the table and grabbed a napkin and began fanning herself too. "Senhor Vasco, I'd like you to meet my new friends, Huw and Sophie."

"I know, I know," said Vasco, "they're renting Armenio's old house."

They sat and watched the dance floor, and Chrissie and China danced by. Chrissie wore heels and tights and a shapeless peasant skirt and a blouse that buttoned up to the chin. China wore a suit. The jacket had lost all its buttons, and the trouser hems were ragged, but a suit it was nonetheless. They danced cheek-to-cheek, China stooping, and moved with no regard for the music, simply swaying and gliding as though rocking each other to sleep.

Maybe, thought Vasco, this evening I will put it to Marco straight. If it is a business partner you are looking for, then, my friend, I am your man.

"Let me ask you something," he said, opening his palm to Huw. "When you come here, what are you looking for? Do you want Internet in the café?"

"Er, not really."

"That is my point exactly. On the one hand, age and experience"—he dropped the palm down low—"on the other, youth and ambition." He opened the other palm. "Which side the scales are tipping? It is not too hard to see."

Vasco looked around to determine if the food had been brought out yet. He saw Marco sitting with Armenio, and Eduardo standing behind Marco's chair, dripping poison, no doubt, in his ear.

Not a crumb of food on the tables. Pathetic, unacceptable, and corrupt. The Junta gave the contract to Armenio, and Eduardo said it had nothing to do with him. Nepotistic, corrupt, and criminal. And Marco could see the result.

Anyway, it was to Vasco's advantage, but if he didn't eat soon, he might faint.

"You would like food?" he said to the Englishwoman, who looked also a little faint.

"It's ready? How wonderful!" she said, sounding truly over-joyed.

Vasco sighed. "No, not ready. But we are all so hungry now."

It was well past nine o'clock when Eduardo took the stage. "Friends," he said. "Good friends, cherished friends . . ."

"He has none," said Vasco in English, "a traitor never does."

"What?" said Eileen. "What was he saying?"

Vasco flapped his hand. "Rest easy. If he utters one word of any importance, I shall faithfully translate."

". . . join together with me in thanking our local musical legend, Senhor Nelson Paulo Cavaco. If anyone would like to hear more from his golden lungs, you can see him in Santiago do Cacém tomorrow evening."

"Still rubbish," Vasco informed the foreigners loudly.

"And in a moment"—Eduardo patted his excuse for a stomach—"we shall all eat, but first I would like, on behalf of the Junta, to thank everyone who worked so hard toward this very special evening. Please give yourselves a clap. . . . And lastly . . ."

"The power," said Vasco, "has gone to his head."

". . . I am sure you will agree that we have here this evening a very special guest. Yes, Marco Afonso Rodrigues, come up here. I propose a toast to my cousin and a friend to every one of you, who has achieved so . . . so many things, and who has finally decided that there is no place like home."

Marco, propelled by many hands, found his way to the foot of the stage.

"To Marco," said Eduardo and raised a glass.

"To Marco."

"We met him last night," said Sophie.

"Why does he shave his head?" said Huw. "Makes him look like a convict."

"It does not," said Sophie. "Don't be an idiot."

Marco weaved back through the tables. Telma Ervanaria blocked his way. "A speech from the honored guest would have been welcome." She folded her arms and trained her formidable breasts directly on the man.

Marco smiled and shook his head. "I'm not one for speeches. I simply extend my humble thanks."

"Marco," said Telma Ervanaria, "when we were children, I used to dangle you upside down by the ankle. Tell me, has such a distance grown between us that you cannot say a single thing?" She smiled too, but, like a dog whose tail has been docked, she seemed ready at any moment to spring.

Those people who were closest tuned in to the conversation. Some stepped a pace or two forward so that Marco and Telma Ervanaria were enclosed. Vasco bashed Bruno on the leg to make him give way, so that he got an unobstructed view from his seat.

"I do not choose to make a distance," said Marco. "I am here with you all."

"Tell us a simple story, then. The story of your life."

Cristina was there and Dona Linda, and Stanton with his hands in his pockets. Eduardo looked on anxiously, bending his hands back and forth at the wrists.

"Is it true," said Vasco, "that you were once in Angola? My uncle Henrique went there."

The party went on around them in the low-ceilinged whitewashed room. There was the muted buzz of adjustment and expectation, as was natural after their attention had been released from the stage.

"A life is never simple," said Marco. "A story is never true."

"Fooey," said Telma Ervanaria. "You went here, you went there, you did this, you did that. Simply give us the facts."

"I could tell you some stories. Stories are what we use to cover things up."

"Nonsense," said Telma Ervanaria, her pug face becoming squarer by the second as she adjusted her chin. "Only if you tell lies."

João came out of the toilet and limped past, smiling left and right, to acknowledge whatever was going on.

Telma Ervanaria seized his arm. "Every honest man will tell you what his life has been. Senhor João here would tell anyone, if he wasn't shy. And those of us who have been abroad are not too proud to speak. Senhor Vasco, I can personally vouch for, is only too happy to talk."

There was laughter and a substantial amount of coughing to disown entirely the laugh.

"What's happening?" said Eileen to Vasco.

"A joke," said Vasco gravely. "Jokes are not possible to translate."

Marco waited a few moments longer, allowing a level of uncertainty to build. "Maybe, then, you know him. Maybe, though, you don't."

Manuel, who had interrupted his pilgrim's progress across the room, drinking to everyone's health, shouted, "I know what he's hiding. He's not rich at all. Look at that old cape he's wearing. The clasp is not real gold."

"No," said Dona Linda, who had learned it from Telma Ervanaria, "that means he's *very* rich. So rich he doesn't have to care."

"No, no, no. A failure, and he doesn't want to say."

"Listen," said Telma Ervanaria, finally releasing her grip on João. "We can see you are a private man."

"That's right," shouted Eduardo.

"Shut up, Eduardo," said Telma Ervanaria. "Let me speak."

Eduardo looked reluctant, but under the circumstances, chiefly of Telma Ervanaria's glare, he gave way.

"As I was saying, you are private about your history, but do please tell us your plans. Those—you cannot deny it—we have a right to know."

Marco shrugged. He gave a laugh. "I have no plans."

"You have no plans."

"No."

"He has no plans."

Until this moment there had been a sense that Marco was carrying the audience with him, all those present eager to hear and see. The mood changed now, swiftly and without commotion, but nevertheless there was a change.

Telma Ervanaria, sensing the turning of tables, strode up and down like a prosecutor with Marco on the stand.

"He denies it. He denies that he has any plans."

"I prefer," said Marco, drawing his cape about him, "to live in the present. This is what I can say I have achieved."

"He says he is living in the present," whispered Vasco to Eileen. "That is the luxury of wealth."

"What about us, senhor?" said Telma Ervanaria, instinctively adopting formality as a method of attack. "We who must look to the future, with families to protect."

"I don't know," said Marco evenly. "Perhaps you should have faith."

"Faith," said Telma Ervanaria with a dangerous rise in her voice. "Our faith is strong."

"Yes?"

"Yes!" Telma Ervanaria wheeled about to target her allies. "Cristina," she called, "come here."

Teresa slipped in with Vicente and leaned against the side door. He picked a white oleander from a chipped vase on the windowsill and tried to fix it in her hair. Teresa witnessed her aunt pushing her mother toward Marco.

"My sister, Cristina, and I myself have never missed Sunday mass. Isn't it true, Cristina? We practically live for the Church."

"I see," said Marco, smiling. "Would you like to speak on your beliefs?"

"Oh, I can do better than that. Father Braga is here. Father! Where is he hiding? Father, come and speak for us."

Father Braga had been loitering at the back of the circle, keeping this little flock under review. He liked, naturally, to speak of faith; indeed, there was nothing he liked more, except perhaps a detective novel and a sheepskin rug in which to bury his feet. But he felt the time was inappropriate, the place was not quite right, and the earnestness of that fellow filled him with deep unease. In any case, he thought, pushing at the door, he had not heard his name called, having been thinking of higher things. By the time he reached the blackly glittering street, he realized also that he had been called away earlier to a neighboring hamlet to minister to somebody very sick. At home he hung up his cassock and thought how pleasant it was finally to be left alone.

"Anyway," said Telma Ervanaria, as Cristina slunk off to the side, "nobody can doubt it. We are certainly devout."

Oh, please, thought Cristina, please don't let her go on. She reflected on *Woman of Destiny,* how the characters said so much with a look.

"We speak of our dear pope and pray for him every day."

"What?" said Senhora Carmona, popping up from behind Eduardo and shuffling through. "What's that about the pope? He's dead, you say?" She put a gnarled hand beneath her ear as though expecting it to fall off.

"We *pray* for him, Senhora Carmona. That is what I said."

"I know that," snapped the old woman. "But is he dead?"

"He's sick again, Senhora Carmona."

"Sick?" snarled the widow. "Of course he's sick. I'm not an imbecile, you know." She had dressed up for the occasion in a gown of shocking pink that gaped fearfully at the front, where her chest had once been, revealing thermals and multiple strings of beads.

"Sit down, Senhora Carmona. Take the weight off your feet."

"Very kind," said the merry widow. "I'll sit with you," she said to Vasco and sat down and patted his knee.

"Anyway," said Telma Ervanaria irritably, hoisting her bosom. She felt she was losing the thread. "Can't you see you make everyone uncomfortable? How do you feel about that?"

Marco took his time. He wasn't a man to be rushed. "I think that it is easier to be with another person who is unhappy. Happiness we always mistrust."

"Santa Maria," cried Telma Ervanaria. "He accuses us of being unhappy!" There was no mistaking now that she might bite; in fact, she showed her teeth. "We are very, very happy, thank you. Thank you for your concern."

Vasco tipped toward the foreigners, who were, like animals or babies, distressed by the atmosphere. He sought to reassure them. "He says that we are all unhappy. But naturally he doesn't include you."

"Happy?" piped up Senhora Carmona. "Who says so? I haven't been happy for fifty years."

"Be quiet," said Telma Ervanaria, hefting her breasts almost up to her chin.

It dawned on Vasco that he would have to do something, especially if they were ever to eat. "Now, now, Senhora Carmona, are you alive—"

"How dare you!" gasped the unmerry widow. She took her rosary from her pocket and waved it around as though she meant to whip his legs.

"Are you alive, Senhora Carmona, to the fact that Telma Ervanaria was simply pointing out that on the whole we are content and that on this evening, of all evenings, we are here to enjoy ourselves?"

Vasco reached around his neck to find his cloth but had to make do without it. "And also that it is high time—past high time, some would say—that dinner was served."

Eduardo clapped his hands and said dinner would have been served long ago, if only *some* people hadn't gotten in the way.

Senhora Carmona turned her little head so that she could view Vasco through the good part of her eye. She removed her vibrating hand from his knee and placed it higher up on his thigh. "When I was young," she confided, "I could make a man like you happy just with a toss of my hair."

Vasco began with fried liver with chili and moved on to the baked tripe. Both dishes he would concede as competent while being in no way inspired. He ate steadily and also ruefully, thinking how little he had eaten today. The *cataplana,* he admitted, was decent, and though he didn't fancy the rice with mixed seafood, he took some so nobody could accuse him of spite. The green beans needed more garlic, and the broad beans were unconscionably tough.

He spied on the gathering between mouthfuls, and it seemed not a person could be still. They passed to and fro through the constellation of tables, the men constantly patting their pockets, the women finding business with hems and jewelry and hair. The children added greatly to the traffic, gnawing barbarously on chicken wings and swinging around grown-ups' legs. The noise level rose and kept rising. Everyone, it seemed, was exceptionally gay.

Some small beast had wormed under the table and was wrestling with Vasco's shoe.

"Excuse me," said Clara, getting down on the floor. "Hugo, come out of there."

There was singing next by the schoolchildren, but they were giddy and out of tune. The adults applauded every song with increasing fervor. The cheers grew so loud they frightened the children, and some began to weep. Mothers stormed the stage to withdraw their offspring and looked about for someone to blame.

The dancing began again, this time to Nelson's recorded interpretation of Rolling Stones and Beatles hits.

Vasco took a deep breath and a gamble. "Dona Cristina, would you consider, by any chance—I hope it is not too unwelcome—that is to say, do me the honor of taking to the floor with me?"

Dona Cristina was pleasingly flustered. She pulled her necklace and twisted it on her finger. The risk of strangulation Vasco assessed as minor, but the emotional turmoil was real.

"Yes," she said eventually, unable to produce more than the one word.

He wiped his fingers on the back of his trousers, even though he'd done a thorough job already with the napkin. Her dress was pale silk, and he was afraid to touch it. He decided it couldn't be helped.

They turned a couple of times in a small circle. He wondered if they would just keep going around. He was pleased that he'd worn his best shirt. It was mustard yellow. The best color for hiding sweat stains.

Dona Cristina seemed to be sagging. He felt like he was holding her up. Lili used to dance like a dervish. She said, "Tarzan, move over. I need space."

"Excuse me, Dona Cristina, do you mind if we stop now?"

"No."

"Oh, you're very kind."

He was feeling, perhaps, a bit queasy. He sought a solution in the buffet. He passed over the salt cod options and sampled the pork and clams, washed down with a glass of sparkling sweet wine. What a good time everyone was having. Even that goat Eduardo and his sinister cousin had not managed to ruin the night.

"Senhor Stanton! I was just thinking what a good time everyone is having."

The writer nodded morosely. "Is that what it is? Having fun."

"Yes," said Vasco expansively. "Now, why do you think it was that Marco refused to speak?"

Stanton smiled with his mouth but not with his eyes. "It's a trick used by old hippies. To make you think they might really have something to say."

"I must ask you," said Vasco, pulling up a chair to the Englishwoman, "about something."

"Oh, dear," said Eileen.

Vasco assured her there was no need to be alarmed. "It's just about what I was reading in the newspaper about your government—"

"I don't know anything about it. Nothing at all, I'm afraid."

"It's about—"

"I definitely don't know about it. The more I read, the less I knew, so I decided to stop reading. It's quite refreshing, you see."

It was a clear rebuff, and Vasco retreated once more to the buffet and consoled himself with goose barnacles and spider crab. The bottle of sparkling wine he had opened still stood on the table, and it seemed a shame to let it go flat.

Picking delicately at his food, he thought of Eduardo and Marco. Marco had shown Eduardo up. No doubt at all about that. Eduardo, he thought, Eduardo, was I not like family to you? They say that blood is thicker than water, but where is the proof? My friend, I always stood by you; now you prepare the dagger for my back.

He couldn't see them anywhere. They were probably plotting outside. They had agreed Marco would say nothing. In business, surprise is a form of attack.

He hurried out to see if he could eavesdrop, plan a counterattack of his own. On the porch Telma Ervanaria was shouting at Bruno, but Eduardo and his son and his cousin were nowhere to be found.

Vasco wandered back to the dance floor, vague thoughts of Dona Cristina taking shape. When he approached her, however, she darted away and made for the door.

The English boy, Huw, was dancing on his own. Vasco was struck by the novelty of it and waved his arms in the air. He felt his stomach wobbling, but for once he gave not a fig. He quickly checked his suspenders, though, and was sufficiently reassured to go on.

"What do you call this music, then?" said Huw, shuffling and nodding his head.

"I believe," said Vasco, breathing quickly, "is called a cover version."

"Uh-huh. What's it a cover of?"

"Your most very British group," said Vasco, surprised, experimenting with a swing of the hips. "The Beatles. You do not know?"

"Yeah, oh, yeah. I know the Beatles. But not when it's sung in Portuguese."

"Portuguese?" squealed Vasco. "Is English, not Portuguese."

He needed something to settle his stomach and selected melon, pineapple, plums, and half a pear. The slice of cake he took was minuscule, and to fill up, he chewed some bread.

He sipped his wine and watched Clara's little brother sleeping across two chairs, beneath some coats. It was amazing how they could sleep like that with the din going on all around. Was it this noisy every year, or was there something different this time?

It took him another few moments to notice there was a fight going on by the stage. Many people had rushed over, and the yelling was catching on across the room.

Vasco got himself upright and saw Antonio and Vicente, locked together, being bundled out the door. Teresa and also Paula were being consoled, or maybe constrained, in opposing camps.

"Did you try the octopus?" said Eduardo, appearing from nowhere, rubbing his nose.

Vasco ignored him. He was about to move away.

"I thought you would like the octopus. It's delicious. Did you try?"

Whatever Eduardo said to Vasco, he clearly meant something else. A man who could not speak straight was an object of contempt.

Vasco was going to let it pass, but he had let it pass so many times. That was why he found himself spoken to like this, of octopus, and in such a sneering tone.

"How dare you?" he demanded. Eduardo would have to answer for his actions now.

Eduardo affected not to know what Vasco was talking about and continued to scratch his nose.

"I will not allow it," said Vasco. "You will not get away with it anymore, you . . ." He searched for a cliché of sufficient magnitude with which to crush his foe.

"Cool it, big man," said Eduardo.

"How dare you!" Vasco put a hand on Eduardo's shoulder to stop him from walking off. He would have liked to seize his throat.

"Get off me," growled Eduardo. His diction was clear enough now.

"Apologize," screamed Vasco.

"For what, you silly man?"

Eduardo knocked Vasco's hand away, and Vasco's rage boiled in his stomach like chilies eaten by the pound.

"What are you doing?" shouted Eduardo as Vasco locked Eduardo's head beneath his arm.

"Traitor," screeched Vasco. "Traitor." He staggered forward. Eduardo kept pushing him in the back.

On the dance floor, people parted to make way for the pantomime horse. Its hindquarters were somewhat stringy, but the front half had had plenty of hay.

"Get off. Get off," yelled Eduardo.

"Don't mumble," said Vasco, squeezing his head.

Eduardo tried to wriggle out but only succeeded in spinning both of them around.

"Don't be stupid, Vasco. Let me go and we'll forget about it. Come on now, let me go."

"Stupid, am I?" squawked Vasco. "Stupid, blubbery octopus."

"Yes, you are," screamed Eduardo. He managed to wriggle free. Eduardo launched a punch, but the blow landed weakly on

Vasco's chest. Vasco grabbed his opponent, convinced he could squeeze him to death. Eduardo clung on grimly with his face pressed to Vasco's neck. The pair waltzed slowly around the dance floor, and all those who had fallen quiet began to shout once more.

Vasco felt he was falling, falling through a big black space. Eduardo was falling with him, and Vasco loved him for that.

He was weightless now in this falling, weightless and totally free. He thought he would tell Eduardo, who was spinning so beautifully with him. He opened his mouth to tell him, and everything spilled out, everything, from the bottom of his stomach it came.

The Potts family sat at their table and watched the chaos erupt. Ruby got up once from her seat but sat down again, shaking her head.

"Mum," said Jay, screwing his nose up. "See what Vasco done?"

"What Vasco did," said Chrissie. "Yes, I saw. But don't stare. It's rude."

Stanton went out and gazed at the North Star, which appeared unaccountably bright. He cupped the back of his head and thought it was time. He wanted to go somewhere cold and preferably Teutonic where writers met in cafés with notebooks and grievances and discourse flowed on the meaning of life and of death. He rather fancied a road trip. He hoped to make it as far as Prague.

The next morning Eduardo went to Vasco's and let himself in at the back. He went upstairs and found Vasco sitting up in bed.

"Octopus," said Eduardo.

"Goat," Vasco replied.

Eduardo sat down and laughed.

"Hand me my puffer," said Vasco. He took two puffs and laughed as well.

"Seems to me that some people are more trouble than they're worth."

"Are you thinking," said Vasco, "of a certain relative of yours?"

They went together to Armenio's house to ask Marco Afonso Rodrigues to leave.

Marco's room was empty. Vasco opened the wardrobe door. "He's gone. The cupboard is bare."

Eduardo went to the bed and picked a sheet of paper off the pillow. "He's left a note," he said.

"Read it, then," commanded Vasco. "What are you waiting for?"

"I've read it. It says, *Peace*."

"Peace? What else does it say?"

Eduardo held out the paper to his friend. "*Peace*. That's all. Just that."

Vasco hurried across and scrutinized the page. He turned it over and turned it back. "You know, the moment I saw him, I said to myself, 'hippie.' And that is what he is."

A few people still spoke of Marco Afonso Rodrigues as winter turned into spring, but many more talked of the price of cork, which had fallen yet again. When the topic was not cork, it was usually drought, which was widely predicted this year. Vasco pronounced on the state of the world, and Bruno readily agreed. And when they were feeling generous, they listened to Eduardo aver at length that Marco was an impostor and not Marco Afonso Rodrigues at all.

João told his pig the story, on a beautiful December day, with the sun shining through the woods and dancing as the leaves danced on the sow's bristling and attentive back.

"Eh, eh," he said, "my beauty. But there's more than one way to look at it." And he began the story again.

Acknowledgments

This is neither a history book nor a travel book, but only a work of fiction. Readers who want to find out more about Portugal might like to turn to two books that combine history and travel to great effect: Paul Hyland's *Backwards out of the Big World,* and *Oldest Ally: A Portrait of Salazar's Portugal* by Peter Fryer and Patricia McGowan Pinheiro. There is not a great deal of literature available, in English, about the Alentejo. Robert and Mary Wilson's excellent *A Short Trip in the Alentejo* focuses on the marble towns of the Alto (Upper) Alentejo, an area that has its own particular character, as does the imaginary corner of the Alentejo about which I have written.

I would like to thank Grant, Wendy, Max, and Maya for introducing me to the pleasures of the Portuguese countryside, Liliana Chachian for her heroic attempts to teach me Portuguese, Nicole Aragi for all her support, and Nan Graham for the continuing education. Most of all I would like thank Simon for telling me to get on with it.

About the Author

Monica Ali lives in London with her husband and two children, and has been named by *Granta* as one of the twenty best young British novelists.

Printed in the United States
By Bookmasters